WANDA & BRUNSTETTER

A Cousin's PRAYER

INDIANA COUSINS | BOOK 2

BARBOUR
PUBLISHING

ISBN 978-1-60260-061-4

Published by Barbour Publishing, Inc., P.O. Box 719, Uhrichsville, OH 44683.

Our mission is to publish and distribute inspirational products offering exceptional value and biblical encouragement to the masses.

ecpa Member of the
Evangelical Christian
Publishers Association

Printed in the United States of America.

Dedication/Acknowledgments

To Mary Alice and Doretta Yoder, two special Amish friends who have patiently answered my many questions.

In appreciation of the Oaklawn therapists who offer spiritual and emotional help to many patients.

With special thanks to Lovina Petersheim for sharing her recipe for Banana Nut Cake.

Peace I leave with you, my peace I give unto you:
not as the world giveth, give I unto you.
Let not your heart be troubled, neither let it be afraid.

JOHN 14:27

PROLOGUE

Katie Miller's stomach churned as she read the letter she'd just received from her cousin Loraine:

> *Dear Katie,*
> *Wayne and I will be getting married the last Thursday of April. I'd like you to be one of my attendants.*

Katie's heart pounded. There was no way she could go to her cousin's wedding, much less be one of her attendants.

"Who's the letter from?" Katie's grandmother asked, taking a seat on the porch swing beside Katie.

"Loraine. She's getting married in April, and she wants me to be one of her attendants." Katie almost choked on the words.

"That's *wunderbaar*. I'm sure you're looking forward to going."

Katie shook her head. "I don't want to go."

"Think how disappointed Loraine would be if you weren't at her wedding."

Katie's gaze dropped to the floor. "I can't go back to Indiana, Grammy."

"Loraine and Wayne have been through so much. Don't you want to be there to share in their joy?"

Katie shivered despite the warm Florida breeze. If Timothy hadn't been killed on their way to Hershey Park last fall, she'd be planning her own wedding right now.

"Katie, did you hear what I said?"

Katie nodded, hoping she wouldn't give in to the tears pushing against her eyelids. "If I hadn't freaked out about a bee in the van, Timothy, Paul, and Raymond would still be alive." Katie drew in a shaky breath. "Jolene wouldn't have lost her hearing, either, and Wayne would still have both of his legs."

"You're not to blame, Katie. It was an accident. It might have happened even if you hadn't been afraid of the bee." Grammy touched Katie's arm. "You need to accept it and go on with your life."

"I—I don't know if I can."

"Timothy wouldn't want you to continue grieving for him. He wouldn't want you to blame yourself for the accident."

"You've said that before."

"Then you ought to listen." Grammy took hold of Katie's hand. "Let's go inside so you can write Loraine and let her know you'll be at the wedding."

"I—I'm afraid to go. The thought of traveling alone scares me. I don't think I can deal with all the painful memories that are there."

"Will you go to Loraine's wedding if I go with you?"

"What about Grandpa? Would he go, too?"

Grammy shook her head. "He has things to do here."

Katie couldn't imagine what things Grandpa would have to do. He was retired and spent a good deal of his time at the beach.

"What about it, Katie?" Grammy asked. "Will you go to the wedding if I go along?"

Katie sat for several seconds, thinking things through. Finally, she gave a slow nod. It would be easier going back to Indiana with Grammy along, and as soon as the wedding was over, they'd come back here.

CHAPTER 1

It sure is good to have you home," Katie's father said as they headed down the road in his buggy toward Uncle Amos and Aunt Priscilla's house. He glanced over at Katie and smiled. "Your *mamm* said Loraine was real pleased when she got your letter saying you'd be one of her attendants."

Katie clutched the folds in her dress as she stared out the window. She didn't know why she felt so edgy. She hadn't felt like this when she was in Florida. She'd been depressed after Timothy died, but not quivery inside the way she'd been since she'd climbed into Dad's buggy. She was grateful they didn't have far to go.

Dad motioned to what was left of the barn they were passing. "Take a look at the devastation from the tornado that hit this past winter. That terrible storm affected nearly everyone around these parts in some way or another."

"No one was killed, though, right?"

"No, but some were injured, and the damage was great. Many, like Wayne's folks, lost their homes, barns, and shops. It's a good thing the house Wayne started building before he lost his leg didn't sustain any damage from the tornado," Dad said. "Several of the men in our community finished it for him, and Wayne's folks have been livin' in it ever since."

"Will they continue living there after Loraine and Wayne get married?" Katie asked.

Dad nodded. "At least until their own house is done."

Katie knew from some of the things Loraine had said in her letters that she and Ada hadn't always gotten along so well. She wondered how things would be with them both living under the same roof.

"Look at the Chupps' place." Dad pointed to the left. "They lost their barn, his buggy shop, and the house. Only those who've actually seen the destruction of a tornado like we had here can even imagine such a sight."

Katie gripped the edge of the seat. "I don't understand why God allows such horrible things to happen."

He shrugged his broad shoulders. "It's not our place to question God. His ways are not our ways."

Katie clamped her teeth together in an effort to keep from saying what was on her mind. Dad wouldn't understand if she told him how angry she was with God for taking Timothy. He'd probably give her a lecture and say it was Timothy's time to die, as he'd said to her on the day of Timothy's funeral.

"Do you know how long you'll be helping at Loraine's?" Dad asked.

"Probably most of the day, since I'm sure there's a lot to be done before the wedding. You can come by sometime before supper and pick me up, or I can ask someone to give me a ride home."

"I don't mind coming back for you. I'll be here around four, okay?"

"That's fine, but if we get done sooner, I'll just ask for a ride home."

"Sounds good." Dad guided the horse up Uncle Amos's driveway and directed him toward the barn. When they stopped at the hitching rail, Dad turned to Katie and said, "Have a good day, and don't work too hard. You're lookin' kind of peaked today."

"I'll be fine, Dad." Katie climbed out of the buggy and headed to the house. She wasn't fine at all. It seemed strange being back here again. She'd only been gone from home a little over six months, but it seemed a lot longer.

She noticed several people in the yard pulling weeds and

planting flowers but didn't see any sign of Loraine or her folks. She figured they must be in the house.

When she stepped onto the back porch, she drew in a shaky breath. She wished Grammy or Mom would have come with her today instead of going shopping in Shipshewana. Katie figured since Mom and Grammy hadn't seen each other for several months, they probably wanted to spend some time alone.

Just as Katie lifted her hand to knock on the back door, it swung open. Loraine stepped onto the porch and gave Katie a hug. "It's so good to have you home! *Danki* for coming. It means a lot for me to have you and Ella as my attendants."

"Danki for asking me." Katie forced a smile. In some ways, it was good to be here, but she felt as out of place as a chicken in a duck pond.

"I just wish Jolene could be here, too."

"She's not coming?"

"Huh-uh. Her aunt's been dealing with carpal tunnel on both of her wrists, and she recently had surgery to correct the problem. Jolene thought it'd be best if she stayed in Pennsylvania to help out."

"That makes sense. But do you think Jolene will ever come back to Indiana?" Katie asked.

"I hope so." Loraine opened the door and motioned Katie inside. "Ella and her sister Charlene are in the kitchen. We decided to have a snack before we head out to the barn to help decorate the tables for the wedding meal."

When Katie entered the kitchen behind Loraine, she saw Ella and Charlene sitting at the table.

Ella jumped up, raced over to Katie, and gave her a hug that nearly took Katie's breath away. "It's so good to see you! We've all missed you so much!"

Katie smiled. "I've missed you, too."

"Would you like a glass of iced tea?" Loraine asked.

Katie nodded and took a seat at the table.

"How about a piece of my sister's *appeditlich* friendship bread?" Charlene motioned to the plate of bread on the table.

"I'm sure the bread's delicious, but I'm not really hungry right now."

"As skinny as you are, you oughta eat the whole loaf." Charlene's eyebrows lifted high. "Are you sure you're not hungry?"

Katie shook her head.

Ella shot her sister a look of disapproval, but Charlene didn't seem to notice. She was busy cutting herself another hunk of bread.

"Didn't you have a birthday last month?" Charlene asked, her mouth full.

Katie nodded. "I turned twenty."

Charlene grabbed her glass and took a drink. "You'd sure never know it. Why, you don't look like you're more than sixteen." She pointed to herself. "I look older than you."

Katie groaned inwardly. She didn't need the reminder that she looked young for her age. She couldn't help it if she was short, petite, and had the face of a teenager. *At least I act more mature than my sixteen-year-old cousin,* she thought.

"I got a letter from Jolene last week," Ella said. "She won't be coming to Loraine's wedding because—"

"She already knows," Loraine interrupted. "I told her about Jolene's aunt when we were out on the porch."

"I wonder if Jolene's using her aunt's surgery as an excuse not to come home. She might be afraid that she won't fit in with the rest of us now that she can't hear," Charlene put in.

Ella shot her sister another look. "I'm sure that's not the reason. Jolene would never make up an excuse not to come to the wedding."

Katie's shoulders tensed as she shifted her gaze to the window. What would her cousins think if they knew she hadn't wanted to come home for the wedding? Did they have any idea how hard it had been for her to make the trip? Even with Grammy along, Katie had felt anxious on the bus ride. Every horn honk and sudden stop had sent shivers up her spine. She knew she couldn't have made the trip home alone. Even though she wasn't looking forward to riding the bus again, she looked forward to going back to Florida where there were no painful reminders of the past.

Loraine stood. "Would anyone like to see my wedding dress?"

Charlene's hand shot up. "I would!"

"Me, too," Ella said.

Katie nodded as well.

"I'll be right back." Loraine scurried out of the room.

Charlene nudged Katie's arm. "What's it like in Pinecraft? That's where your *grossmudder* lives, isn't it?"

Katie nodded as she fiddled with the edge of the tablecloth. "As you know, Pinecraft is the section of Sarasota where many Plain People have homes or come to rent. It's a nice community."

"Is it true that there are no horses and buggies?" Charlene asked.

Katie nodded. "Unless they're going out of the area and need to hire a driver, everyone either walks or rides a bike."

"Do you go to the beach very often?" Ella questioned.

"*Jah*. Grandpa and I go there a lot. We enjoy looking for shells, and Grandpa likes to fish."

Charlene sighed. "I wish I could visit Florida sometime. I'm sure I'd enjoy being on the beach."

"Maybe you can visit me there sometime."

Ella's eyes widened. "You're going back?"

"Of course. My home's in Pinecraft now."

The room got deathly quiet. Ella and Charlene stared at each other as though in disbelief.

Katie figured it was time for a change of subject. "Who did Wayne choose to be his attendants?" she asked.

"Jolene's *bruder*, Andrew, and Freeman Bontrager," Ella replied. "Wayne and Freeman have become good friends since Freeman and his sister, Fern, moved back to Indiana a few months ago."

"Freeman opened a bicycle shop," Charlene added. "Mom and Dad bought me a new bike for my birthday in February."

"Oh, I see." Katie stifled a yawn. She'd had trouble falling asleep last night.

"Freeman won't be helping here today because he has lots of work at the shop." Charlene sipped her iced tea. "You should see all the bikes he has. I'll bet he'd do real well if he had a shop in Sarasota, since so many people ride bikes there."

"Here it is," Loraine said, sweeping into the room with a khaki green dress draped over her arm. "I'll wear a full white apron over the front of the dress, of course." She held it out to Katie. "What do you think?"

With trembling fingers and a wave of envy, Katie touched the smooth piece of fabric. "It—it's very nice."

"Are you okay?" Loraine asked with a look of concern. "Your hand's shaking."

Katie dropped both hands into her lap and clutched the folds in her dress. "I'm fine. Just a bit shaky because I didn't have much breakfast."

"Then you oughta have a piece of this." Charlene pushed the plate of friendship bread toward Katie. "You'll blow away in a strong wind if you don't put some meat on your bones."

Katie ground her teeth until her jaw began to ache. One of the first things Mom had said to her when she'd arrived home was that she needed to gain some weight. Of course, Dad had mentioned it, too.

"Charlene's right." Ella spoke up. "If you're feeling shaky, then you should eat something."

"Maybe you're right." Katie grabbed a piece of bread and took a bite. Then she washed it down with a sip of iced tea.

Bam! The screen door swung open, causing Katie to nearly jump out of her seat. Walking with a slow, stiff gait, Wayne entered the room. His face broke into a wide smile when he saw Katie. *"Wie geht's?"*

"I'm fine." The lie rolled off Katie's tongue much too easily. She was getting used to telling people what she thought they wanted to hear.

Wayne moved across the room and stood beside Loraine's chair. "We're sure glad you could come for the wedding."

Katie forced a smile and nodded.

"Would you like to see my new leg?" Before she could respond, Wayne pulled up his pant leg, exposing his prosthesis.

Katie bit back a gasp. "D—does it hurt?" She could hardly get the words out.

"It did at first, but I've pretty well adjusted to it now." Wayne took a seat beside Loraine. "It could have been worse, and I'm grateful to be alive."

Uneasiness tightened Katie's chest, and she blew out a slow, shaky breath. Seeing him like this was a reminder of what she'd caused—and what she'd lost.

Wayne reached around Ella and grabbed a piece of bread. "Looks like you've been baking again, huh, Ella?"

She nodded. "It keeps me busy when I'm not helping my *daed* in his business."

"Those wind chimes he makes are so nice," Loraine said. "I might buy one soon, to hang on our porch."

"You won't have to do that," Charlene said. "Dad and Mom are planning to give you one of his nicest sets of wind chimes for a wedding present."

Ella poked her sister's arm. "It was supposed to be a surprise."

Charlene covered her mouth. "Oops."

Loraine poured another glass of iced tea and handed it to Wayne. "How are things going outside?"

"Pretty good. By the end of the day, I think your folks' yard will look like a park." He grinned and lifted his glass to take a drink. "This sure hits the spot. It's getting mighty warm out there. Much warmer than normal for April, I think."

"That's fine with me," Loraine said. "A warm spring day is exactly what I wished we'd have on our wedding day. I hope the weather stays just like it is—at least until Thursday."

Katie stared out the kitchen window, blinking back tears of envy and frustration. *I'd give anything if it were me and Timothy getting married in two days. Oh Lord, please give me the strength to get through Loraine's wedding.*

CHAPTER 2

Katie squinted against the sunlight streaming through the open window of her bedroom. Today was her cousin's wedding day, and no matter how much she dreaded going, she knew she was expected to be there on time.

Forcing herself to sit up, she swung her legs over the edge of the bed. Shuffling across the room, she peered out the window. The sky was a deep indigo blue, and the sun shone so brightly she had to shield her eyes from its glare. Loraine had gotten her wish—it was going to be another warm day. Katie wished she could spend the day sitting on the grassy banks by the pond behind their house instead of going to the wedding and putting on a happy face. No matter how bad she felt, though, she couldn't let on to Loraine or anyone else in her family. Only Grammy knew that Katie hadn't fully recovered from Timothy's death, and even she didn't know the full extent of Katie's emotional state.

She sighed and turned away from the window. It was time to get dressed and help Mom with breakfast.

❧ ❧

"Are you sure you really have to leave the day after tomorrow?" Katie heard Mom say as she approached the kitchen.

"Jah, I need to get back home in time for my friend Anna's birthday," Grammy said. "Anna's a recent widow, and several of her friends are getting together to take her out for lunch, and then I'll need to. . ." Grammy's voice lowered, and Katie couldn't hear the rest of what she said. Well, it didn't matter; Katie was relieved to know they'd be returning to Sarasota soon. Even though she didn't look forward to riding on the bus again, it would be a welcome relief to get back to a place where she felt free from so many reminders of the past.

When Katie stepped into the kitchen, she was greeted by a friendly smile from Grammy, who stood at the sink filling the coffeepot with water.

"Didn't you sleep well, Katie?" Mom asked, moving away from the stove, where she'd been frying a slab of bacon. *"Du bischt awwer verschlofe heit."*

Katie yawned and stretched her arms over her head. "I guess I am sleepyheaded. I had trouble sleeping."

"You were probably excited about the wedding today, jah?"

Katie nodded and forced a smile. She felt nervous about being one of Loraine's attendants, but if she admitted that to Mom, she'd probably be given a bunch of suggestions on how to relax.

"I know I've said this before, but it's awfully good to have you home." Mom gave Katie a hug. "Your daed and I have missed you so much. So have your brothers and their families."

"I. . .I missed you all, too." Katie looked around, anxious for something to do—anything to keep her hands busy. "Is there something you'd like me to do?" she asked.

"Why don't you scramble up some eggs?" Mom pointed to the refrigerator. "Your daed brought in some fresh ones earlier, so there should be plenty."

Katie took a carton of eggs from the refrigerator and set it on the counter. When she removed a bowl from the cupboard she bumped her arm. The bowl slipped out of her hand and crashed to the floor.

"*Ach*, Katie, watch what you're doing!" Mom's forehead wrinkled. "Are you feeling *naerfich* about the wedding? Your hands are sure shaking."

"Guess I am a little nervous. This is the first wedding I've been asked to take part in."

Katie went down on her knees to pick the bowl up, relieved that it hadn't broken.

When she stood, Mom said, "Are you okay?"

"I'm fine."

"I've got the coffee going now, so Katie, why don't you let me scramble the eggs?" Grammy smiled. "Then you can have a seat at the table and visit with your mamm and me until your daed comes in to eat."

Katie shook her head. "I don't need to sit. I want to help with breakfast."

"Then why don't you run down to the basement for me? I'd like to have a jar of my homemade salsa to put on the table." Mom smiled. "You know how much your daed likes salsa on his eggs."

"Okay." Katie grabbed a flashlight from a wall peg near the door and hurried from the room. When she reached the basement, she lit a gas lamp and made her way to the area where Mom kept all her canning goods. Several shelves were loaded with an array of jars filled with peaches, pears, beets, carrots, and several other fruits and vegetables, as well as the salsa. As she reached for some salsa, something furry brushed her bare foot.

Katie jumped as a little gray mouse skittered past her and ducked into a hole across the room. *Calm down*, she told herself. *It's just a little* maus.

She grabbed the jar of salsa, turned off the gas lamp, and hurried up the stairs.

"I think Dad needs to set some mousetraps in the basement," Katie said to Mom when she entered the kitchen. "I saw a maus down there."

Mom pursed her lips. "I thought he had set some traps. Guess he'll need to set a few more."

"A few more what?" Dad asked, walking through the doorway.

"Mousetraps," Mom said. "Katie saw a maus in the basement."

"I'll take care of it after we get home from the wedding." Dad hurried to the sink and washed his hands. "Is breakfast ready? We'll need to get going soon."

Mom nodded. "Sit yourself down, and we'll put things on the table."

After everyone was seated, they bowed their heads for silent prayer. Katie prayed for strength to get through the day and asked God to calm her racing heart.

When the prayer was done, they hurried through their meal, although Katie only picked at the food on her plate. How could she eat when it felt as if a brigade of butterflies was fluttering around in her stomach?

She pushed her chair away from the table and was about to grab her plate when Mom said, "You'd better eat more than that if you're going to make it through the day, Katie."

"I can't eat any more."

"It'll be a long time until the first wedding meal's served. I really think you should—"

"Let the girl be, JoAnn," Dad said. "If she's hungry, she'll eat."

Katie was relieved when Mom didn't press the issue. It was bad enough that her stomach was tied in knots; she didn't need Mom pestering her to eat.

When the kitchen had been cleaned up and dishes were done, Katie and her family hurried outside and climbed into Dad's buggy.

The buggy horse stamped nervously, obviously anxious to be on his way. Katie sure wasn't anxious to go. The more she thought about her part in Loraine's wedding, the more nervous she became. The only thing that might make it a little easier to get through the day was knowing that in just a few days, she and Grandma would be on their way to Florida.

~❧ ❧~

"Are you naerfich?" Freeman asked Wayne when he joined him and Loraine's cousin Andrew outside the Hershbergers' buggy shed where the wedding service would be held.

Wayne gave a quick nod and clasped his hands together. "I've never felt more nervous, but I'm feeling *glicklich* to be marrying the woman I love."

17

"So if you're feeling lucky, then you must not be gettin' cold feet."

"Just one cold foot." Wayne pointed to his artificial limb. "This foot doesn't feel anything at all." He chuckled and punched Andrew's arm.

Andrew snickered. "I've never known anyone who liked to joke around the way you do."

"What about Jake? He always has lots of funny stories."

"Speaking of Jake," Freeman spoke up, "will he be coming today?"

Wayne shook his head. "I got a letter from him last week. Said he was busy at the horse ranch in Montana and wouldn't be able to make it to our wedding."

Freeman had a feeling the reason Jake wasn't coming to this special event had more to do with the fact that he used to date Loraine than it did with him being too busy. He couldn't really blame him. It would be hard for any man to watch the woman he loved marry someone else. Not that Freeman knew anything about that personally. He was twenty-two years old but had only had a couple of girlfriends so far. He'd never been serious about either of them.

"Looks like Loraine and her attendants are heading this way," Andrew said, nudging Wayne's arm.

Freeman glanced to his left. Ella walked beside Loraine, and he recognized Katie Miller, the shorter of the two, walking with her. He hadn't seen Katie since he'd moved to Ohio with his family several years ago, but he didn't think she'd changed much. Same emerald green eyes, shiny brown hair, and turned-up nose. She was only two years younger than him, but she looked more like a fifteen-year-old girl than she did a woman.

"Are you ready for this?" Loraine asked, stepping up to Wayne.

He grinned down at her. "I'm a bit naerfich, but I'm more than ready to make you my *fraa*."

Loraine's cheeks turned pink when she smiled at her groom. Then she turned to Freeman and said, "You remember my cousin Katie, don't you?"

"Of course." He smiled at Katie. "It's good to see you again."

She gave a nod but averted her gaze.

Freeman remembered how when they were children, Katie had been a little chatterbox. She'd always asked their teacher a lot of questions and often whispered to her friends when she should have been paying attention.

Freeman heard some laughter and glanced to his right. Eunice Byler was walking across the yard with her parents and twelve-year-old brother, Richard. The Bylers had moved to Indiana a few weeks ago, after leaving Pennsylvania in search of more land. Eunice's dad had stopped by Freeman's bicycle shop a few days after they'd moved and purchased bikes for Eunice and Richard. Since that time, Eunice had come by the shop a couple of times to ask Freeman some questions about her bike.

"It's time for us to go in now." Wayne leaned closer to Loraine. "Just think, by this time next year, we'll be celebrating our first anniversary."

"You might even have a *boppli* by then," Ella said with a twinkle in her eyes.

※ ※

The wedding service seemed to drag on and on as the congregation sang songs and listened to the messages being preached by some of the visiting ministers. It was so hot inside the building that steam had formed around the edges of the windows.

When Loraine and Wayne finally stood in front of the bishop to say their vows, Katie noticed that Wayne's eyes glistened with tears, although his face wore a broad smile, as did Loraine's.

"Can you confess, brother, that you accept this, our sister, as your wife, and that you will not leave her until death separates you?" the bishop asked Wayne.

Without hesitation, Wayne nodded and said, "Yes."

Katie blinked against a rush of tears as a sense of unease grew within her like a gathering storm. She attempted to focus on what the bishop was saying to Loraine, but the rapid rhythm of her heartbeat made if difficult to stay focused. The unexplained fear she felt increased, and a nauseous bile rose in her throat.

I need to concentrate on something else. Katie glanced to the other side of the room where several young boys sat. They looked bored. One of them chewed gum. Another twiddled his fingers. A third boy stared out the window with a look of longing on his face. Did he wish to be outside as much as Katie did?

She looked at the section where the men sat. One young father held his sleeping young son in his lap. Another sat with a restless baby in his arms.

Her gaze swung to the other side of the room. Some of the younger girls sat quietly whispering to one another, and a few of them held their dolls in their laps.

Hearing a baby cry, Katie's attention was drawn to the benches where some of the young mothers sat. One woman held a baby against her shoulder and was gently patting its back. Another, whose baby had fallen asleep, stroked the infant's flushed cheek with her thumb.

" 'Husbands love your wives, even as Christ also loved the church, and gave himself for it,' " the bishop quoted from Ephesians 5:25.

Katie's face heated up then broke into a cold sweat. Her hands felt frozen, yet the air in the room was stifling. It felt as if something heavy was pushing on her chest. Her stomach clenched. She needed some air. She needed to get out of this room!

With no thought of what anyone might think, Katie jumped up and raced out the door.

CHAPTER 3

Katie's legs shook as she stood outside the Hershbergers' buggy shed trying to cool off and calm her racing heart. The fresh scent of earth coming from the first warm days of spring offered little comfort. She couldn't believe she'd gotten up in the middle of Loraine and Wayne's wedding vows and rushed outside. She couldn't believe she was such a ball of nerves.

There must be something wrong with me. Am I losing my mind? A shudder rippled through Katie. When she had been sitting in that buggy shed, she'd felt as if she was going to die. Was that how Timothy had felt right before his life was snuffed out?

A gentle hand touched Katie's shoulder, and she whirled around. Ella stood behind her with a worried expression.

"Are you okay? You look *umgerennt.*"

Katie shook her head. "I'm not upset. It was so hot in there, and I—I needed some fresh air." She fanned her face with her hands and blew out a quick breath.

"Your face looks flushed. Maybe you should go up to the house and get a drink of water."

"I'm okay now. I just need to stay out here awhile so I can cool down."

"The wedding will be over soon, and then we'll be heading over to Aunt Priscilla and Uncle Amos's place for the first meal of the day. Maybe you'll feel better once you've had something to eat."

"Jah, maybe so." Katie wished she didn't have to go to even one of the wedding meals, but with her being one of Loraine's attendants, she didn't see any way she could get out of it.

Ella slipped her arm around Katie's waist. "Are you sure you're all right?"

"I'm fine. I just need to be alone for a while."

Ella looked stunned. "You're not going back inside for the rest of the wedding?"

"No."

"I'll wait out here with you then."

Katie shook her head. "It wouldn't look right if we both stayed out here. Everyone will wonder what's going on."

"You're probably right. Guess I'd better get back inside."

When Ella left, Katie decided to start walking up the road to Uncle Amos and Aunt Priscilla's house. Maybe her help would be needed in the kitchen. At least that would occupy her hands and hopefully keep her from thinking too many negative thoughts.

～❦❦～

"How come you left the wedding?" Loraine asked when she stepped into her mother's kitchen and found Katie mixing a fruit salad.

"It was too warm in there, and I needed some air." Katie glanced past Loraine's shoulder. "Where's Wayne? Shouldn't the two of you be seated at your table by now?"

Loraine nodded. "And so should our attendants."

Katie's face flamed. "I'm—uh—busy helping here."

"You're not one of the cooks, you know. You're supposed to be with the wedding party."

Katie dropped her gaze to the floor. "I'll be there as soon as I'm done with the salad."

"I can do that for you." Selma Hershberger scurried across the room and took the spoon from Katie.

As Loraine followed Katie out the door, she felt concerned. Not only had Katie run outside in the middle of the wedding, but she was acting awfully strange. It seemed as though she'd rather be helping in the kitchen than joining the others at the wedding meal. What happened to the old Katie who used to be full of laughter and enjoyed being with people?

When they entered the barn where the tables had been set up a few days before, Loraine took a seat on the left side of her groom, while Ella seated herself beside Loraine, with Katie next to her. Andrew and Freeman took seats on the right side of Wayne.

Loraine looked over at Ella and said, "I've smiled so much already today that the muscles in my cheeks are beginning to ache."

"It's been a happy, blessed day, and you have every right to smile." Ella squeezed Loraine's arm. "Seeing two people I care so much about come together as husband and wife brought tears to my eyes."

"It brought a few tears to my eyes as well," Loraine said.

"Same here." Wayne leaned closer to Loraine. "When the bishop asked if I'd accept you as my wife and never leave until death separates us, I got so choked up I wasn't sure I could answer his question."

Loraine reached under the table and clasped Wayne's hand. "When I think of how close I came to losing you, I get choked up, too."

He squeezed her fingers in response. "I hope we never take each other for granted. I want us to teach our *kinner* to appreciate their family and live each day to the fullest."

"I agree with that." Loraine glanced over at Katie. She still seemed sad and nervous. She hadn't said more than a few words to anyone since they'd sat down at the table. Was she missing Timothy? Was she thinking about the wedding they'd never have?

As they bowed their heads for silent prayer before the meal began, Loraine thanked God for her new husband and asked Him to bless all of her family—especially Katie.

⊱ ⊰

"With all this food being served here, I hate to think of how full we'll be by the end of the day," Freeman said to Andrew.

Andrew chuckled and reached for the bowl of fruit salad

one of the waiters had just put on the table. "Think maybe I'll run around awhile between each of the meals that will be served throughout the day. When I get tired of that, I might make some animal balloons for some of the kinner."

Freeman's interest was piqued. "I didn't know you could do that. Is it hard to learn?"

"Some of the basic balloon animals are fairly easy, but a few of them are pretty difficult to make." Andrew shoveled a heaping spoonful of fruit salad onto his plate. "The hardest part of making balloon animals is blowing 'em up."

"Does it take a lot of air?"

"Sure does, which is why I usually use the hand pump when I've got a lot of balloons to blow up."

"Making balloon animals sounds like fun," Freeman said as Andrew passed him the salad bowl.

"It is, and so are balloons I make look like flowers. The beagle on a bike is my favorite one, though."

"Beagle on a bike, huh? Now that sounds like the kind of balloon I should to learn to make."

"I'd be glad to show you sometime," Andrew offered.

Freeman shrugged. "Guess we'll have to see how it goes. Between my job at the bike shop and your job at the harness shop in Topeka, neither one of us has a lot of free time."

"That's true, but I'll make the time if you're interested."

"I'm definitely interested, so I'll let you know when we can." Freeman glanced at the tables where some of the young women sat and caught Eunice looking at him. He smiled and gave her a nod. She returned his smile with one of her own. Her shiny blond hair and vivid blue eyes made her stand out in the crowd. He figured it wouldn't take her long to find a boyfriend. Next year at this time, she could even be the one getting married.

He looked past the bridal couple and noticed Katie. There wasn't much food on her plate, and what was there looked like it had hardly been touched. *I wonder if she's on a diet.*

Freeman shook his head. Katie Miller didn't need to lose any weight. If anything, she needed to gain a few pounds. He had a feeling something was going on with Katie. She'd been acting kind of strange all day. The way she'd run out during the wedding made him wonder if she might be sick.

"Here you go," Andrew said, handing Freeman a platter of fried chicken.

"Danki." Freeman forked a piece onto his plate and handed the platter to Wayne. Then he turned his attention back to Katie again. She fidgeted in her chair, and her hand shook as she reached for her glass of water and took a drink.

She's either sick or nervous about something, he decided. *The way she's acting makes me think. . .*

"Here's some more food to put on your plate." Andrew handed Freeman a bowl of mashed potatoes and then some gravy and bread filling.

Freeman helped himself and passed the bowls along. As he ate his meal, he kept glancing at Katie. She didn't look well at all.

～≈ ≈～

The napkin in front of Katie bore nothing but crumbs, and she didn't even remember eating the roll that had been on her plate. That same panicky feeling she'd had during the wedding was coming over her again. She didn't want to make a fool of herself by rushing outside, so she reached for her glass of water and took a drink. *I'll never make it through the rest of the day. Help me, Lord.*

She glanced at the smiling newlyweds and wondered how she could make her escape without arousing too much suspicion. Leaning close to Ella, she whispered, "I'm not feeling so well. I think I'd better go home."

Deep wrinkles formed across Ella's forehead. "What's wrong. Are you *grank*?"

Katie's chin quivered, and her throat felt so clogged she could barely speak. "I. . .I'm not sure."

"Do you want me to see if I can find your folks?"

"No, I can do that. Please explain things to Loraine for me, would you?"

"Sure." Ella patted Katie's arm in a motherly fashion. "I hope you feel better soon."

Katie was on the verge of saying she hoped so, too, when she was hit by a sudden wave of nausea. She covered her mouth, jumped up, and bolted from the room.

Outside, she drew in a couple of deep breaths and was relieved when the nausea finally subsided. Then her head started to pound. Maybe she really was sick. She might be coming down with the flu.

She glanced around the yard and spotted her father standing near the barn talking to Uncle Amos. She hurried over to him and said, "Can you take me home, Dad? I'm not feeling well."

"Are you grank?" he asked with a look of concern.

She nodded. "I've got a *koppweh,* and my stomach's upset."

"Maybe it's one of those sick headaches," Uncle Amos spoke up. "My fraa gets 'em sometimes when she's feeling stressed out."

"Are you feeling stressed?" Dad asked Katie.

She shook her head. "I think I might be coming down with the flu."

"I'd better take you home then." Dad motioned to the long line of buggies parked in the field. "You can wait in our buggy while I get your mamm and grossmudder."

"Why don't you let them stay awhile? You can take me home and then come back here to enjoy the rest of your day."

Dad frowned. "Your mamm wouldn't like the idea of you goin' home alone if you're sick."

"I'm not that sick, and there's no reason for her to know."

"You sure about that? I mean, if you think you need—"

"I'll be fine once I'm home and can lie down awhile."

"Okay." Dad started walking toward the horses, and Katie sprinted for their buggy. She could hardly wait to get home.

As they headed down the road, Katie spotted an Amish couple sitting under a gazebo in their front yard. Two small children played nearby. Katie's heart ached at the sight of them. She longed to have a husband and children of her own.

When Dad turned off the main road and into their driveway, the horse picked up speed and headed straight for the barn. As soon as the buggy came to a stop, Katie hopped out. "I'll see you later, Dad!"

Her feet churned against the grass as she raced for the house. Flinging the door open, she leaned against the wall and drew in a couple of deep breaths. Her head still hurt, and her stomach hadn't completely settled, but she felt safer and calmer than she had all day.

The stairs creaked as Katie made her way up to her room. When she opened the door, a blast of warm air hit her full in the face. She hurried to open the window, and when a trickle of air floated into the room, she breathed deeply. She stood there several seconds then flopped onto her bed.

Plumping up the pillow, she closed her eyes and tried to relax. She hoped Loraine wasn't too upset that she'd skipped out like that. She'd really had no other choice, for if she'd stayed at the table, she might have thrown up or even passed out.

Uninvited tears seeped from under Katie's lashes. She'd never felt sick enough to run away from a gathering like that, and the fearful thoughts she'd had today made no sense at all.

She opened her eyes and dabbed at the wetness beneath them. She tried to pray, but no words would come. Looking ahead to the future caused Katie's feelings of anxiety to return. After all, what kind of a future was there for someone like her?

CHAPTER 4

When Katie came downstairs the following morning, she heard whispered voices coming from the kitchen. A sense of dread balled in her stomach when Grammy said, "I agree with you, Jeremy. Katie's been living with us long enough. Under the circumstances, I think it's best if she remains here with you and JoAnn."

Katie rushed into the kitchen, but before she could open her mouth to protest, Mom turned in her chair and said, *"Mir hen yuscht vun dir ghat."*

Katie's head bobbed up and down as she swallowed around the lump in her throat. "I know you were talking about me. I heard Grammy say she didn't want me to go back to Florida with her."

Grammy shook her head. "I never said that, Katie. I said I thought under the circumstances that you need to stay here."

"What circumstances?"

Grammy rose from her chair and slipped her arm around Katie's waist. "Grandpa and I won't be living in Florida much longer, so—"

Katie's mouth fell open. "What? Where are you going?"

"We're moving to Wisconsin to be closer to my sister, Mary. She's been widowed for sometime and is having some health problems, so we've decided to move there and help her out."

"That's the reason my daed didn't come to Indiana with my mamm," Mom said. "He needed to stay in Sarasota and get the

28

house ready to rent out."

Katie groaned as she sank into a chair at the table. "Why wasn't I told about this sooner?"

Grammy's face turned crimson. "We didn't want to upset you. Your grandpa and I thought that after you came back here and saw everyone again, you'd be more receptive to the idea of staying."

Katie folded her arms and frowned. "I was looking forward to going back to Florida. I. . .I like it there."

"We know you do, but we're not going to be there, and it's best that you stay here with your folks."

Katie gave a woeful shake of her head. "I can't stay. There are too many painful memories here."

"You can't run from the past for the rest of your life," Mom said.

Katie clasped Grammy's arm. "Can't you just go to Wisconsin to help Mary for a while and then move back to Florida when she's better?"

"I'm not sure she'll ever be better, and we're going to do what we think is best for Mary," Grammy said.

Doesn't anyone care what's best for me? Katie bit her bottom lip in an effort to keep from crying. She knew she was being selfish, but the thought of Grandpa and Grandma leaving Florida, where she'd felt safe these last several months, made her nausea return. She'd be happier in Florida. She'd even made a few friends there. How could they expect her to stay here with all her painful memories?

"Maybe I could get a job and rent your house in Pinecraft," Katie said, feeling more desperate by the minute.

Grammy shook her head. "We've already found someone to rent it."

"Now that we've got everything settled," Dad said before Katie could protest further, "let's eat breakfast so I can get to work making windows in my shop, and you and your mamm can open your stamp shop."

Mom looked over at Katie. "I was hoping you could work by yourself for a few hours this afternoon while I go to my dental appointment."

A sense of panic seized Katie, and she gripped the edge of her chair. "You want me to work there alone?"

Before Mom could reply, Grammy spoke up. "If there's anything I can do at the shop, I'd be happy to help out."

Katie breathed a sigh of relief. She hadn't worked in the stamp shop for several months. The thought of waiting on customers made her feel apprehensive. "I'd appreciate the help," she said with a nod.

❧ ❧

"Would you like some more eggs?" Freeman's grandmother asked, smiling at him from across the table.

He shook his head. "No thanks. I've got lots to do today, so I'd better get out to my shop." He stood.

"How late do you plan to work today?" Grandma asked.

Freeman shrugged. "Don't know. Guess that all depends on how much work I get done."

"I hope you'll be finished in time for us to take Fern out to supper like we'd planned."

Freeman's forehead wrinkled. "We're taking Fern to supper?"

Grandma sighed. "I'm glad she went to town early this morning to do some shopping. I wouldn't want her to hear that her bruder has obviously forgotten that today's her birthday."

Freeman's face heated up. "Oh, that's right. Guess it must have slipped my mind."

Grandma held up her hand. "No need to offer an excuse. Just make sure you're done working in time to take us to supper."

"Okay." Freeman started across the room and was about to pluck his hat off the wall peg when he turned back around. "Do you have any idea what Fern might like for her birthday? Has she dropped any hints?"

Grandma shook her head. "She's given me no hints, but I know she's been working on a scrapbook the last few months. Maybe some rubber stamps would be appreciated."

"Is that what you planned to give her?"

"No. I made her something for her hope chest." Grandma sipped her coffee. "If you can spare the time, why don't you go over to the Millers' stamp shop today and see what you can find."

Freeman nodded. "I'll try to do that during my lunch hour."

Grandma smiled. "Would you like me to take a sandwich out to you shortly before noon so you can eat while you're riding over to the Millers'?"

"That won't be necessary. I'll pick something up on my way back home." Freeman plopped his hat on his head and hurried out the door.

When he entered his shop a few minutes later, he lit the gas lamps then quickly set to work on a bike one of their English neighbors had brought in for repairs.

He'd only been working a short time when the shop door opened and Eunice stepped in.

"Wie geht's?" she asked with a cheerful smile.

"Can't complain. How about you?"

"I'm doing well." Her smile widened as she moved closer to him. "Looks like you're hard at work."

He nodded. "Always have something to do, it seems."

"I'm still enjoying the bicycle my daed bought for me."

"Glad you like it."

She squatted down beside him and leaned so close that he could see the smattering of light-colored freckles on her nose. "The bike you're working on looks like a nice one. How many speeds does it have?"

"It's a 21-speed, just like yours."

"What's wrong with it?"

Freeman motioned to the back of the bike. "The wheel's bent, the chain's messed up, and one of the pedals is broken."

"What happened?"

"Wally Andrews, the owner of the bike, took a bad spill the other day."

"Was he hurt?"

"Just a few scrapes and bruises." Freeman grimaced. "The bike took the worst of it."

"You sure seem to know what you're doing. How long have you been repairing bikes?"

31

"Since I was sixteen. My uncle in Ohio trained me well." Freeman reached for the wrench lying on the floor beside Eunice. "The last time you were here, you mentioned that you'd been looking for a job. Have you found one yet?"

She shook her head. "No one seems to be hiring right now. Things are tight all over."

"I know. Hopefully, once the tourists begin pouring into Shipshewana when the flea market opens next month, some jobs will come open."

"I hope so." Eunice offered him another pleasant smile. "If you're not too busy this afternoon, would you like to come over to my house for lunch? My mamm fixed too much chicken corn soup for supper last night. You'd be doing us a favor if you helped us eat some of it for lunch."

"I appreciate the offer, but I have an errand to run during my lunch hour."

Her pale eyebrows furrowed. "That's too bad. If you came for lunch, it would give us a chance to get better acquainted."

"Maybe some other time."

A light danced in her eyes. "You mean it?"

He nodded.

"How about coming over for supper this evening?"

"I can't. Today's my sister's birthday. I'll be taking her and my grossmudder to supper."

"Oh, I see." Eunice sighed. "I'm going to be busy helping my mamm with the garden the first part of next week, but what about Saturday? Would you be free to have lunch with me then?"

Freeman shook his head. "That's the day of the school program and potluck meal. Since my sister's one of the teachers, I think she'd like me to be there."

"Oh, that's right, I'd forgotten about the program. When would you be free?"

"How about the following Saturday?"

"All right then." Eunice stood and smoothed the wrinkles in her dress. "Guess I'd better let you get back to work. See you at church tomorrow, Freeman."

As the door shut behind Eunice, Freeman slapped the side of his head. "I hope she doesn't think we're a courting couple just because I agreed to have lunch with her in a few weeks."

~❦ ❦~

By the time Katie and Grammy had been working in the stamp shop a few hours, Katie had begun to relax. She'd almost forgotten how much she enjoyed the work.

Grammy placed a stack of off-white cardstock on one of the shelves. "There are so many interesting things in this shop. I think it must be a fun place to work."

Katie nodded. "I was just thinking that. When I worked here with Mom before I went to Florida, and we weren't waiting on customers or stocking shelves, we used to take a few minutes out to work on our own scrapbooking projects. We also liked to make cards that we could give to our friends and family on special occasions."

Grammy nodded. "Your mamm has sent me several of her homemade cards over the years, and I've always enjoyed getting them. I think a homemade card's so much more personal than one that's bought in a store."

Katie was about to comment when the bell above the shop door jingled and Loraine walked in. "How are you today?" she asked, stepping up to Katie. "I was worried when you left the wedding meal."

"Didn't Ella tell you I left early because I wasn't feeling well?"

Loraine nodded. "But I wanted to come by and find out if you're okay."

"I'm fine now."

"Glad to hear it." Loraine slipped her arm around Katie's waist. "It's good to see you working in the stamp shop again."

"Looks like I'll be working here from now on, because Grammy and Grandpa are planning to rent their place out and move to Wisconsin. That means I won't be going back to Sarasota."

Grammy explained about her sister's ill health then turned to Katie and said, "It's almost lunchtime. If you don't need me for anything right now, I think I'll go up to the house and fix us something to eat."

"That's fine," Katie said with a nod. "We can eat it out here so I won't have to close the stamp shop."

Grammy smiled at Loraine. "If you're not here when I get back, I'll see you at church tomorrow. I'll be leaving for Florida on Monday morning to finish getting ready for the move, so Sunday will be my last chance to say good-bye to everyone."

"It's been nice seeing you again," Loraine said. "I hope things go well with your move."

After Grammy left the shop, Katie started putting some stamps on the shelves. "Are you and Wayne getting settled into your new house?" she asked Loraine.

"Pretty much. We moved our wedding gifts over there yesterday after we'd finished helping clean things up at my folks' place. You probably heard that Wayne's parents lost their house when the tornado hit last winter, so they've been living in Wayne's house ever since. They'll continue to do so until their new house is finished."

"How long do you think that will be?" Katie asked.

Loraine shrugged. "Don't know. Crist and Wayne have been so busy in the taxidermy shop that they haven't had much free time to work on it. Now that spring's here, many of our Amish neighbors are busy planting their fields, so I doubt they'll get much help on the house from them, either."

"I hope it goes okay with you and Ada living under the same roof. I know you two didn't always get along so well."

"Things are better between Ada and me now. I don't think it should be too difficult to have her and Crist staying with us."

Katie motioned to the stamps she'd put on the shelf. "Mom said these recently came in, so if you need any new stamps, you might wanna choose 'em now before they're all picked over."

"Actually, I need to run some errands in Shipshe right now," Loraine said, "but maybe I'll come by sometime next week and take a look."

"Okay. I'm sure they won't all be sold by then."

Loraine gave Katie a hug. "I'm glad you're feeling better, and I'll see you at church tomorrow morning. It'll be at Ella's folks' place."

Katie nodded. She hoped sitting in her uncle's barn with a crowd of people wouldn't bother her as much as it had during Loraine's wedding.

Loraine waved as she went out the door. A few minutes later, the bell above the door jingled again. Thinking it might be Grammy with their lunch, Katie continued to stock the shelves and didn't look at the door.

"Can ya help me find something my sister might like?" a deep voice asked.

Startled, Katie dropped the stamps she'd been holding. When she turned and bumped into Freeman, she gasped.

CHAPTER 5

I...I didn't realize you were here," Katie stammered. "I mean, I thought it was my grossmudder who'd come into the shop."

Freeman smiled. "Nope, just me. Today's my sister's birthday, so I came in to see if I could find her a gift."

Katie's hand shook as she motioned to the stamps she'd already put on the shelf. She didn't know why she felt so nervous all of a sudden. She'd been perfectly calm a minute ago. "We just got in a new supply of stamps. Maybe she'd like one of them."

"This one's kind of nice." Freeman picked up a large rubber stamp with a hummingbird on it. "Ever since Fern was a *maedel,* she's liked to feed the hummingbirds that come into our yard. I'm thinkin' she'd probably like this."

"There're a couple other hummingbird stamps over there." Katie pointed to the shelf a few feet away. "They're older ones, though, so she may already have them."

"She couldn't have gotten much, since we've only been back in Indiana a few months ourselves," he said.

"My mamm's not working here today, but if you'd like to come back tomorrow, we can ask if she knows what stamps Fern has bought."

"I can't wait that long. We're going out to celebrate Fern's birthday this evening, and I'm sure she'd be real disappointed if I didn't have a gift to give her."

"Guess you'd better buy one of the newer ones then."

"I'll take the humming bird stamp, and also this one," he said, reaching for one of the larger stamps with a sunflower on it.

The bell above the door jingled once more, and Katie turned. Rita Howard, one of their English neighbors, stood in the doorway. Rita was a robust woman with curly red hair and deeply set blue eyes. As she ambled across the room toward Katie, the floor vibrated.

"I left my boys outside to play while I look around," Rita said. "I hope that's okay."

"It's fine." Katie figured having the rambunctious boys playing outside would be better than having them in the shop where they were likely to run all over the place and mess with things.

"When I was in here on Monday, your mother said she'd be getting some new stamps by the end of the week. Did they come in yet?" Rita asked.

Katie motioned to the shelf she'd been stocking. "They're right here."

"Oh good." Rita rushed toward Katie, nearly knocking her over.

Katie stepped back and bumped into Freeman. "Excuse me."

Wham! A baseball crashed through the window and hit one of the shelves, knocking several stamps to the floor. Katie screamed, and Rita rushed outside. At least no one had gotten hurt, and from what Katie could tell, nothing had been damaged, but her legs shook so badly she could barely stand.

Freeman grabbed Katie's arm. "You're trembling like a newborn colt tryin' to stand. Maybe you ought to sit down."

Feeling very unsteady, Katie wobbled across the room and sank into the chair in front of her mother's desk.

"I'll get you something cold to drink." Freeman hurried into the bathroom and returned with a paper cup full of water. "Here you go," he said, handing it to Katie.

"Danki." She took the cup and gulped down some water.

"Feel better?"

"A little."

"Take a few deep breaths. That should help you relax."

Katie did as Freeman suggested.

Ding! The shop door opened and Rita stepped in. "Sorry about the broken window," she said, stepping up to the desk where Katie sat. "Guess my boys were playing too close to the store." She reached up to rub her forehead. "I should have left 'em home with their dad today."

"Other than the broken window, no harm was done," Katie said.

"I'm glad of that, and I'll pay for whatever it costs to replace the window." Rita glanced toward the door. "I'd better gather up my boys and head for home. I'll come by sometime next week when the kids are in school and look at the new stamps you got in. Maybe by then you'll have a new window and will know how much I owe you." Without waiting for Katie's reply, Rita scurried out of the store.

Katie remained at the desk while Freeman picked up the stamps that had been knocked to the floor. When he was done, he handed Katie the stamps he'd chosen for Fern. "I'd better pay for these and get back to work. I've been gone longer than I'd planned."

Katie rang up his purchase and had just put the stamps in a paper sack when Grammy burst into the room. "A *deichel* broke, and there's water running all over your mamm's kitchen floor!"

"What pipe?" Freeman asked.

"It's under the sink. I tried to shut it off, but the valve wouldn't budge, and I don't know where Katie's daed keeps his tools."

"I'd better take a look." Freeman rushed out the door, and Grammy and Katie followed.

When they entered the house, Grammy halted inside the utility room. "We'd better take off our shoes. The kitchen's turned into a flood zone."

Katie slipped off her shoes, and when she entered the kitchen, she gasped. Water shot out from under the sink, and the floor looked like a small lake.

"You two had better wait out here while I check things out,"

Freeman said. "It wouldn't be good for either of you to slip and fall on the floor." He plodded through the water and squatted in front of the sink. "Ah, I see the problem. The pipe has a huge hole in it. Must have rusted out." He glanced over his shoulder at Katie. "If you'll find me a wrench, I'll get the water turned off."

Katie sloshed through the water and opened the drawer where Dad kept his tools. She grabbed the wrench, sloshed back, and handed it to Freeman.

"If your daed has another pipe and some plumbing supplies, I think I can fix this," he said after he'd shut off the water.

"I think there might be some plumbing tools in the shed, but I don't know if there's any pipe or not," Katie said.

"Shouldn't we get this water cleaned up first?" Grammy asked, sticking her head through the open door.

Katie nodded. "I'll work on getting the water off the floor while Freeman looks for the plumbing supplies."

Freeman hurried out the door, and Katie got out the mop. By the time he'd returned to the kitchen, she had some of the water mopped up.

"Found a pipe that I think will work," he said, going down on his knees in front of the sink.

While Katie finished mopping and towel-drying the floor, Freeman installed the new pipe.

Grammy stepped into the room and pointed to the water marks that had been left on the wall. "Your daed will have a conniption when he gets home and sees this, not to mention the broken window that'll have to be replaced in the stamp shop."

"You're right," Katie agreed. A horse and buggy pulled into the yard, and she glanced out the window. "Someone just pulled up in front of the stamp shop. Guess I'd better go see who it is." She hurried out the door and stepped onto the porch in time to see Ella climb down from her buggy.

"What happened to the window in the stamp shop?" Ella asked when Katie joined her on the lawn.

"Rita Howard was here with her boys. She left them outside to play while she came in to look at stamps." Katie grimaced.

"Between that and a broken pipe under our kitchen sink, this has not been a good day."

Ella draped her arm across Katie's shoulders. "You look upset. Don't let a few mishaps ruin your day."

"My day's not ruined. I'm just frustrated, that's all."

Ella motioned to the other horse and buggy tied to the hitching rail near the shop. "Whose rig is that?"

"It belongs to Freeman Bontrager. He came by to get some stamps for his sister's birthday. He's in the house putting a new pipe under the sink."

Ella smiled. "I'm surprised Freeman isn't married already. A man as helpful as him will probably make someone a real good husband."

Katie stared at Ella. "Are you interested in Freeman?"

Ella's mouth opened wide. " 'Course not. I was just saying that he'll make a good husband." She motioned to the stamp shop. "Are you open yet, or have you closed for the day?"

"We're still open. Is there something you need?"

Ella nodded. "I need a stamp pad with blue ink for my daed's business invoices."

"No problem. We have plenty." As Katie led the way to the stamp shop, she thought about Ella's comments concerning Freeman making a good husband. *I hope she wasn't hinting that I should take an interest in him, because I'm not interested in any man.* Uninvited tears blurred Katie's vision. *I'm in love with Timothy, and I always will be.*

CHAPTER 6

When Fern entered the hardware store in Shipshewana, she noticed Eunice standing in front of the book rack.

"Is there anything new to read?" Fern asked, stepping up to Eunice.

Eunice pointed to one of the books. "I thumbed through several pages of this children's book. It's about a young Amish girl and her brother who live in Pennsylvania. I think it might be something your scholars would enjoy reading."

Fern picked up the book and read the description on the back cover. "You're right. This could be a nice addition to the fiction I have available at the schoolhouse. Since school will be out for our summer break next week, I may as well wait and get the book when it's closer to the next school term in August."

"I guess that makes sense." Eunice smiled. "I understand that the end-of-the-year school program is next Saturday. Your bruder mentioned that he plans to attend."

Fern nodded. From the hopeful expression she saw on Eunice's face, she had a suspicion that Eunice might have more than a passing interest in Freeman. "As far as I know, my bruder and our grossmudder are both planning to go to the program."

"I hope to come, too, since my brother, Richard, will no doubt have a part in the program."

"Good, I'd like you to come."

41

Eunice gave Fern's arm a gentle squeeze. "By the way, happy birthday!"

"How'd you know?"

"When I spoke with Freeman this morning, I invited him to come over to our place for supper this evening. He said he couldn't, though, because he was taking you out to celebrate your birthday."

"Why don't you join us?" Fern suggested. "We're going to Das Dutchman, and we could pick you up on our way there."

Eunice's face broke into a wide smile. "Danki for inviting me; I'd love to go!"

～❧ ❧～

After Freeman left and Katie was sure that all the water was off the kitchen floor, she and Grammy ate a quick lunch; then Katie returned to the stamp shop while Grammy did the dishes.

Katie flopped into the chair at her mother's desk and yawned. She felt weak and kind of shaky and wished she could close the shop and take a nap. She stared at the stack of invoices lying on the desk. She should file them away but wasn't in the mood. *Maybe I'll make a few cards instead.*

She'd just pushed back her chair when the shop door opened and Mom stepped in.

"What happened to our window?"

Katie quickly explained and then told Mom about the broken pipe in the kitchen.

Deep wrinkles formed above Mom's brows. "Were you able to get the water shut off?"

Katie nodded. "Freeman Bontrager was here, so he turned off the valve and put a new pipe under the sink."

"That's good to hear." Mom smiled. "Freeman's such a nice man. I wouldn't be surprised if some young woman doesn't come along soon and snag him for a husband."

"Well, it sure won't be me!"

Mom looked at Katie as if she'd taken leave of her senses. "I wasn't suggesting that at all. Why are you acting so defensive?"

"Sorry," Katie mumbled, "but I think you should know that I'm not interested in any man. I'm still in love with Timothy."

Mom pursed her lips. "Timothy's dead, Katie, and you need to—"

"I'll never stop loving Timothy, and you can't make me!" Katie rushed out of the shop and raced to the house, leaving Mom to manage the stamp shop by herself.

~≈ ≈~

When Freeman entered the house, he found Fern and Grandma sitting at the kitchen table.

"Are you two ready to head out for supper?" he asked.

"In a minute. Let's give Fern her gifts before we leave." Grandma gestured to Freeman. "Do you want to go first, or shall I?"

He shrugged. "Doesn't matter to me."

"I'll go first then." Grandma stood, pulled open one of the kitchen drawers, and removed a package. She placed it on the table in front of Fern.

Fern grinned. "I may be a twenty-four-year-old woman, but I still like getting presents." She pulled the tissue off and removed two embroidered pillowcases and a quilted table runner. "They're beautiful, Grandma. Danki."

Grandma's pale blue eyes twinkled as she patted Fern's hand. "I made them for your hope chest."

Fern smiled. "That's a nice thought, but I'll probably never get married."

"What makes you say that?" Grandma asked.

Fern shrugged. "Just don't think I will, that's all."

"You're not pining for your old boyfriend, I hope." Grandma's brows furrowed when she frowned. "Wayne chose Loraine, and you need to come to grips with that."

Fern shook her head. "I'm not pining for Wayne. I just have no interest in getting married."

"Don't you want to have kinner someday?"

"I'm happy being a schoolteacher; the scholars are almost like having my own kinner."

Grandma shook her head. "It's not the same as having your own, and I'm sure you'll change your mind about marriage some-day when the right man comes along. In the meantime, if you want to make use of the pillowcases and table runner, that's fine with me."

Freeman stepped forward and handed Fern a paper sack. "Here you go. Happy birthday."

Fern opened the sack, and a smile spread across her face as she pulled out two rubber stamps. "These are so nice. I'll use them when I do scrapbooking. Danki, Freeman."

"You're welcome." Freeman moved toward the door. "Now can we go eat? I didn't have any lunch today, so I'm starving."

"How come you didn't eat?" Grandma asked.

"Because I ended up replacing a broken pipe during my lunch hour."

Fern's eyebrows puckered. "Was it a pipe in your bike shop?"

"No, it wasn't. I'll tell you about it on our way to Das Dutchman." Freeman grabbed his hat and hurried out the door with Fern and Grandma following.

They were almost to Freeman's buggy when Andy Weaver, one of Fern's students, walked into the yard carrying a cocker spaniel puppy in his arms. "We had five *hundlin* at our house, and this one's the last to go." He held the pup out to Fern. "Happy birthday, Teacher!"

Fern's eyes widened, and she looked over at Freeman as if she hoped he'd come to her rescue.

Freeman just shrugged and folded his arms.

"I named the *hundli* Penny 'cause she's copper-colored like a penny." Andy grinned up at Fern. "I hope you'll take good care of her."

Fern nodded and took the puppy from him. "Danki, Andy."

"You're welcome." Andy gave Penny a quick pat then headed down the driveway. "See you at school, Teacher."

"What are you going to do with the dog while you're teaching school?" Grandma asked. "I hope you don't expect me to care for it, because I've got enough to do already."

Fern looked at Freeman. "Will you keep an eye on Penny for me when I'm away from home?"

"I guess the mutt can hang around with me in the bike shop, just as long as she doesn't cause any trouble." He took the pup from Fern. "In the meantime, I'll put her in the barn where she'll be safe while we're gone to supper."

"Danki, Freeman."

Freeman grunted in reply. He wasn't thrilled about babysitting the puppy but didn't have the heart to tell Fern no. As soon as he had some free time, he'd build the pup a dog run; then he wouldn't have to worry about playing babysitter.

He hurried to the barn and put Penny in one of the empty horse stalls. When he went back outside, he found Fern and Grandma sitting in his buggy.

"Oh, I almost forgot to mention something," Fern said after Freeman had climbed into the driver's seat.

"What's that?"

"I ran into Eunice when I was in Shipshe earlier today, and I invited her to join us for supper." Fern smiled. "I said we'd pick her up on the way to the restaurant."

"How come you invited her to go along?" Freeman asked.

"Eunice told me she'd invited you to her house for supper tonight, but you said you couldn't go because you were going out with Grandma and me. I figured I was doing you a favor by asking Eunice to join us."

"You did it as a favor to me, huh?"

"That's right, and I hope you don't mind."

Freeman shrugged and guided the horse and buggy down the driveway. "It's your birthday, so you can invite whomever you please."

As they headed down the road, Freeman told Grandma and Fern about the broken window in the Millers' stamp shop and the broken pipe in their kitchen.

"Sounds like you had an interesting, busy day," Fern said.

"Guess you could say that." Freeman grunted. "It was busy, at least."

Grandma reached across the seat and patted Freeman's knee. "It was nice of you to help out at the Millers. You've turned into a fine young man."

"I sure couldn't leave 'em with water running all over the kitchen floor." Freeman flicked the reins to get the horse moving faster. "Katie acted real nervous after the ball sailed through the shop window. If she'd had to deal with the broken pipe on her own, she'd probably have fallen apart."

Fern leaned over the seat and poked his shoulder. "Don't *iwwerdreiwe* now."

"I'm not exaggerating; it's the truth. Katie was shaking so badly I was afraid she might cave in."

"As I recall, Katie took it real hard when her boyfriend died," Grandma said. "I spoke to Katie's mamm at Loraine and Wayne's wedding, and she said Katie's still having a hard time with it."

"That's too bad, but what I saw today seemed like it was more than just somebody grieving over someone who'd died."

"Did you do anything to try and calm Katie?" Fern asked.

Freeman nodded. "Told her to take a couple of deep breaths, and I got her a glass of water. Guess there might have been more I could have done, but it felt kind of awkward, and I really wasn't sure what to say or do."

"When put in the position of comforting someone in pain, what often needs to be said can best be said with a listening ear or a comforting touch." Grandma smiled. "It might not seem like much to the person offering comfort, but it can be more effective than you may ever know."

"Grandma's right," Fern agreed. "When one of my scholars gets hurt on the playground or becomes upset over something, I give them a hug and let them know that I care. It seems to help a lot."

Freeman grunted. "Jah, right. Like I was gonna give Katie a hug. She probably would've thrown me out of the stamp shop if I'd tried something like that."

"I wasn't suggesting that you hug her," Fern said. "I was merely saying that a person doesn't always have to say something to make someone who's hurting feel better."

"That's right," Grandma agreed. "But I'm sure you handled it the best way you could."

As they approached the driveway leading to Eunice's house, Freeman's hands grew sweaty. The way Eunice had looked at him this morning made him wonder if she had more than friendship on her mind.

CHAPTER 7

Everything we ordered sure looks good." Eunice smiled so sweetly at Freeman that he couldn't help but be drawn to her luminous blue eyes.

"You're right; it does." He reached for a roll from the bread basket and slathered it with apple butter.

"Did you get any more bikes in for repair today?" Eunice asked Freeman.

He nodded and forked some mashed potatoes into his mouth.

"I'm glad you're keeping busy with work," Grandma said. "Some folks in our area aren't so fortunate right now."

Fern nodded. "That's true. When I was at the hardware store in Shipshe today, Esther mentioned that several of the trailer factories have shut down. That means many of our Amish friends are now out of work."

"You're fortunate to have a business of your own," Eunice said to Freeman. "Especially one that seems to be doing so well."

He nodded. He hoped his business would continue to do well, but with the economic slump, there were no guarantees.

"After I left the hardware store, I did some shopping in the fabric store," Fern said. "I found some material for a new dress, and then..."

Freeman listened halfheartedly as Fern told about the events of her day. He was really more interested in filling his empty stomach than engaging in idle chitchat. As he continued to eat his meal, he glanced at Eunice and noticed that she seemed to be watching him. Was she expecting him to say something to her? Maybe when he was done eating, he could think of something to talk about, but right now he needed to eat.

"Oh, I almost forgot. I have a birthday present for you." Eunice reached into her purse and handed a small package to Fern.

Fern smiled. "You didn't have to get me anything."

"I know, but I wanted to." Eunice motioned to the gift. "I hope you like it."

Fern opened the package and removed a leather journal. "Danki, it's very nice. I'll use this to record my thoughts about teaching school."

"I'm glad you like it." Eunice looked over at Freeman and smiled. "You mentioned earlier today that you plan to be at the school program next Saturday."

Freeman nodded.

"I wanted you to know that I'll be there, too. Your sister said she'd like me to be there."

"I'm sure you'll enjoy it." Freeman grabbed a chicken leg and took a bite. First Fern had invited Eunice to join them for supper, and now the school program. He wondered if she'd decided to play matchmaker all of a sudden. Maybe Fern thought he and Eunice would make a good pair. The question was, did he think that, too?

~⋇ ⋇~

Loraine smiled at Wayne as the two of them sat at the kitchen table drinking coffee. Wayne's dad had gone to the barn after supper to feed the horses, and his mother was in the living room doing some sewing. It was the first chance Loraine had had to be alone with her husband all day, and she was glad they could spend a few minutes alone.

"I stopped by the stamp shop today to check on Katie," Loraine said. "I'm worried about her."

"How come?"

"She seems sad and kind of jittery."

He nodded soberly. "I noticed that on our wedding day. Do you think seeing us get married brought back memories of Timothy?"

"I'm sure it did, but she wasn't herself at the stamp shop today, either."

"Maybe she just needs more time to adjust to being home again. She might miss Florida and those sunny beaches."

"I suppose that could be part of it, but I think there might be more going on with Katie than we know."

"Like what?"

"I'm not sure." Loraine sighed. "I just wish there was something I could do to help her, but if she won't open up and tell me what's wrong—"

"My advice is to give her some time and be as supportive as she'll let you be." Wayne took hold of Loraine's hand. "Remember how things were with me when I first lost my leg?"

"Jah."

"Even though it took me awhile to work through the pain and frustration of it all, with God's help and the support of my family, I came through it, and I believe my faith was strengthened, too."

"I know it was, and so was mine." Loraine gave his fingers a gentle squeeze. "I'm glad I married such a *schmaert* man."

Wayne chuckled. "I'm smart all right. Smart because I woke up and realized I was going to lose you to Jake Beechy if I didn't let you know how much I loved you."

Loraine leaned her head on his shoulder. "If I'd had my way, we would've been married even sooner." She glanced around their cozy kitchen. "I'm glad you had this house started and that it didn't take long to finish it after the tornado struck."

He nodded. "My folks were glad, too, because if we hadn't invited them to move here after their place was destroyed, they wouldn't have had a place to live."

"Do you think they'll be here much longer?"

Wayne shrugged. "My daed wants to start working on their new house again, but my mamm says they should wait until they have more money to finish the house. I've heard 'em go back and forth about it several times."

"Every couple disagrees sometimes, but they need to work things out so no misunderstandings occur."

Wayne grunted. "Tell that to my mamm. You know how determined she can be."

Loraine wondered if Ada and Crist were having marital problems. She was about to ask when Crist entered the room. "Sorry to bother you, but I could use your help with something in the barn," he said to Wayne.

"Okay." Wayne stood, dumped the rest of his coffee in the sink, and left the room with his dad.

Loraine closed her eyes. *Lord, if Crist and Ada are having marital problems, then please help them work things out on their own or seek help through one of our ministers.*

❦ ❧

"Supper's going to be awhile yet, so if you want to go out and feed the cats now, go ahead," Mom said after Katie had finished setting the table.

"All right, I'll do it now." Katie slipped out the door.

As she stepped onto the porch, a gentle breeze caressed her face. She breathed deeply, listening to the sounds of the night: an owl hooting from a nearby tree; their hound dog's loud snores coming from his pen; and a chorus of sweet music from crickets and frogs settling in for the night.

Unexpectedly, the breeze turned blustery as it whipped through the trees and under the eaves of the house. Katie hurried across the yard and into the barn. A fluffy gray cat darted out from behind a bale of hay as soon as she poured food into one of the feeding dishes. A few seconds later, two more cats showed up.

Katie put the food away and took a seat on a bale of hay. A shaft of light filtered through the beams above, but it seemed dark inside the barn.

She leaned her head back so it touched the wall and closed her eyes. For an unguarded moment, she allowed herself to imagine what it would be like being married to Timothy. She could see herself sitting with him on the sofa, holding a baby boy in her lap. He looked like Timothy.

Tears pushed against Katie's eyelids, threatening to spill over, while a surge of frustration washed over her like angry waves on the beach.

"I still love him," Katie murmured, "but he's gone, and wherever he is, he's not coming back." She drew in a deep breath and hiccupped on a sob when she released it. *What a battle I'm having with bitterness, guilt, and confusion.* Katie wished she could share her deepest feelings with someone, but there was no one she felt she could trust.

The wind howled, and Katie found the drumming of the rain against the roof to be an annoyance.

She stood. *Mom's probably got supper ready by now, so I'd better get inside.*

She left the barn and headed for the house, stepping carefully around the mud puddles that had already formed. The wind blew against her back like an angry crowd pressing her forward, and her stiff white *kapp* hung limp against her head from the rain.

When Katie stepped into the kitchen, the strong smell of onions fastened itself to her face, and she nearly gagged. "What kind of onions are you using? They smell so strong."

"They're yellow onions. The smell lingered even after I added them to the stew." Mom pointed to Katie's dress. "From the looks of your clothes, I'm guessing it must be raining pretty hard."

Katie nodded. "It came up quick, too."

"Supper's almost ready, but I think you'd better change before we eat."

Katie started for the steps but turned back around. "It's fine if you and Dad want to start without me."

"There's no need for that. Your daed's still taking a shower."

Katie hurried up the stairs, relieved that Mom hadn't noticed her tears. The last thing she needed was a bunch of questions.

As Freeman helped Eunice into the buggy, she shivered with excitement. The tingle she felt when his hand touched hers made her want to be his girlfriend.

If Fern and Freeman's grandma weren't with us tonight, this would seem like a real date, she thought. *Freeman acted as if he was having a good time during supper, and he kept looking at me. Maybe he is interested in me.*

Eunice smiled to herself and settled against the seat. *If I can get Freeman to ask me out, by this time next year we might be married.*

CHAPTER 8

The tantalizing aroma of bacon and eggs floated up to Freeman's nose, and he sniffed appreciatively. He enjoyed having breakfast out with his friends and hoped they could do it on a regular basis.

Freeman looked across the table at Wayne and Andrew. They seemed as eager to eat their breakfast as he was.

"Let's pray so we can eat," Wayne said. "I'm as hungry as a mule that hasn't been fed for a week."

Freeman chuckled then bowed his head. *Dear Lord, bless this food to our bodies, and be with those who are in need.*

An image of Katie Miller popped into his head. *And please give Katie a sense of peace today. Amen.*

"How are things going at your place?" Andrew asked Wayne. "Are you happy being married? Is my cousin treating you okay?"

Wayne nodded and reached for his glass of juice. "Loraine's a good wife, and I couldn't be happier." A smile stretched across his face as he winked at Andrew and then Freeman. "I'd recommend married life to both of you."

"Gotta find the right woman first." Andrew bumped Freeman's arm. "How about you? Is there anyone special in your life these days?"

Freeman's face heated up. "Uh, no, not really." He wasn't about to admit that he might be interested in Eunice. There'd be no end to the teasing he'd have to put up with from these two.

Wayne dipped the end of his toast into the egg on his plate. "From the looks of your red face, I'm guessing there's someone special in your life. Come on now, *raus mitt*!"

"Jah, out with it now." Andrew bumped Freeman's arm again. "Don't keep us in suspense. Who is she?"

Freeman took a bite of his toast and washed it down with a drink of juice. "I don't have an *aldi,* but I probably could have if I wanted one."

Andrew leaned his elbows on the table and looked at Freeman with interest. "Who is she—this aldi you don't have but could?"

"Eunice Byler." Freeman reached for the jar of apple butter and slathered some on his toast, thinking he ought to come up with something else to talk about real quick.

"So tell us, what's going on with you and Eunice?" Wayne chuckled.

"Nothing's going on. I just have a feeling that she likes me."

"How do you know?" Andrew asked.

Freeman told them how Eunice had come by his shop a couple of times, and how she'd joined them for supper on Saturday evening.

"Maybe she likes bikes," Andrew mumbled around a mouthful of bacon.

"That could be, but why'd she accept Fern's invitation to join us for supper?"

"Maybe she enjoys your sister's company." Andrew added some salt and pepper to his eggs. "Just because she's been to your shop a few times and went out to supper with you doesn't mean she wants to be your aldi."

"Well, she invited me to her house for supper, too." Freeman rubbed the bridge of his nose. "And you should have seen the way she looked at me when we were at the restaurant."

"How was that?" Wayne asked.

"Like she wanted to be my aldi." Freeman groaned. "Eunice seems nice enough, and she looks pretty good, but I'm not sure if I'm interested."

Wayne chuckled again, a little louder this time. "I'll just bet you're not sure."

Freeman shook his head. "I really don't have time to be courting anyone right now. I've got a business that needs my attention, not to mention a little thing named Penny."

"Who's Penny?" Andrew asked.

Glad for the change of subject, Freeman explained how the cocker spaniel pup had come to live at their house. "She spent the last two nights in an empty stall in our barn, but I'll have to make the hundli a pen pretty soon, I expect."

"That's probably a good idea," Wayne agreed. "A horse stall's really not the place for a growing puppy."

"Fern expects me to babysit the dog while she's teaching school, but I'm not sure I want a lively little mutt underfoot in the bike shop." Freeman shook his head. "My customers might not like it, either."

"You never know," Wayne said. "It might bring in more customers if you have a cute little pup for folks to pet."

A shrill horn honking, followed by screeching brakes, drew Freeman's attention to the window.

"Looks like someone riding a bike got hit!" Wayne pushed back his chair and stood. Freeman and Andrew did the same.

They and several others in the restaurant hurried outside to see what had happened.

A young English man lay in the middle of the road, his mangled bike nearby. Several people were gathered around, and the English driver stood beside his car with a cell phone up to his ear.

"Can you tell what's going on?"

"Is he hurt bad?"

"Did you see how it happened?"

Everyone spoke at once, until a middle-aged man who said he was a doctor pushed his way through the crowd.

Freeman stood on the sidewalk with the others, watching as the doctor checked the injured biker. "Has someone called 911?" the doctor asked.

"I just did," the English driver said. "An ambulance is on its way." He slowly shook his head. "That fellow was weaving in and out of traffic. He obviously doesn't know a thing about bicycle safety."

Freeman thought about how Wayne's mother had been riding her bike a few months ago and had skidded in some gravel. She'd fallen and broken her leg. Then a few weeks ago, a young Amish girl had lost control of her bike and run into a tree. She'd been lucky to have endured only a mild concussion.

As Freeman heard the wail of sirens in the distance, he made a decision. If Fern was agreeable, he planned to give her scholars a lesson on bicycle safety.

~*~

As Katie stood with Grammy on the porch waiting for Marge Nelson to take Grammy to the bus station in Elkhart, a lump formed in her throat. "I wish you didn't have to go. I wish you and Grandpa were moving here instead of Wisconsin."

Grammy reached for Katie's hand. "We'll come for visits whenever we can, and you and your folks can visit us, too."

Mom nodded as she and Dad stepped onto the porch. "We haven't been to Wisconsin for a long time, so we'd enjoy a trip there."

Marge Nelson's car came up the driveway just then, and Dad picked up Grammy's suitcase. "Looks like your ride's here, so I'll carry this out to the car for you."

Grammy hugged Mom and Dad; then she turned to Katie and said, "I love you. Take care of yourself, you hear?"

Katie nodded. "I. . .I love you, too. Write to me, okay?" She nearly choked on the words, holding back her tears.

"Of course I will, and I expect you to do the same." Grammy gave Katie a hug and hurried toward the car.

Katie's shoulders tensed as she watched Marge's car pull away. She was trying not to cry, but when she heard Mom sniffle, she finally gave in and wept.

"It's been good having my mamm here for a visit, even though it was just a short one." Mom dabbed at her tears.

All Katie could do was nod.

Dad stepped back onto the porch and slipped his arm around Katie's shoulders. "How'd you like to take a ride with me?"

"Where to?" she asked.

"I have some errands to run in Topeka today. Thought you might like to go along." He looked over at Mom. "Can you get by without Katie's help in the stamp shop for a few hours?"

"I managed on my own while she was living in Florida, so I'm sure I can manage fine now." She touched Dad's arm. "Oh, and since you'll pass by Clara Smucker's place on the way to Topeka, would you mind dropping off a couple of things she ordered from the stamp shop? I left a message on her answering machine the other day, but she hasn't returned my call."

"Sure, we can do that." Dad stepped off the porch behind Katie. "I'll hitch my horse to the buggy while you get Clara's stuff put together. I'll be ready to go in ten minutes."

~≈ ≈~

Loraine plunged her hands into the dishpan full of soapy water and sloshed the sponge across a plate coated with sticky syrup. It had just been her, Ada, and Crist for breakfast this morning, since Wayne had gone out to eat with Andrew and Freeman. Both Ada and Crist had been unusually quiet during the meal, and Loraine wondered if her suspicions were right about them having marital problems. She'd intended to talk to Wayne more about it but hadn't had the chance. She'd thought she could bring up the subject last night before bed, but Wayne fell asleep before she'd been able to say anything. Then this morning, he'd left early to have breakfast at a restaurant in Middlebury.

The *clip-clop* of horse's hooves and the rumble of buggy wheels drew Loraine's attention to the window. She smiled when she recognized her mother's horse and buggy pulling up to the hitching rail.

Loraine dried her hands on a towel and hurried to the door.

"Wie geht's?" Mom asked as she stepped onto the porch a short time later.

"I'm fine. How are you?"

"Other than sniffling because of my spring allergies, I can't complain."

Loraine opened the door and motioned Mom inside. "Come on in, and let's have a cup of tea."

"That sounds good." Mom followed Loraine into the kitchen and took a seat at the table. "Where's Ada? Isn't she going to join us?"

"She had an appointment with her chiropractor this morning, and I think she planned to do some shopping afterwards." Loraine's forehead wrinkled. "I'm worried about her and Crist. I think they're having marital problems."

Mom sucked in her breath. "Ach, my! Do you know what the problem is between them?"

"Not really, but they were both very quiet during breakfast this morning, which is unusual, especially for Ada."

Mom blew on her tea and took a sip. "Communication is the key to a successful marriage. Maybe I should talk to the bishop's wife and see if she knows anything. She and Ada have been good friends for a long time. Ada might have confided in her."

Loraine nodded. "That's a good idea. In the meantime, we'd better both be praying."

~ ❦ ~

As Katie and her father headed for Topeka, her head lolled against the seat, and she closed her eyes. Ever since the accident, riding in any vehicle made her feel nervous. She wished she could make the anxious feelings stop, but she didn't know how. "You're awfully quiet." Dad nudged Katie's arm. "Are you sleeping?"

Katie opened her eyes. "I'm awake; just trying to relax."

"Are you still feeling sad about your grossmudder and *grossdaadi* moving to Wisconsin?"

"Jah." No point in telling Dad that she was nervous about riding in the buggy. She was sure he wouldn't understand.

They traveled in silence until they came to Clara's driveway. When Dad pulled the buggy up to the hitching rail, he motioned to the package sitting on the floor by Katie's feet. "Would you mind taking Clara's things in to her?"

"Okay." Katie picked up the package, sprinted for the house, and knocked on the door.

When Clara didn't answer, she knocked again.

Still no response.

The door squeaked when she opened it and poked her head inside. "Clara, are you at home?"

No reply.

Figuring Clara might be upstairs or out back in the garden, Katie decided to leave the package on the kitchen table. She stepped into the room and halted when she saw Clara lying on the floor. Katie's heart pounded. She was sure the woman must be dead!

CHAPTER 9

Katie raced outside, hollering, "*Kumme,* Dad, *schnell!*"

"What's wrong?" Dad asked as he scrambled out of the buggy. "What are you hollering about?"

"Clara's lying on the kitchen floor, and I...I'm sure she's dead!" Katie shook so hard that her teeth chattered.

Dad quickly tied his horse to the hitching rail and raced for the house.

Katie lowered herself to the grass and drew in a couple of deep breaths, hoping to calm her racing heart.

Several minutes passed before Dad came out of the house and hurried toward Katie. "Clara's not dead. She was only sleeping."

Katie's brows furrowed. "Why would she be sleeping in the middle of the kitchen floor?"

"She said she'd been mopping the floor and got a kink in her back. Said it hurt so bad she had to lie down on the floor and ended up falling asleep."

"If she was only sleeping, why didn't she hear me knock or call out to her?"

"Said she didn't have her hearing aid in."

"Will she be all right?"

Dad nodded. "I helped her up, and she's resting on the sofa. We'll stop by her daughter's place on the way home and let her know what happened. I'm sure she'll see that Clara gets to the chiropractor's right away." He untied the horse and motioned to the buggy. "We'd better get going."

∽≈ ≈∾

Woof! Woof!

Freeman glanced down at the eager-looking pup staring up at him and groaned. When he'd returned from having breakfast with Wayne and Andrew, he'd brought Penny out to the bicycle shop, but all the dog had done since then was either whine or bark. Freeman had quit working to take the dog outside a few times, and he'd stopped to pet the mutt more times than he cared to admit.

Woof! Woof! Woof!

"Go lie down; I've got work to do." Freeman pointed to the braided throw rug across the room.

Penny looked up at him and whimpered pathetically.

Freeman knelt on the floor to begin work on a bike that had been brought in last week. He should have finished it by now.

Slurp! Slurp! The puppy swiped Freeman's hand with her warm pink tongue.

Freeman picked Penny up, carried her across the room, and placed her on the rug. "Now go to sleep!"

The pup wagged her tail and pawed at Freeman's leg.

Freeman grimaced. If he couldn't get the pup to settle down soon, he'd never get any work done. "Maybe I should put you back in the barn."

"Put who in the barn?"

Freeman whirled around and was shocked to see Eunice standing there. He hadn't even heard her come in.

"I'm babysitting the pup Fern got for her birthday." Freeman motioned to the dog. "The little *pescht* won't let me get any work done."

"What's the puppy's name?" Eunice asked.

"Penny."

"She's sure a cute little thing." Eunice bent over and scooped the pup into her arms. "If you like, I'll keep an eye on her for you."

"Do you want to take her home?"

Eunice shook her head. "I thought I'd stay and keep the pup occupied right here."

Freeman gulped. If Eunice hung around his shop all day, he'd never get anything done. "I appreciate the offer, but I think I'll put Penny back in the barn."

"You don't want me to stay?"

"It's not that. I'm sure you have better things to do with your time."

"Not really, but do whatever you think's best with the dog." She stood and brushed a clump of dog hair off her dress. "The reason I came by is because my bike's been making a strange grinding sound when I try to shift gears. I was wondering if you could take a look at it."

"I guess I could do that right now. Why don't you bring the bike in?"

"I don't have it with me. I walked over here."

"Oh, I see. Well, whenever you can bring in the bike, I'll take a look and see if I can locate the problem."

"I thought maybe you could come over to my house this afternoon. Afterwards, you can stay for supper."

A trickle of sweat rolled down Freeman's forehead. He was attracted to Eunice, but things were moving a bit too fast. Besides, he'd already agreed to have supper at her place next Saturday, so he didn't see why she was asking him to go there today.

He motioned to the line of bikes that had been brought in for repair. "I appreciate the offer, but I have a lot of work to do, and I'll probably be working late every night this week. If you're not able to bring the bike into my shop, then when I come for supper next Saturday, I'll take a look at it."

Eunice dropped her gaze to the floor. "I don't want to ride the bike the way it is, and I don't want to wait that long, so maybe I'll just ask my daed to haul it over here. See you later, Freeman." Eunice hurried out the door before he had a chance to respond.

Woof! Woof!

Freeman looked down at Penny and slowly shook his head.

"Some women are sure hard to figure out. That goes for you, too."
He leaned over and patted the dog's head.

※ ※

JoAnn glanced out the kitchen window. It was nearly lunchtime,
and still no sign of Jeremy and Katie. *I wonder what's taking them
so long.*

She moved away from the window and over to the stove to
check on the chicken soup that was heating.

She hoped nothing had happened to them. There'd been
several buggy accidents on the stretch of road between their
place and Shipshewana lately, and she couldn't help feeling some
concern.

The whinny of a horse drew her attention back to the window,
and she breathed a sigh of relief when she saw Jeremy's horse and
buggy roll into the yard.

A few minutes later, Katie entered the house, her face as pale
as fresh-fallen snow.

"What's wrong, Katie?" JoAnn asked. "Aren't you feeling well?"

"I've got a koppweh, and I feel kind of shaky."

"Maybe some food will make your headache better." JoAnn
gestured to the stove. "The soup should be hot enough now, so as
soon as your daed comes in, we can eat."

Katie shook her head. "I'm not hungry. I need to lie down."
She hurried up the stairs to her room.

※ ※

A cool breeze trickled through the open window in Katie's bedroom as she sat on the edge of her bed. She wished she could tell
someone what was on her mind, but no one would understand.
How could they when Katie herself didn't?

She flopped onto the pillow and released a puff of air as she
thought about finding Clara on the kitchen floor. What if she had
been dead? What if she'd died with no one with her? What if—

Katie rolled onto her side and squeezed her eyes shut. She
didn't want to think about death. She didn't want to think about

anything at all. She just wanted to sleep.

An image of Timothy popped into her head, so real she could almost feel his warm breath on her face and see the twinkle in his eyes when he teased her.

Tears stung Katie's eyes, and she clutched the edge of her mattress. It was bad enough when a person got old and died, but to have someone snatched off the earth in the prime of life wasn't fair! How could God be so cruel? Why did bad things happen to good people?

Katie curled into a tight ball and sobbed until no more tears would come.

❦

JoAnn sighed as she stood at the stove stirring the soup. It upset her that Katie didn't want to eat lunch. She'd been eating like a bird ever since she came home, and she was too thin for her own good.

The back door swung open, and Jeremy stepped into the room. He sniffed the air. "Somethin' smells good in here. I hope whatever you've fixed is ready, because I need to eat and get out to my shop and start workin'."

"The soup's ready, and I'll dish it up while you wash your hands."

When they were seated at the table a few minutes later, Jeremy looked at Katie's empty chair and frowned. "Where's our *dochder?*"

"Our daughter's upstairs in her room. She said she had a koppweh and wasn't hungry." JoAnn slowly shook her head. "I'm worried about her, Jeremy. I don't think she's happy being home. Maybe we should have sent her back to Florida with my mamm."

"But your folks are moving to Wisconsin."

"I know, but maybe Kate could have moved there with them."

Jeremy shook his head. "We've had this discussion before, and I don't think Katie's behavior has anything to do with her not being happy here. I think she's still grieving over Timothy."

"How do you know?"

"There was an incident over at Clara's place this morning. Seeing how shaken Katie was made me realize that she's not come to grips with Timothy's death."

"What are we going to do about it?"

"If she doesn't snap out of it soon, we might have to make her an appointment to see one of the counselors at the mental health facility." He bowed his head. "In the meantime, we need to pray and eat our lunch."

CHAPTER 10

Katie squinted against the intense morning sun as she stepped into the yard to feed the chickens Saturday morning.

The hens followed her, clucking in anticipation of what was to come.

"You're all greedy, you know that?" Katie mumbled as she threw some corn on the ground.

Weep! Weep! She looked up and spotted a cardinal in the tree overhead. It amazed her how cheerful the birds in their yard seemed to be. She wished she could sing the way they did when she really felt like crying.

She threw out some more food for the chickens then headed for the house.

When she stepped into the kitchen, the fragrant aroma from whatever Mom was baking lingered in the air.

Mom gestured to the teapot on the table. "Pour yourself a cup of tea, and we can visit while my cookies are baking."

Katie thought it was too warm for tea, so she filled a glass with water and took a seat at the table.

"You haven't forgotten about the program and potluck lunch at the schoolhouse, I hope," Mom said, taking a seat beside Katie.

"No, I haven't forgotten." Truth was Katie wasn't in the mood to go to the program, but she knew if she didn't go, Mom would pressure her.

"We'll leave in about an hour," Mom said. "I should be done with my baking by then."

A trickle of fear meandered through Katie's mind until it turned into a torrential flood of negative thoughts. She hated feeling so nervous about things. She wished she could be strong, confident, and happy again.

"Don't look so down-in-the-mouth," Mom said. "Today will be fun. You'll see."

~❦ ❦~

When Katie and her mother stepped into the schoolhouse, Katie quickly found a seat near the back of the room. She wanted to be close to the door in case she felt the need to escape.

She looked around and spotted several people she knew—Loraine and Wayne; Ella, Charlene, and their folks; Freeman and his grandmother; and her cousin Andrew.

Katie wondered if being here today and seeing Fern at the front of the room, taking the place of his sister, made Andrew feel sad. It made Katie sad. The accident she and her cousins had been in had turned everyone's lives upside-down. It must be awful for Jolene to have lost her hearing, as well as her job. She'd been forced to move away so she could learn to read lips and talk with her hands. Then there was Ella's family, Timothy's family, and Paul's wife, who had each lost a loved one because of the accident. Katie hadn't suffered physically, but she wasn't sure her emotions would ever be the same.

"Before we begin our program today," Fern said, drawing Katie's attention to the front of the room, "my brother, Freeman, has asked if he can speak for a few minutes about bicycle safety." She smiled at the scholars seated on one side of the room. "Many of you own bikes and will be riding them a lot this summer, so please listen to what Freeman has to say."

Fern took a seat, and Freeman walked to the front of the room. "All bicycles should be adjusted to the size of the rider, and the bike should have properly adjusted brakes and a bell that can be heard from one hundred feet away," he said. "Red reflectors should be mounted on the rear of the bike, as well as the spokes of the rear wheel. White reflectors should be mounted on the front of the bike and also in the spokes of the front wheel. During low-light situations, the bike should have a white lamp visible from five hundred feet to the front, and a red lamp visible from five hundred feet to the rear."

Katie tuned Freeman out as she glanced at the closest window. It was warm and stuffy in the building. *I wish someone would open at least one of the windows. I feel like I can't breathe.*

She looked around the room, wondering if anyone else felt the way she did. Everyone seemed to be listening to what Freeman had to say. Everyone appeared to be calm and relaxed. Everyone but her.

Katie looked out the window again, praying for the strength to stay in her seat. She couldn't embarrass herself by getting up and leaving before the program had begun. *I can do this. I just need to think about something else.*

A pesky fly buzzed overhead, and when it landed on Katie's arm, she flicked at it.

The fly zipped across the room and back again; then it landed on the windowsill behind Katie. Wayne must have spotted it there, for he turned and opened the window.

Katie breathed deeply as a breeze floated into the room. It smelled as if rain might be coming soon. Hopefully, not until later in the day, as she knew the older scholars had planned a game of baseball with some of the men.

Katie turned her attention to the front of the room. Freeman had finally finished his talk, and several of the younger students had begun reciting poems. Katie thought about the programs she'd taken part in as a girl. School days had been fun and carefree, and when she'd graduated after eighth grade, she'd been happy to help Mom in the stamp shop full-time. Soon after Katie had turned sixteen, she and Timothy had begun dating.

Katie closed her eyes as she thought about Timothy and how happy they'd been together. He'd always been able to make her laugh and had treated her as if she was someone special. He'd teased her a few times about looking like a little girl, but it was only in fun. How she missed his dimpled smile and laughing blue eyes.

Someone poked Katie's arm, and her eyes snapped open.

"Katie, wake up. The program's over," Mom whispered.

"I wasn't sleeping. I was just resting my eyes."

Mom motioned to the back of the door leading to the basement. "Let's go downstairs and help set out the food."

Katie followed Mom out of the room. The sooner they ate, the sooner they could go home.

~ ❧ ~

After the meal was over, Freeman wandered outside to watch the baseball game the older boys and some of the men had begun playing.

"Aren't you gonna join us?" Andrew called from where he stood near second base.

Freeman shook his head. "I have to leave soon, so I'll just watch until it's time for me to go."

Andrew shrugged. "Suit yourself."

Freeman heard voices nearby and noticed Ella and Loraine visiting a few feet away.

"What's Wayne have to say about his folks having marital problems?" Ella asked Loraine.

Loraine shrugged. "I was finally able to talk to him about it the other night, but he said he doesn't think it's anything serious and that he's sure they'll work things out." She clutched Ella's arm. "I've heard Ada raise her voice at Crist several times in the last few weeks, and I can't help but be concerned."

Freeman wondered if he ought to say something to Wayne about what he'd heard but decided it was none of his business. Besides, whatever Loraine had witnessed between Crist and Ada might be nothing more than a little spat.

Freeman was about to walk away when Eunice showed up.

"The program went well, didn't it?" she asked, smiling up at him.

He nodded. "I thought all the scholars did a good job with their parts."

"I was hoping to talk to you after lunch, but you got away too quick."

"It was hot and stuffy, even in the basement, and I was anxious to get some fresh air." Freeman glanced to the left and saw Wayne heading his way. "I'd better go. I've got a customer coming to the bike shop soon." The last thing he needed was more ribbing from his friend about him being sweet on Eunice.

"Oh, okay." Eunice turned with the grace of a bluebird floating on the wind and walked away.

Freeman was halfway to his buggy when he spotted Fern trying to convince one of her students to join the water balloon game. "Why don't you let the little fellow alone?" He stepped up to her. "It upsets a man to be ordered about, so just let go of his hand and let him decide for himself if he wants to play the game or not."

Fern squinted as she pursed her lips. "I think I know the best way to handle things with my students."

Freeman shrugged. It was obvious that Fern wasn't going to listen to anything he had to say. Even when they were kinner, she thought she knew more than him and often bossed him around. "I'm leaving now," he mumbled.

"So soon? But we're having ice cream after the games, and I'd hoped you could help me with the water balloons."

"I've got a customer coming to pick up a bike this afternoon. I need to be there when he shows up." Freeman hurried off before she could say anything more.

He found Grandma sitting in a chair on the lawn, visiting with a couple other women her age. "I'm heading for home," he told her. "Do you want to come along, or would you rather stay and ride home with Fern?"

Grandma smiled sweetly. "I think I'll ride home with Fern. I'd like to stay and watch the kinner play their games."

"Okay, I'll see you later on." Freeman hurried toward his buggy, anxious to be on his way.

❦

As JoAnn sat on a bench outside the schoolhouse with several other women, she glanced across the yard and noticed Katie sitting on the lawn by herself. She'd been quieter than usual today and hadn't eaten much lunch or visited with her cousins during the meal. JoAnn figured Katie ought to be with Ella and Loraine right now as they sat on the grass watching the younger children toss water balloons back and forth. For some reason, she obviously preferred to be alone.

I remember when my daughter was a little girl, JoAnn thought. *She used to be a happy, curious child, full of fun and looking for adventure around every corner. She's changed since the accident. Makes me wonder if she'll ever be the same.*

She tapped her chin. *If what Jeremy said about Katie grieving for Timothy is true, then it might be good for her to visit his grave. Hopefully, it'll help Katie come to grips with Timothy's death.*

An unexpected puff of wind rattled the leaves on the trees, and the next thing JoAnn knew, a few sprinkles of rain fell. She knew if she was going to stop by the cemetery she'd better do it soon before the rain got any worse.

She hurried over to Katie. "We'd better go. I think we might be in for some heavy rain."

Katie followed JoAnn to their buggy and climbed in without a word.

JoAnn untied the horse from the hitching rail and took her seat on the driver's side. As she headed the horse in the direction of the cemetery, she glanced over at Katie. "You seemed awfully quiet today and kept to yourself. Didn't you visit with any of your friends?"

"Not really."

"How come?"

"I didn't have anything to say."

"Did you enjoy the program?"

"It was okay."

"I thought the skit the older scholars put on was quite funny, didn't you?"

"Uh-huh."

JoAnn sighed. She'd hoped going to the program might give

her daughter a reason to smile, but it seemed as if Katie didn't want to have a good time.

As they pulled onto the grassy spot outside the cemetery, Katie stiffened. "What are we doing here?"

"I thought it would be good for you to visit Timothy's grave."

"I don't want to."

"It's stopped raining now, so let's take a walk over there."

Katie shook her head.

"I really think it will help you—"

"What I've lost will never be returned." Katie's voice shook as she stared at the graveyard.

"You're right," JoAnn agreed. "Timothy's not coming back, but your life's not over, Katie. God might have someone else for you in the days ahead."

"I don't want anyone else!"

JoAnn touched her daughter's trembling shoulder. "It's perfectly normal for a person to grieve when they lose someone they love, but it's not normal to carry on like this for such a long time. I'd hoped that the months you spent with my folks in Florida would help you come to grips with your pain, but apparently it did no good at all."

Katie shook her head in short, quick jerks. "That's not true. I felt a lot more peaceful when I was living with Grammy and Grandpa than I do here."

"Why don't you feel peaceful here?"

"Because there are too many reminders of Timothy."

JoAnn felt deeply troubled by her daughter's dark mood and wished there was something she could do or say to make things easier for Katie, but she didn't know what. It might have been better for Katie if she could have stayed in Florida, but she was here now, and they'd need to find a way for her to work things through.

CHAPTER 11

Katie squinted against the invading light shining in her bedroom window. It had rained most of the night. Now her room felt hot and sticky. She hadn't slept well last night and wished she could spend the day in bed. But this was Sunday, and she was expected to go to church with her folks.

Katie rolled out of bed, plodded across the room, and opened her window, hoping to let in a cool breeze. What she got was a blast of hot air. The sun had risen over the horizon like a giant ball of fire.

Last spring they'd had some muggy days like this, with high temperatures in the eighties. She wondered if it would be like that again and whether it meant they were in for a very hot summer.

With a weary sigh, Katie moved away from the window. She needed to get dressed and go downstairs to help Mom with breakfast. She picked up the hand mirror on her dresser and grimaced. Her eyes had an almost distant look to them. Her face looked thinner than it used to be. Her hands shook as she placed the mirror back on the dresser.

There must be something wrong with me. Should I talk to Mom about it?

Katie shook her head. *Bad idea. Mom will probably say I need to eat more and get out of the house more often. She might even make me go to the doctor. If that happens, the doctor might run all sorts of tests.*

If he finds something seriously wrong with me, he'll say I'm going to die, and then—

Tap! Tap! Tap! "Katie, are you up?" Dad hollered through the closed door. "Your mamm's got breakfast ready."

"I'm coming!" Katie pinched her cheeks to give them more color and set her covering in place.

When she stepped out of the room, the aroma of sausage and eggs floated up the stairs to meet her. She would force herself to eat something this morning even if she didn't feel hungry.

As Katie descended the stairs, she heard whispered voices coming from the kitchen. She halted on the bottom step and tipped her head and listened.

"I can't help but be worried about Katie," Mom said. "She's been acting so strange since she got back from Florida. She didn't visit with anyone at the school program yesterday, and when I took her by the cemetery, she refused to get out of the buggy." She made a clicking noise with her tongue. "She'll hardly eat a thing and jumps at the slightest noise. I want to help her, but she won't open up to me."

"Do you think it's something physical going on with her, or is it a mental problem she's dealing with?" Dad asked.

"I don't know. It could be either or both."

"Maybe we should take her to see Dr. Baker and ask him to run some tests. If he doesn't find anything, then we'd better see about getting her some counseling at the mental health facility." Dad grunted. "If you'll recall, I suggested taking her there after Timothy died, but you insisted on sending her to your folks, for all the good it did."

Katie froze as a wave of nausea rolled through her stomach. She couldn't let them send her there. She didn't want to know what was wrong with her, and she didn't want anyone to think she was crazy. She'd do whatever she could to make Mom and Dad think she was okay. No matter how nervous or sickly she felt, she would pretend that she felt fine.

❧ ❧

During the church service that morning, which was held in

the Lehmans' buggy shop, the room had become so warm that someone finally passed out the lids from ice cream pails to use as fans. Even with the makeshift fans, Katie felt hot, confined, and woozy.

She gripped the edge of her bench and forced herself to focus on the message the bishop was giving. She couldn't give in to these feelings, so she would remain seated instead of rushing outside for fresh air like she wanted to do. Katie had noticed Mom watching her and knew if she did anything out of the ordinary it might be just what Mom needed to haul her off to the doctor's office. Worse yet, Mom might insist that Katie see someone at the mental health facility where she'd be expected to tell them things she didn't understand and could barely deal with herself.

A wave of dizziness washed over Katie, and she grabbed the edge of her bench for support. *I can do this. I can do this. The service is almost over. I can make it through okay.*

Katie blinked a couple of times as the bishop's face began to blur. Her head tingled, and she felt as if she were being pulled into a long, dark tunnel. She swayed unsteadily; then everything went black.

CHAPTER 12

Wake up, Katie. Can you hear me? Are you all right?"

Katie blinked as her mother's face came into view. She saw Dad, Ella, and several others looking down at her, too. "Wh–what happened? Where am I?"

"You passed out just as church was about to end." Dad's forehead wrinkled as he stared at Katie. "Are you feeling grank?"

Katie shook her head and slowly sat up. "I'm not sick. It was hot in there, and I felt kind of woozy."

"I think you'd better see the doctor tomorrow," Mom said. "You haven't felt well since you got back from Florida, and something could be seriously wrong."

Katie's heart pounded, and her mouth went dry. She didn't see how she could be seriously ill when she'd felt fine while she was in Sarasota. But then there had to be something wrong with her, or she wouldn't keep having these strange attacks.

"You didn't eat a lot for breakfast this morning," Dad said, helping Katie to her feet. "Maybe that's the reason you passed out."

She nodded, hoping that was all there was to it.

Mom slipped her arm around Katie's waist and led her toward the Lehmans' house. "I think you ought to lie down awhile. I'll come and get you after lunch is set out."

Katie didn't argue. The way her legs were shaking and her heart was pounding, she knew she really did need to lie down.

Soon after the common meal had been served, Loraine sought out Ella and suggested that they check on Katie. "I haven't had a chance to speak with her since we ate lunch," she said to Ella. "I want to see how she's doing."

"That's a good idea. She's sitting under the maple tree over there."

They headed across the yard, and when they reached the tree, they knelt on the ground beside her.

"Mind if we join you?" Ella asked.

Katie smiled, although her expression appeared to be forced. "'Course not."

"It really scared us when you passed out during church," Loraine said. "How are you feeling now that you've had something to eat?"

"I'm better."

Ella touched Katie's shoulder. "Your daed said he thinks you didn't have enough to eat for breakfast. What do you think?"

Katie shrugged. "I guess that might have been part of the problem, but I was doing okay until the room got so warm."

"Have you ever passed out like that before?" Loraine asked.

"Huh-uh, but I've felt dizzy a couple of times."

Ella and Loraine's worried expressions made Katie wish she could put their minds at ease, but that was hard to do since she was worried herself.

"Are you going to see the doctor like your mamm suggested?" Ella questioned.

"Not if I can help it."

Tiny wrinkles formed in Loraine's forehead. "Why not? Don't you want to find out what's wrong with you?"

Katie shook her head.

Ella looked at Katie as if she'd lost her mind. "You're kidding, right?"

"No, I'm not. If there's something seriously wrong with me, then I don't want to know about it." Katie sighed. "Now, can we please change the subject?"

Ella looked at Loraine as if she was hoping she might say something more, but Loraine just shrugged and looked away.

"Let's talk about the stamp shop then," Ella said. "Are you and your mamm keeping busy there, or are you getting fewer customers now that jobs are scarce and money's tight for so many people?"

"We're still busy," Katie said. "I think more people are making cards rather than buying them. Since we have a good variety of rubber stamps and other card-making supplies, we're hoping the business will keep going."

"Say, I have an idea," Loraine said. "Why don't the three of us get together one of these days and do some stamping like we did when we were teenagers?"

Ella nodded. "That sounds like fun. What do you think, Katie?"

"I guess it would be all right, but it'd have to be after the shop's closed for the day. I don't think my mamm would appreciate me fooling around with stamping projects when I'm supposed to be working."

"Aren't there days when you're not so busy?" Loraine asked.

"Jah, but Mom usually finds something for me to do."

"That's fine," Ella said. "We can get together some evening."

As they continued to visit, Loraine was pleased that Katie seemed more talkative, even though she did seem to be on edge.

"I got another letter from Jolene yesterday," Ella said. "She's doing well with her classes on sign language and thinks when she's done she might want to teach deaf children."

"That'd be good," Loraine said. "I know how much she's missed teaching school, and she really does need a purpose."

"Speaking of purpose," Ella said, "I need to buy a few things in Goshen later this week, and I was wondering if you two might be free to go with me. We can have lunch afterwards—maybe go to that restaurant where they serve barbecued ribs."

Loraine nodded. "Sounds like a fun day to me."

Ella turned to Katie. "How about you?"

Katie shook her head. "I don't think my mamm can spare me that long."

Just then Eunice showed up. "I hope I'm not interrupting anything," she said.

"We were just catching up with each other's lives." Loraine patted the ground beside her. "Have a seat; you're welcome to join us."

"I think I will." Eunice lowered herself to the ground. "Are you okay?" she asked, looking at Katie. "You gave us all a scare when you fell off the bench like that."

"I'm fine."

"Are you sure? Your face still looks awfully pale."

Katie's lips compressed together. "I'm feeling much better now."

"Glad to hear it."

"We've been talking about getting together to do some stamping," Ella said. "If you like to stamp, maybe you'd like to join us."

"That sounds like fun. When did you plan to get together?"

"We haven't picked a date yet," Katie said, "but we'll let you know when we do."

Loraine smiled. It was good to see Katie taking an active part in their conversation. She'd been quiet and kept to herself much of the time since she'd been home. Maybe she was beginning to adjust.

When Loraine heard her name being called, she glanced over her shoulder and saw Wayne heading her way.

"My mamm's got a headache and wants to go home," he said when he approached her. "Since my folks rode in our buggy today, we're kind of obligated to take them home."

Loraine stood and pressed the wrinkles from her dress. "That's fine. I'm ready for a little nap myself." She said her good-byes and hurried off with Wayne.

❧ ❦

Eunice leaned back on her elbows and stared at the sky. "It's another warm day—too warm for spring, if you ask me."

Ella nodded. "Makes me wonder what summer will be like."

Katie grimaced. "Probably hot and sticky."

"After living in Florida, I'd think that you'd be used to hot and sticky," Ella said.

"It was different there. I could cool off whenever I went to the beach."

"I've never been to Sarasota, but I hear the sand is white, and someone told me that there are lots of interesting shells on the beach," Eunice said.

Katie nodded. "I would have brought some home with me, but I didn't know I'd be staying."

"You were planning to go back?" Eunice asked.

"Jah, but things have changed."

Eunice glanced over her shoulder and saw Fern standing near the Lehmans' back porch. When Fern motioned to her, she clambered to her feet. "Fern's waving at me, so I'd better go see what she wants. Let me know when you're ready to do some stamping."

Ella smiled. "We will."

Eunice hurried off and took a seat beside Fern on the porch.

"I was hoping to talk to you after the program yesterday," Fern said when Eunice joined her. "But things got busy with the games, and you left before I had the chance to say anything."

"Was there anything in particular you wanted to talk to me about?" Eunice asked.

"I wanted to see if you'd be free to come over to our place for supper tomorrow evening."

"I'd like that." Eunice moistened her lips with the tip of her tongue. "Will Freeman be there?"

Fern nodded. "I thought it would give the three of us a chance to get better acquainted. I think our grossmudder would enjoy visiting with you, too."

"That'd be great." Eunice didn't know if she'd enjoy visiting with Fern's grandmother, but she was eager to spend more time with Freeman. Even though he'd be coming to her place soon, she wasn't about to turn down Fern's invitation.

❧ ❧

"That was a real good service we had today," Grandma said as Freeman drove their buggy toward home later that day. "I enjoyed visiting afterwards, as well."

"It was a nice day," Fern agreed. "I had a short visit with Eunice Byler, too." She tapped Grandma lightly on the shoulder. "I invited Eunice to join us for supper tomorrow night. I hope that's all right with you."

"Won't bother me any," Grandma said with a chuckle, "because I won't be at home."

Freeman gave her a sidelong glance. "Where will you be?"

"Several of us widows are going out for supper. I thought I'd mentioned that to you both a few days ago."

"Guess we forgot," Fern said.

Freeman glanced over his shoulder. "What made you decide to invite Eunice over for supper, Fern?"

"She seems like a nice person, and I thought it would give us a chance to get to know her a little better."

"Hmm. . .I see." Freeman had to admit the idea of spending the evening with Eunice held some appeal, but he'd promised to have supper at her place next Saturday and hadn't expected they'd be getting together quite so soon. He had a feeling Eunice might be looking for a husband, and since he wasn't ready to settle down yet, he hoped it wasn't him she had in mind for the job.

"I don't know about you two, but I'm feeling hungry," Grandma said when Freeman guided the horse and buggy onto their driveway. "Think I'll fix myself a little snack."

Freeman chuckled. Grandma might be a small woman, but she could pack away food like a full-grown man. It seemed as if she was always snacking on something.

"I'll drop you off here, and then I'll put the horse and buggy away," Freeman said, pulling the buggy up close to the house. "Oh, and Grandma, if you want to fix a snack, I think I could manage to eat a little something, too."

"Will do." Grandma climbed down from the buggy with the ease of a woman much younger than her seventy years. Fern stepped out behind her.

When they stepped onto the porch and opened the back door, Grandma let out a high-pitched screech. "Ach, what a *marascht*!"

Freeman jumped out of the buggy and sprinted for the house.

"What's a mess?" he asked, leaping onto the porch.

"Come in here and look for yourself," Grandma hollered from the kitchen.

Freeman rushed in and screeched to a stop just inside the door. Grandma and Fern stood there shaking their heads.

Penny lay curled up on the braided throw rug by the kitchen sink, sleeping peacefully. The room, however, was a disaster! A box of cereal must have fallen off the table, for the contents were dumped on the floor. Several plastic sacks that had been in a box in the utility room were ripped up and strewn about. Some of Grandma's dish towels were shredded, and a wad of napkins lay clumped together on the floor near the pup.

"This doesn't set well with me at all," Grandma grumbled. She pointed to Freeman. "I want you to get that hundli out of my kitchen right now!"

When Freeman started across the room, Penny's eyes snapped open. She leaped up and darted under the table.

"Nemm ihn fescht!" Fern hollered.

"Penny's a she, and I'm trying to take hold of her like you asked." Freeman lunged for the pup, but she slipped through his fingers. The pup's toenails clicked against the linoleum as she raced out of the room.

Freeman tore after the animal, hollering, "Come back here, you troublesome mutt!" He rounded the corner just in time to see Penny collide with the cardboard box on the utility porch.

Yip! Yip! Yip! The pup shook her head and looked up at Freeman with a pathetic whimper.

Freeman bent down and scooped Penny into his arms. "You're nothing but trouble; you know that? How'd you get in the house and manage to make such a mess?"

Slurp! Slurp! The pup swiped her tongue across Freeman's chin.

"You're going back to the barn!" Freeman pushed the screen door open with his knee. "I'll be back to help clean up the mess in a few minutes," he called over his shoulder. "First thing tomorrow morning, I'm gonna build this mutt a dog run with a sturdy gate!"

CHAPTER 13

Katie picked up the heavy braided throw rugs she'd taken from the living room and lugged them out to the porch. She'd been cleaning the house while Mom did the laundry. Because the stamp shop was always closed on Mondays, it was the best time to get things done around the house. She'd been relieved this morning at breakfast that neither Mom nor Dad had said anything more about her seeing the doctor. Since she'd eaten most of the food on her plate and had forced herself to smile and appear relaxed, maybe they'd decided there was nothing wrong with her and she didn't need to see the doctor.

Katie draped the rugs over the porch railing and beat them with a broom. Dust flew in all directions, causing her to sneeze. She set the broom down, leaned against the railing, and sighed. It was too warm to be cleaning house.

The back door opened, and Mom stepped onto the porch holding a basket of laundry. "If you feel up to it, would you mind hanging these clothes on the line for me while I wash another load?"

"Sure, I can do that." Katie took the basket and plodded down the stairs. She trudged across the lawn and set the basket under the clothesline.

By the time she'd hung the last sheet, she was sweating, and her back ached from stretching to reach the line.

Bzz. . .bzz. . .

Katie looked up and gasped. A swarm of bees was heading her way!

Bzz. . .bzz. . .

They landed on the sheet overhead.

Katie raced across the yard, screaming, "*Iemeschwarm!*"

The back door flew open, and Mom rushed outside just as Katie leaped onto the porch. "What's going on, Katie? What swarm of bees are you hollering about?"

"Th–they landed on one of the sheets!" Katie's voice trembled, and so did her legs. She leaned against the porch railing and drew in a shaky breath. "I. . .I feel sick to my stomach, and I can hardly breathe."

Mom took hold of Katie's arm. "This has gone on long enough. I'm making you a doctor's appointment today!"

Katie shook her head. "I don't want to see the doctor, and you can't make me go!"

She dashed down the stairs and raced into the field.

With tears coursing down her cheeks, she ran until her sides began to ache. She stopped at the edge of the road and sucked in several deep breaths of air. Then she started walking along the shoulder of the road.

The sun burned furiously, but Katie hurried on, paying no attention to where she was going. When she came to the entrance of their Amish cemetery, she halted. *Should I go in? Would I feel better if I visited Timothy's grave like Mom wanted me to do? Would seeing it again make me feel better or worse?*

Katie stood several minutes, shifting from one foot to the other. Finally, she gathered up her courage, opened the gate, and stepped inside. When she found Timothy's grave, she dropped to her knees. It didn't seem possible that the man she loved and had been planning to marry was lying dead beneath the mound of dirt by his headstone.

Katie's eyes and nose burned; she held her breath until her lungs screamed for air.

Where are you, Timothy? Where'd your spirit go when it left your body?

A strange prickling sensation came over Katie, and her heart started to pound. Suddenly, everything seemed unreal—as if she no longer existed.

Katie jumped up and started to run. She needed to get away. Needed to find a place where she felt safe.

～～

When JoAnn entered the health food store, she noticed Eunice Byler talking to one of the English women who worked there, so she decided to look around on her own, hoping to find a remedy that might help Katie relax. There was no doubt in JoAnn's mind that Katie had some sort of physical or emotional health issue. But if Katie refused to see the doctor, what could be done for her? Katie was a woman now, and JoAnn couldn't force her to go to the doctor. Maybe, though, she could convince Katie to take one of the natural remedies found here.

As JoAnn headed down the aisle where the herbs and homeopathic remedies were displayed, she spotted Loraine's mother, Priscilla.

"Wie geht's?" JoAnn asked when Priscilla stepped up to her.

"I'm fine, but Amos isn't doing so well. He's come down with a cold." Priscilla frowned. "Told me this morning that he felt stuffed up like a rag doll, so I came here to see what I could find to help with his symptoms. What brings you here today? Is someone in your family grank?"

"I'm not sure. Katie might be, but she refuses to let us take her to see the doctor."

"Is she still feeling dizzy like she was on Sunday?"

"I don't think so, but this morning she freaked out over some bees that landed on one of the sheets hanging on the clothesline. Said she felt sick to her stomach and could hardly breathe. She got real upset when I tried to talk to her and ran off into the field." JoAnn motioned to the bottles of herbs. "I figured if I could get her calmed down, she might listen to reason about seeing the doctor, so I came here looking for something that might help."

"Maybe you should try this." Priscilla handed JoAnn a bottle of valerian root. "This herb is supposed to act as a natural sedative.

There's also a remedy in the homeopathic section that's used for calming."

"I appreciate the suggestions, and I'll see if Katie's willing to try them." JoAnn smiled. "How are things with Loraine and Wayne? Are they enjoying married life?"

"Except for Loraine's concerns over Crist and Ada, I believe things are going well."

"What concerns? Are there problems between Loraine and Ada again?"

Priscilla shook her head. "From what I understand, Crist and Ada are having marital problems."

"What a shame. Has our bishop or one of the other ministers counseled with them?"

"Not that I know of. I'm not sure any of the ministers knows about the problem."

"Divorce is not an option for Ada and Crist, so I'd think they would seek help if their marriage is strained."

"I'm not sure Crist would admit to such a thing, and you know how stubborn Ada can be."

"You're good friends with Sadie," JoAnn said, thinking of their bishop's wife. "Maybe you should talk to her about the situation with Crist and Ada."

Priscilla nodded. "I've thought of that, and I may drop by to see her on my way home."

"I think you should. No point in letting this go on until things get worse."

"You're right. It's stressful enough for the newlyweds to be sharing their house with Wayne's folks. They don't need any arguing going on."

"Let me know how it goes." JoAnn turned toward the counter where the cash register sat. "Guess I'd better pay for my things and be on my way. Hopefully by the time I get home, Katie will be there, too."

❦

Freeman whistled as he headed for home with his horse and

buggy. He'd just come from Shipshewana, where he'd picked up the things he needed to finish the dog run he'd started building. He'd be glad to get it done so the pup could be in a safe place, away from the house and his bike shop.

Freeman glanced to the right and was surprised to see Katie Miller running along the shoulder of the road. He guided his horse and buggy alongside of her and stopped. "What are you doing out here so far from home?" he called.

She didn't answer, just kept on running.

Freeman followed her down the road and stopped his horse again when he got ahead of her. This time he got out of the buggy and waited for her. "Katie, what's wrong?"

She finally stopped running and stared up at him like a frightened child. "I. . .I'm going home."

"You're a long ways from home. Where have you been?"

She dropped her gaze to the ground and kicked at the pebbles beneath her feet. "I was out for a walk and ended up at the cemetery."

Now it made sense. Katie's strange behavior had something to do with her visit to the cemetery. "Did you go there to visit Timothy's grave?"

She nodded slowly, and when she lifted her head, tears gathered in her eyes. "I. . .I started to feel funny while I was there, and I knew I needed to go home."

"Funny in what way?"

She shrugged. "Just funny, that's all."

It was obvious that she didn't want to talk about it, so Freeman decided not to press the issue. He motioned to his buggy. "I'm on my way back to my shop, so why don't you let me give you a ride?"

She shifted uneasily but finally nodded.

When they climbed into his buggy, Freeman noticed that Katie had started to shiver. He reached under the seat and pulled out a buggy robe. "If you're cold, here's something you can wrap around your shoulders."

She took the robe but gave no reply.

As they rode along, Freeman asked God to give him the right

words to say to Katie. She was clearly upset, and he didn't want to say anything that might upset her even more.

"Do you have a dog?" he asked.

She gave a quick nod.

"Full grown or still a pup?"

"Full grown."

Not much information, but at least she was talking.

"What kind of dog do you have?"

"Just an old hound, but he's really my daed's dog."

"One of Fern's students presented her with a cocker spaniel puppy for her birthday. She's real cute but can sure be a pescht." Freeman grimaced. "One of us must have left the back door open yesterday morning, because the pup got into the house without our knowing it. When we came home from church, she was in the kitchen and had made a big mess."

"Puppies are known for that. Timothy had a puppy that chewed nearly every one of his socks." Katie's chin quivered. "I. . .I miss him so much."

"I'm sure you do. It's always hard to lose a friend or family member."

"We were going to be married this fall." Katie's voice broke, and she covered her mouth with the back of her hand.

Freeman reached across the seat and touched her arm. "I'm sorry, Katie."

"Can we talk about something else?"

"Jah, sure. If you'd rather, we don't have to talk at all."

She nodded and sighed.

Lord, please be with Katie, Freeman prayed. *I can see that she really does need a friend.*

～≈ ≈～

"Danki for the ride," Katie said when Freeman pulled his horse and buggy to a stop near their barn.

"You're welcome."

She slipped the buggy robe he'd given her under the seat and stepped out of the buggy.

"Take care, Katie," Freeman called as she sprinted toward the house.

When Katie entered the kitchen, she found Mom making a sandwich. "Where have you been, Katie? I've been so worried about you."

"I went to the cemetery."

"On foot?"

Katie nodded.

"But that's a long way to walk."

"I needed to be alone, and I wasn't thinking about how far it was." Katie glanced out the window and watched as Freeman's buggy headed down the driveway. "As I walked home, Freeman came along and offered me a ride."

"That's good. I'm glad you didn't have to walk all that way." Mom moved closer to Katie. "You still look distressed. Are you still upset over that swarm of bees, or is it because you went to the cemetery?"

Katie nodded. "It was a mistake to go there. I won't go again."

"Avoidance isn't the answer, Katie." Mom opened one of the cupboard doors and took out two bottles. "I went to the health food store while you were gone and got these."

"What are they for?"

"One's valerian root, and the other's a homeopathic remedy. Both are supposed to have a calming affect, and I thought they might help you feel better."

Katie shook her head. "I won't take them."

"Why not?"

"Because I don't need them; I'm fine."

"You don't look fine to me. Your face looks strained, and I can see from the red around your eyes that you've been crying."

"I don't need any herbs or homeopathic remedies. I just need to be left alone!"

"You're being stubborn," Mom said. "Just because you still look like a little girl doesn't mean you have to act like one."

"I'm not a little girl, but you're treating me like one!" Katie turned and dashed up the stairs.

When Eunice returned home from the health food store, she found her mother sitting in a chair on the front porch with a basket of mending in her lap. "Here's the chickweed salve you asked me to get for Richard's poison ivy." She handed the paper sack to her mother and took a seat in the chair beside her.

"Danki. I appreciate your going after it. I'm sure your little bruder will, too."

"While I was at the health food store, I heard Priscilla and JoAnn talking about a couple of things that were very surprising."

"Like what?"

Eunice leaned closer to Mom. "For one thing, Priscilla said that Ada and Crist Lambright are having some marital problems."

"Are you sure?"

Eunice nodded. "Priscilla said she's planning to speak with the bishop's wife about it."

"You shouldn't listen to idle chitchat, Eunice."

"It wasn't chitchat. Loraine's mamm is worried about Crist and Ada."

"Even if it's true, it's none of our business."

"You want to know the other thing I heard that really surprised me?"

"What was that?"

"JoAnn was talking to Priscilla about Katie, and she said that she needed to get a remedy to help Katie calm down." Eunice crinkled her nose. "You know what I think, Mom?"

"What's that?"

"I think Katie might be pregnant."

CHAPTER 14

Supper's ready," Mom called through Katie's bedroom door.

Katie groaned. She'd been taking a nap and didn't want to be disturbed.

Tap. Tap. Tap. "Katie, are you awake?"

Katie nestled under her covers like a kitten burrowing into a pile of straw. She didn't want to eat supper, but she knew if she didn't, Mom would probably badger her some more about taking the remedy she'd bought at the health food store.

Tap. Tap.

"I'll be right there!" Katie pushed the covers aside and climbed out of bed. Using her fingers, she tried to smooth the wrinkles from her dress, but it was no use; she looked a mess. She was tempted to change clothes but figured that if she took the time to do that, Mom would knock on her door again.

She set her head covering in place, tucked a few stray hairs under the sides, and left her room. Pulling her shoulders back, she hurried down the stairs.

When she entered the kitchen, she couldn't help but notice the impatient look on Mom's face.

Dad tapped his foot a couple of times. "It's about time," he mumbled. "I'm hungry, and the food's gettin' cold."

"Sorry." Katie slipped into her chair and bowed her head.

After their time of prayer, Dad looked over at Katie and said,

"Your mamm told me what happened earlier today. You shouldn't have run off the way you did. Don't you know how worried your mamm was when you didn't come back right away?"

"I didn't mean to make her worry; I just needed to be alone."

"Jah, well, you could've gone to your room instead of takin' off like that." Dad helped himself to a slice of ham. "And what's all the fuss about a few bees?"

"It wasn't a few bees, Dad. It was whole swarm." Katie forked a piece of ham onto her plate and handed the platter to Mom. "I'm sorry for not helping with supper. I fell asleep in my room."

"Don't worry about it," Mom said with a wave of her hand. "When we're finished eating, you can clear the table and wash the dishes."

Dad looked over at Katie and frowned. "Your mamm also said that she bought something at the health food store to help calm your nerves, but you refused to take it."

Katie slowly nodded. She didn't like being questioned like this. It made her feel like a little girl.

"Why didn't you give one of the remedies a try?"

"I didn't think I needed it. I just needed to rest awhile." Katie took a drink of water. "I feel much better after my nap."

"Glad to hear it." Dad shoveled some mashed potatoes onto his plate and dropped a pat of butter on top. "Your mamm and I have been very worried about you, Katie."

She gave a shaky laugh. "Well, you don't need to be. I'm fine."

"Are you sure about that?"

Katie nodded.

"You weren't fine when you passed out during church," Dad said.

"That was because it was so warm in the buggy shop, and it may also have been because I hadn't had much breakfast."

"What about how upset you got today?" Mom asked. "You sure weren't fine when you ran off the way you did."

"I was upset about the bees, and I'm sorry if I upset you."

Mom's disbelieving look made Katie even more determined

to prove to her folks that she didn't need any kind of remedy to settle her nerves.

~¾ ¾~

Loraine had just set a kettle of water on the stove to boil when Wayne stepped into the kitchen.

"What's for supper?" he asked, sniffing the air. "I don't smell anything cooking."

She pointed to a package of noodles on the counter. "I'm just getting started. We should be ready to eat in a half hour or so."

"I'm surprised my mamm's not in here helping. Where is she anyway?"

"She spilled coffee on her dress and went to her room to change."

Wayne's forehead puckered. "I hope she didn't burn herself."

Loraine shook her head. "It was a cup she'd forgotten to drink, so it wasn't hot."

"That's good." Wayne looked over his shoulder. "My daed came in behind me, but I think he headed down the hall to the bathroom."

Loraine lowered her voice to a whisper. "By the way, have you had a chance to speak to your folks about their problem?"

"What problem?"

"Their marital problem."

Wayne shrugged. "I'm not sure they're having a problem. I mean, I haven't heard them raise their voices for a couple of days."

"*Absatz!* Stop badgering me, Ada!" Crist rushed into the kitchen, his face bright red. He halted in front of Wayne. "Your *mudder* just won't leave me alone!"

"That's because he won't listen to reason!" Ada shouted as she followed him into the room. She frowned at Crist. "If he *could* listen, that is."

Crist took a step back from her. "You don't have to yell! I'm standing right here!"

"If I didn't yell, you wouldn't hear what I was saying!"

Wayne held up his hand. "Don't you two realize how it makes us feel when you argue like this?"

"We wouldn't argue if your daed wasn't so stubborn." Ada motioned to Wayne. "Can't you talk him into getting his hearing tested?"

Wayne's eyes widened. "Is that why you've been hollering at each other so much lately?"

Ada nodded. "I'm surprised you and Loraine haven't been yelling so your daed could hear you, too."

Wayne gave a nod. "Now that you mention it, I have had to repeat myself to Pop several times lately."

Ada nudged Crist's arm. "Uh-huh, I knew it."

Loraine heard a buggy rumble into the yard, and she glanced out the window. "Looks like we've got company."

"Now who's come here this close to supper? I hope it's not someone bringing another dead animal hide to your taxidermy shop." Ada craned her neck to look around Crist. "Ach, it's the bishop! I wonder what he wants."

Loraine's mouth went dry. *What if Mom spoke to the bishop's wife like she said she might do? What if Sadie told James, and he's come here to speak to Ada and Crist about their marital problems?*

"There's only one way we'll know what Bishop James wants, and that's to open the door and let him in." Wayne ambled out of the room and, moments later, returned with the bishop.

The bishop pulled his fingers through his thick, full beard and looked right at Crist. "I heard some rather distressing news today. Figured I'd better come over here and find out if it's true."

"What good news did you hear?" Crist asked.

The bishop's bushy eyebrows shot up. "I said *distressing* news, not *good* news."

"What distressing news?" asked Ada.

Loraine's heart started to pound, and she stepped between Ada and the bishop. "I. . .uh. . .think there's been a mistake."

"What kind of cake?" Crist scratched his head. "Are we having cake for dessert tonight?"

Ada groaned. "No one said anything about cake." She turned

to the bishop. "What kind of distressing news did you come to give us?"

The bishop shook his head. "Didn't come to give you any news. Came to see if I could help with your marital problems."

Ada's mouth formed an O. "Crist and I aren't having marital problems. Who said we were?"

The bishop motioned to Loraine. "Her mamm told my fraa that you and Crist have been hollering at each other a lot lately."

"I holler because he can't hear." Ada needled Crist in the ribs. "He needs to get his hearing tested, but he refuses to go."

"That's all there is to it?"

Ada nodded.

A look of relief flooded the bishop's face. "You come with me later this week," he said to Crist. "I'll take you to my doctor to get your hearing tested."

Crist moved closer to the bishop. "What was that?"

"Said I'll be by later this week, and we'll get your hearing tested!"

Crist nodded and smiled. "Jah, sure; I'd be happy to go along when you get your hearing tested."

Loraine looked at Wayne; Wayne looked at Ada; and they all laughed. It was a relief to know that Ada and Crist's marriage wasn't in trouble. And if the bishop could get Crist to have his hearing tested, then Loraine was sure all the shouting would end.

※ ※

"Where are you going?" Fern called to Freeman as he started out the back door.

"I'm headin' to the phone shed to call a few customers. Need to let 'em know that their bikes are ready."

"Well, don't be too long. Eunice will be here soon, and supper's almost ready."

"No problem. I'll be back in short order. Wouldn't risk missing out on your baked ham and mashed potatoes." He winked at Fern and went out the door.

As Freeman headed down the path leading to the phone shed,

he thought about Katie and wondered how she was doing. After seeing how she'd acted this afternoon, he was sure something was weighing on her mind besides missing Timothy. If there was just some way he could get her to open up about her feelings. If he could get her to do that, maybe he could find out what was at the root of her nervousness.

I'll just have to keep praying for her, and whenever I get the chance, I'll offer an encouraging word, he thought as he stepped into the phone shed.

Since the small building had no windows, it was dark inside. Freeman left the door open and turned on the battery-operated lantern sitting on the small table beside the phone. Then he took a seat in the folding chair, placed his notebook on the table, and punched in the phone number of the first customer he needed to call.

He got a busy signal, so he tried the next number. There was no answer there, so he left a message on the customer's voice mail.

He'd just started dialing the third number, when a gust of wind came up. *Bam!* The door blew shut.

A sense of uneasiness tightened Freeman's chest as he thought about the discomfort he felt whenever he was in a confined place like this.

He moved away from the phone and grabbed the doorknob. When he turned it, the knob fell off in his hand.

"Oh no!" Sweat beaded on Freeman's forehead and ran down his nose. His shoulders tensed, and he drew in a quick breath.

Don't panic. Relax. Stay calm.

He placed the doorknob on the phone table, took a couple more deep breaths, and closed his eyes.

An image from the past leaped into his head. He'd been seven years old and had gone down to the cellar to get a jar of peaches for his mother. He hadn't been afraid at first—not until he couldn't get the door open. Then when his flashlight batteries died, Freeman had panicked. He'd pounded on the door and hollered until his throat hurt, certain that no one would find him and he'd die in the cellar. By the time Mom realized he was missing and come looking for him, he was bawling like a newborn calf.

Freeman's eyes popped open, and his mind snapped back to the present. *I'm not a little boy anymore. I'm a grown man, and I know how to diffuse my fear.*

Breathe deeply. . .move through the anxiety. . .float with it. . .get mad at it. . .do whatever it takes.

He stared at the doorknob, wishing he had the tools to put it back on. "This is really dumb," he muttered. "All I need to do is call someone and say I'm locked in the phone shed."

He dialed the number of their closest neighbor, got their answering machine, and left a message. Then he called another neighbor, but there was no answer there, either.

After making five calls and getting nothing but voice mails and answering machines, he was more than a little frustrated.

Stay relaxed, he told himself. *If someone gets my message soon, they'll rescue me. Or else when supper's ready and I'm not at the house, Fern will come looking for me.*

Freeman drew in another deep breath and rested his head on the table. *While I'm waiting, I may as well try to take a nap.*

CHAPTER 15

As Eunice guided her horse and buggy in the direction of the Bontragers' house, her excitement mounted. She could hardly wait to see Freeman again and hoped he would enjoy the pie she'd brought for dessert.

An unexpected gust of wind pushed against the buggy, and it started to rain.

She leaned forward, straining to see through the rain-spattered windshield. At this rate, it would take forever to get to Freeman's house.

Eunice didn't like driving in the rain, but fortunately she didn't have far to go. She hoped that by the time she was to return home this evening the weather would improve.

A pair of wide-beamed headlights went by; then she saw the red taillights as the car disappeared. Eunice leaned over and flipped the button to turn on the windshield wipers, keeping her focus on the road.

As Eunice passed the Millers' place, she thought about Katie and the way she'd fainted in church. Between that and the things she'd heard Katie's mother say at the health food store, Eunice was almost sure Katie must be pregnant. She wondered if anyone else thought that, too. Mom had cautioned her not to mention her suspicions to anyone since she didn't know for sure that Katie was pregnant, but it was going to be hard to keep quiet about this.

Soon the Bontragers' place came into view, and she breathed a sigh of relief. She turned up the driveway, drove past the phone shed and the bike shop, and halted the horse near the barn. Then she climbed out of the buggy, unhitched the horse, and put him in the corral.

Returning to the buggy, she grabbed the plastic container with her pie inside and sprinted for the house.

When she stepped inside, she was greeted by Fern.

"It's good to see you; you're right on time," Fern said, glancing at the clock on the kitchen wall.

Eunice smiled and handed her the container. "I brought a strawberry-rhubarb pie for dessert."

"Umm. . .that sounds good. Strawberry-rhubarb's one of Freeman's favorites. It's also one of mine."

Eunice glanced around. "Where is Freeman? I didn't see any light coming from his shop, so I figured he must have quit working and was here at the house."

"He was here, but he went out to the phone shed to make a few calls." Fern's forehead wrinkled as she looked at the clock again. "That was quite awhile ago. He should have been back by now."

"Maybe he went out to his shop after he made the phone calls."

"That could be."

"Want me to go check?"

"If you don't mind going back outside. It's raining pretty hard out there."

"It started coming down soon after I left home." Eunice motioned to her rain-soaked dress. "I'm already wet, so I guess a little more rain won't matter."

"There's an umbrella hanging on the wall peg by the back door," Fern said. "You can borrow that if you like."

"Danki." Eunice grabbed the umbrella and scooted out the door.

She'd only made it halfway to the bike shop when a gust of wind came up and turned the umbrella inside-out.

"I don't need this kind of trouble," she mumbled as she hurried along.

Her feet slipped on the wet grass, and she went down on her knees. With a sense of determination, she scrambled to her feet. When she finally reached the bicycle shop, she discovered that the door was locked. Freeman was obviously not inside.

He must still be in the phone shed. Eunice quickened her steps and headed in that direction.

~≪ ≫~

Freeman lifted his head from the table and stared at the phone, wondering if he should make another call. He was sure someone would eventually hear one of the messages he'd left, but in the meantime, his rumbling stomach kept reminding him that it was time for supper.

I wonder if Eunice has arrived yet. He hadn't heard her horse and buggy come up the driveway, but then the wind and rain were making so much noise, he probably couldn't have heard a dump truck if it had roared past the shed.

A knock on the door pulled Freeman's thoughts aside. "Are you in there, Freeman?"

Freeman was relieved to hear Eunice's voice. "Jah, I'm here. The doorknob came off, and I'm trapped."

He heard a rattling noise; then a few seconds later, the door opened. When Eunice stepped inside, he noticed that her dress was sopping wet and her kapp had gone limp from the rain. Even so, he thought she looked like an angel.

"How long have you been in here?" she asked.

He shrugged. "Too long. I don't like small places."

She motioned to the phone. "Why didn't you call someone for help?"

"I did, but all I got were folks' answering machines or voice mails." Freeman groaned. "I was beginning to think I'd have to spend the night out here."

She snickered. "I'm sure your sister would have eventually come looking for you."

"Jah, I suppose."

"We'd better get up to the house right away, or she'll probably come looking for both of us."

Freeman pointed to the doorknob lying on the phone table. "Guess I'll worry about fixing that later. It's not likely that anyone will come by wanting to use the phone shed in this crummy weather."

As they stepped outside, Freeman wrapped his hand around hers and gave it a gentle squeeze. "Danki, for coming to my rescue, Eunice."

"You're welcome," she said smiling up at him sweetly.

They hurried across the yard, and when they entered the house, Fern gave Eunice one of her dresses to change into.

While Eunice changed clothes, Freeman told Fern about his ordeal in the phone shed.

"I had no idea you were trapped in there. I wondered why it was taking so long for you to make a few calls." Fern touched his shoulder. "Did it bother you being stuck in that small shed?"

"It did at first, but I worked through it okay."

Fern smiled. "And then Eunice came along and rescued you."

"That's right, and I'm grateful she did."

Fern gestured to the stove. "Supper's ready now, so as soon as Eunice comes out of the bathroom we can eat."

⚜

Freeman stared into his nearly empty glass. Throughout the meal he'd become acutely aware that Fern approved of Eunice and was making every effort to get them together. No doubt that was the reason she'd invited Eunice to join them for supper this evening. Well, that was okay with Freeman. He could enjoy Eunice's company, even though he had no plans to settle down to marriage for a good long while.

"Now it's time for us to eat the dessert I brought." Eunice smiled at Freeman, her eyes sparkling in the light of the gas lamp hanging above the table.

He patted his full stomach and groaned. "I ate so much supper,

I'm not sure I have any room for dessert."

Eunice's chin jutted out, and her nose crinkled. "You have to try some of my strawberry-rhubarb pie. I baked it just for you."

Freeman smiled. "That's my favorite kind of pie, so I guess I can't say no."

～ ❧ ～

"You ought to see how hard the wind's whipping the trees in our backyard," Katie's mother said, staring out the kitchen window. "I hope your daed's not having any trouble getting the horses put in the barn."

Katie stepped up beside Mom and peered out the window. It was hard to believe the warm weather they'd been having had changed so drastically and in such a short time.

She caught sight of Dad struggling to get one of their horses into the barn. If Katie's four brothers weren't married and still lived at home, they'd be outside helping him right now.

Maybe I should go out and help. Katie hurried across the room and plucked her jacket off the wall peg near the back door. "I'm going out to help Dad," she called to Mom before she rushed out the door.

Katie fought against the harsh wind as she made her way to the corral. Two of Dad's newer horses that weren't fully trained hadn't gone into the barn yet. They stamped their hooves, reared up, and kicked out their back legs, obviously frightened by the howling wind.

Dad had a rope and was trying to fasten it around one horse's halter, while the second horse ran around the corral in circles.

Katie darted into the buggy shed and grabbed a buggy whip. Dad never used a whip on any of his horses unless it was absolutely necessary. Katie figured she could put the whip to good use without hitting the horse, so she snapped it behind the horse a couple of times, and that did the trick.

By the time they got both horses into the barn, Katie was out of breath, and her dress was soaking wet from the rain.

"Danki for your help." Dad gave Katie an appreciative smile.

"I think those two were really spooked by this nasty weather."

Katie nodded. "The wind and rain are enough to spook anyone."

"I'd better get the door shut or we'll have rain and wind in here." Dad grabbed the handle of the barn door and gave it a tug. He almost had it closed when a gust of wind whipped against the door, and it slammed shut, smacking him in the head.

Dad let out a moan and crumpled to the floor.

CHAPTER 16

I wish I could stay and visit awhile longer," Eunice said, rising from the sofa. "But since there's a break in the rain, I'd better get home before it starts up again."

"That's probably a good idea. I'll get the rest of your pie for you to take home," Fern said, heading for the kitchen.

"No, that's okay. You can keep what's left of the pie." Eunice looked over at Freeman and smiled. "Maybe I'll bake another pie when you come over for supper on Saturday."

"That'd be nice."

Eunice started for the door but turned back around. "Oh, I almost forgot. . . I left my dress hanging in the bathroom. I'd better check and see if it's dry so I can give you back your dress, Eunice."

"It's probably still wet, but you can wear my dress home. I'll get it from you later in the week." Fern gave Eunice a hug. "I'm glad you were able to join us for supper."

"Me, too. Well, I'll get my dress and put it in a plastic bag, then I'll be on my way." Eunice hurried down the hall to the bathroom.

When she returned to the living room a short time later, she was disappointed to see that Freeman wasn't there.

"Freeman's outside getting your horse hitched to the buggy," Fern said. "You might want to wait in here until it's ready."

"It shouldn't take him too long, so I'll wait out on the porch.

Thanks again for supper. It was delicious." Eunice smiled and scooted out the door.

She was pleased when Freeman brought the horse and buggy close to the house and called, "He's hitched up for you and ready to go!"

Eunice left the porch and hurried up to Freeman, who stood by the horse stroking it behind the ears. "Seems like a nice mare," he said. "What's her name?"

"Dolly."

He grinned. "Did you name her that, or did she already have the name when you got her?"

"Dolly was her name when my daed bought her for me." Eunice put her purse and the bag with her dress in it inside the buggy; then she turned to face Freeman. "I appreciate your getting my horse and buggy ready. Danki."

He pulled his fingers through the sides of his hair and gave a quick nod. "Sure, no problem."

She hesitated, hoping he might say something more, but he just stood, scuffing the toe of his boot on the ground.

"Guess I'd better go." Eunice stepped into the buggy and took up the reins.

"I'll see you next week," he called as she turned toward the driveway.

She smiled and lifted her hand with a wave.

～≪ ≫～

When Freeman returned to the house, he found Fern sitting at the kitchen table drinking a cup of tea.

"Would you like another piece of pie?" she asked.

He shook his head.

"How about some tea?"

"No thanks."

Fern motioned to the chair beside her. "Then have a seat, and we can visit while I drink my tea."

Freeman bristled. He didn't care for her bossy tone.

As if sensing his irritation, Fern said in a much softer tone,

"Please, have a seat. I'd like to talk to you a minute."

The chair scraped against the linoleum as Freeman pulled it away from the table. "What'd you want to talk about?"

"Eunice."

"What about her?"

"I think she's nice, don't you?"

He nodded.

"She's very pleasant and easy to talk to."

Freeman propped his elbows on the table. "Are you trying to make a point?"

Fern took another sip of tea. "Grandma and I were talking the other day, and we're both hoping you'll join the church this fall."

"Uh-huh, I probably will."

"We're also hoping that you'll find the right girl, and that you might—"

"Get married and settle down?"

"Jah."

"Don't tell me—you think Eunice is the girl I should marry."

Fern nodded. "From what I can tell, I think she'd make a good wife."

Irritation welled in Freeman's chest. He didn't appreciate his sister trying to choose a mate for him. If and when he felt ready for marriage, he'd do his own choosing.

He glanced at the clock above the refrigerator. "It's getting late. Shouldn't Grandma be home by now?"

Fern shook her head. "She told me this morning that after she was done eating supper with her widowed friends, she'd be going to Sharon Hershberger's to spend the night."

"How come?"

"Because Sharon's feeling very lonely—it's only been a month since her husband died. Some of Sharon's friends and relatives have been taking turns spending the night with her. Tonight is Grandma's turn."

"Oh, I see. That's nice of her."

Fern nodded. "Getting back to Eunice, what did you think of her pie?"

"It was good. If you'll recall, I had two pieces." Freeman pushed his chair away from the table. "I'm tired; think I'll go on up to bed."

Fern opened her mouth as if to say something more, but Freeman hurried from the room.

≈ ❧ ↢

Katie squirmed in her chair as she sat beside her mother in a waiting area outside the emergency room at the hospital in Goshen, awaiting some news on her dad's condition.

Please, God, Katie prayed, *don't let my daed die.*

Tears stung her eyes, and she could barely swallow because her throat burned so much. Even though this wasn't the same hospital she and her cousins had been taken to after their accident last fall, she felt as if she were reliving the moment. She could see herself sitting in the waiting room after she'd been given the news that Timothy was dead. She could hear Loraine's voice as she tried talking to her, and she remembered how unresponsive she'd been.

Katie could almost smell the hospital smells and feel the cold metal of the chair she'd been sitting in. She'd withdrawn into her own little world and hadn't emerged until she'd move to Florida to be with Grammy and Grandpa.

Mom touched Katie's shoulder. "Did you hear what I said?"

"What was that?"

"I asked if you'd like something to drink."

Katie shook her head. "I just want to know how Dad is doing. I hope he's not going to—" Her voice faltered, and she nearly choked on a sob.

Mom grasped Katie's hand. "We have to trust God and keep praying for your daed."

I prayed for Timothy, and what good did that do? Katie thought bitterly. She glanced at the clock on the far wall. It had been almost two hours since Dad had been taken in to be examined. What could be taking so long?

At the sound of a siren approaching, Katie jumped up. She went to the window and looked out. An ambulance had pulled

108

up to the emergency room entrance. Two paramedics rushed in, pushing a man on a gurney. He was covered in blood!

A rush of heat flooded Katie's face, her heart thudded, and a wave of nausea rolled through her stomach. Everything felt unreal—as if she no longer existed. She could see and hear what was going on around her, but it felt as if it were all a dream. She whirled around and raced out the door.

Leaning heavily against the side of the building, she closed her eyes and gulped in some air. Her legs wobbled, and she felt weak and light-headed, as if she might pass out.

The rain had stopped, and a cool breeze blew, but it didn't help at all. She wanted to run and keep on running but didn't know where to go.

"Katie, are you all right?"

Katie's eyes snapped open, and she blinked a couple of times. She could see by the pinched expression on Mom's face that she was worried about her.

"I. . .I'm fine. The sight of all that blood made me feel woozy." No point in telling Mom about the feeling of unreality that had converged on her. Mom wouldn't understand. Besides, the strange feelings Katie had experienced were too difficult to explain.

Mom slipped her arm around Katie's waist. "I just spoke with one of the doctors."

"What'd he say?"

"He said your daed has a mild concussion, but he's going to be okay. The doctor wants to keep him overnight for observation, so I'll call our driver to take us home, and then we'll come back tomorrow to get your daed."

Katie nodded as a sense of relief flooded her soul. Dad wasn't going to die. At least one of her prayers had been answered. Now if God would only answer her most recent prayer and take away the anxious feelings she'd been having since she had returned home.

CHAPTER 17

The month of June brought hot days and humid nights, causing Loraine to feel wet and sticky. That, coupled with nausea, made it hard not to be cross. But this morning, as she returned home from her doctor's appointment, she felt better than she had in days. Her heart pulsed with joy as she held both hands against her stomach. She was carrying Wayne's child. In seven months she was going to be a mother. She could hardly wait to see Wayne and share the good news.

Loraine was tempted to go out to the taxidermy shop where Wayne was working with his dad, but she didn't want to disturb them. Besides, what she had to say was for Wayne to hear in private. He had the right to know he was going to be a father before his parents heard the news. She hoped he'd be as happy about becoming a parent as she was but was worried that he might not feel ready to take on the responsibility. With their business slacking off some in the last few weeks, he might feel that they couldn't afford to have a baby right now.

Well, it's too late for that, Loraine thought as Marge Nelson pulled up in front of the house. She paid Marge for the ride, said good-bye, and hurried up the stairs.

When Loraine entered the kitchen, she found Ada filling a cardboard box with dishes and towels. "What are you doing?" she asked.

Ada smiled. "Since Crist and I will be moving next week to the little house we found to rent, I figured I'd better get some things packed up."

"Are you getting tired of waiting for your new house to be built? Is that why you've decided to rent?"

Ada nodded. "That, and we came to the conclusion that it's time for us to leave you and Wayne alone to enjoy each other and raise your family without us in the way."

"You're not in the way," Loraine said with a shake of her head.

"That's nice of you to say, but we feel that moving into the rental will be best for all." Ada pulled out a chair at the table and sat down. "How'd your doctor's appointment go? Did you find out why you've been feeling sick to your stomach so often lately?"

Loraine's face flamed. "You know about that?"

Ada chuckled. "You can't hide things like that from a woman who's had a boppli herself."

"No, I suppose not."

"So what'd the doctor say?"

"I'd like wait and talk to Wayne about my appointment before I say anything to you and Crist," Loraine said.

"I understand. Sorry for putting you on the spot like that. Sometimes I shoot off my big mouth before I think about what I should say."

Loraine smiled. Wayne's mother had changed in the last several months. There was a day when Ada wouldn't have admitted to any of her shortcomings. She wouldn't have spoken so kindly to Loraine before, either.

"How's Crist adjusting to his new hearing aid?" Loraine asked. "I haven't had the chance to ask him about it."

"He's hearing much better these days, although there are times when I think he turns it off so he won't have to listen to me."

Loraine chuckled. Ada had even developed a sense of humor that she hadn't had before.

She took a glass from the cupboard and filled it with water. "Do you think Crist will move the taxidermy shop to one of the buildings on your property when your new house is finally finished?"

Ada shrugged. "I don't think so. Crist mentioned keeping the shop here because it's closer for Wayne. After all, he'll be taking it over someday."

"Did Wayne tell you that?"

"Tell me what?" Wayne asked as he stepped into the kitchen.

"We were just talking about the taxidermy business," Loraine said. "Your mamm mentioned you'll be taking it over someday."

"Maybe so, but there's still a lot I don't know about the business, and I hope Pop will be working with me for a long time." Wayne joined Loraine in front of the sink. "How'd your doctor's appointment go? Did you find out why you've been feeling so tired and queasy?"

Loraine glanced over at Ada, hoping she wouldn't say anything about what she suspected.

"Think I'll leave you two alone while I take something cold to drink out to your daed." Ada opened the refrigerator and removed a container of lemonade. Then she grabbed two paper cups and scurried out the door.

Loraine motioned to the table. "Let's have a seat, and I'll tell you what the doctor said."

Wayne pulled out a chair for Loraine, and after she sat down, he seated himself in the chair beside her. "You look so solemn. Please don't tell me there's something seriously wrong."

She shook her head. "No, no, I'm fine." She placed both hands on her stomach. "I'm in a family way, that's all."

Wayne's eyebrows met between the bridge of his nose, and he stared at her with a look of disbelief.

Loraine wondered if he was unhappy about becoming a father. She remembered how reluctant he had been to marry her after he'd lost his leg. Maybe he was afraid his disability would keep him from being the kind of father he felt he needed to be.

"Are you disappointed?" Her question came out as a squeak.

Wayne shook his head. "Of course not; I'm just surprised. We've only been married a few months, and I didn't think we'd be starting our family so soon." He sat motionless for several seconds, then reached for her hand. "I'm glad you're with child. I can't wait to be a father."

She leaned her head on his shoulder and breathed a sigh of relief. Now they could tell the rest of their family.

❦

As Freeman sat on the Bylers' back porch with Eunice's twelve-year-old brother, he couldn't help but smile. The boy was a regular chatterbox, and he couldn't sit still for more than a few minutes. Freeman remembered Fern mentioning that she'd had trouble dealing with Richard in class. Watching the way the boy carried on, Freeman could understand why. He didn't envy Fern her job as Richard's teacher.

"Sure is hot out tonight." Richard swiped at the sweat rolling down the side of his face. "Makes me wish I could go swimmin' in our pond." He frowned. "I'll probably have to spend my whole summer workin' for Papa in the fields. Probably won't get to do much swimmin' at all."

"I'm sure you'll get some time off so you can have a little fun." Freeman leaned back in his chair, put both hands behind his head, and rested his head in his palms. He knew how important it was for a young boy to have some time to himself. Even though Freeman had enjoyed working in his uncle's bike shop when he was a teenager, he'd anxiously awaited his days off so he could fool around and have some fun.

Freeman reached into his pocket and pulled out a long, slender yellow balloon. Andrew had come by the bike shop a few days ago and taught Freeman how to make a few simple animal balloons, like a giraffe and a weiner dog.

Richard tipped his head. "Whatcha doin' with that balloon?"

"I'm gonna blow it up and make a giraffe for you."

"Oh, ya mean like Andrew Yoder does?"

Freeman nodded and stretched the balloon. "It takes a lot of air to blow one of these up, but it helps if the balloon's stretched well first."

"I'll bet I could blow the balloon up without stretchin' it."

"You think so?"

Richard bobbed his head. "Sure do."

"All right then." Freeman pulled another balloon from his pocket and handed it to Richard. "Here you go."

Freeman quickly blew up his balloon; then he sat back and waited to see what the boy would do.

Richard put the end of the balloon between his lips and blew. Nothing happened. He blew again and again until his face turned red. Finally, he stretched the balloon a few times and tried once more. The balloon still didn't inflate.

Freeman chuckled. "Looks a lot easier than it is, doesn't it?"

With a look of sheer determination, Richard blew again. Finally, the balloon inflated.

"Now watch what I do with my balloon and then try to do the same with yours." Freeman twisted a bubble for the giraffe's head. When that was done, he twisted several more bubbles, until the balloon looked like a giraffe.

"Whew! That was hard work," Richard said once his giraffe had been formed. "Sure hope Mama and Eunice have supper ready soon, 'cause I'm more hungry now than I was before!"

Freeman laughed as he nodded his head. "Me, too. I'm lookin' forward to trying out some of your sister's cooking."

"*Sie is en gudi koch,*" Richard said.

"I'm sure she is a good cook. I had some of her strawberry-rhubarb pie last week, and it was wunderbaar."

"Sure hope Mama don't fix her green bean casserole." Richard wrinkled his nose. "I don't like green beans!"

Freeman leaned closer to the boy and lowered his voice. "Can you keep a secret?"

"Sure can, but if you've got a secret, then you'd better not tell Eunice, 'cause she blabs everything she hears."

"I do not!"

Richard's face blanched, and Freeman whirled around at the sound of Eunice's shrill voice. He'd been so engrossed in his conversation with her brother that he hadn't heard her come out to the porch. He'd never heard her shout like that, either. It made him wonder what kind of a mother she would make.

Eunice gave her brother a nasty look then quickly covered it with a smile in Freeman's direction. "What was the secret you wanted to tell my little bruder?"

"It's not really a secret," Freeman said. "I was just going to say that I don't care much for green beans."

A look of relief spread across Eunice's face. "No problem. There will be no green beans on the table this evening."

Richard clapped his hands. "That's a relief!"

"I came out here to tell you that supper's almost ready." Eunice looked over at Richard. "Run out to the barn and tell Papa that we'll be ready to eat in five minutes."

The boy frowned. "Can't ya just ring the dinner bell? Freeman's been showin' me how to make an animal balloon." He held up the giraffe. "And we've also been busy gabbin'."

Eunice shot him another look. "Do as I asked or I'll tell Mama that you're being uncooperative again! You know how she feels about kinner who don't listen. If you're not careful you might get a *bletsching*."

"Don't want no whippin', so I'll be goin' right away!" Richard jumped out of his chair, leaped off the porch, and raced for the barn.

Eunice shook her head as she lowered herself into the chair he'd been sitting on. "That ornery bruder of mine has a mind of his own."

"I think most boys his age do," Freeman said.

"Maybe so, but he's more headstrong than most boys his age." Eunice gave Freeman a heart-melting smile. "I'm glad you were able to come for supper this evening."

He returned her smile. "I hear you're a good cook, so I'm sure it was well worth the wait."

≈≫≈

"Are you sure you won't change your mind and come with us to Ohio for my cousin's funeral?" Mom asked when she stepped into the garden where Katie had been weeding.

Katie shook her head. "You and Dad will be gone several days, and someone needs to be here to run the stamp shop."

Mom's eyebrows furrowed. "We can close the shop if you'd like to come along. It's not like we're running a business that requires someone to be here all the time."

"No, that's okay; I'd rather stay here and keep working."

Mom squatted beside Katie. "I'm worried about you staying here by yourself."

"I'll be fine. I'm looking forward to some quiet time on my own." Katie hoped Mom believed her. She needed her folks to think she was doing okay, and she was determined to put on a brave front. Besides the fact that Katie couldn't deal with the thought of going to another funeral, she really did look forward to being alone for a few days. It would be a welcome relief not to have Mom fussing over her all the time, asking how she felt, and suggesting that she see a doctor or take some herbs.

Katie brushed the dirt from her hands and stood. "You and Dad go on to Ohio and stay as long as you need to. I'll be fine on my own while you're gone."

As Katie thought about spending the next several nights alone, a ripple of apprehension shot up her spine. *At least I hope I'll be fine.*

CHAPTER 18

Breathing the damp aroma of the moist soil where she'd been pulling weeds, Katie let her fingers trail along the stem of a flower. She lifted her head and watched as the puffy clouds shifted across the sky. Simple pleasures, she knew, were the most satisfying, and working in the garden was a simple pleasure.

An oppressive hot wind whipped against Katie's face, but she kept pulling weeds. She wanted to get this done before it was time to fix supper, and she hoped, if there was enough time before it got dark, she could take a walk out back to the pond.

The *clip-clop* of horse's hooves drew Katie's attention to the road. When a horse and buggy started up their driveway, Katie slapped her hands together to remove the dirt and stood. She figured it was someone coming to the stamp shop, and she'd need to tell them that the shop was closed for the day.

Katie was surprised when the buggy pulled up to the barn and Loraine and Ella got out.

"We heard your folks had gone to Ohio and that you'd stayed here by yourself," Ella said when Katie stepped up to Loraine's buggy.

Katie nodded. "They left this morning after breakfast."

"Ella and I decided to come by and see if there was anything you needed," Loraine said.

"That's nice of you," Katie replied, "but I'm getting along fine on my own."

117

Ella handed Katie a small paper sack. "I brought you some of my friendship bread. Should we go inside and have a piece?"

Katie hesitated but finally nodded. "Jah, sure. It'll be good to get out of this heat for a while."

They hurried into the house, and while Loraine and Ella took seats at the table, Katie washed her hands and then poured them each a glass of iced tea and cut Ella's bread.

They sat across from each other, talking about ordinary things like the hot, humid weather and Ella's job doing the books at her dad's wind chime business.

"There's another reason we came by," Ella said.

"What's that?" Katie asked.

Ella looked over at Loraine. "You'd better tell her. After all, it's your surprise."

Loraine's cheeks turned pink as she placed both hands against her stomach. "Wayne and I are expecting a boppli."

"A baby? When?"

"It's not due until the end of February, but we can hardly wait."

"I'm looking forward to being a second cousin." Ella reached for another piece of bread. "I think it'll be fun to have a sweet little boppli we can all fuss over."

Loraine chuckled. "Between Wayne's mamm and my mamm, we might have to stand in line to hold the boppli."

Katie sipped her iced tea as she listened to her cousins talk about the baby. She was happy for Loraine but couldn't help feeling a bit envious. She longed to be a wife and a mother, but that dream had been snatched away the day Timothy died. She'd have to spend the rest of her life enjoying other people's babies.

Loraine pushed her chair away from the table and stood. "I think we'd better go. It'll be time to start supper soon, and I should be there to help Ada."

Ella nodded. "My mamm will be expecting my help, too."

Katie followed them to the door. "Danki for coming by. It was nice to take a break from what I was doing."

As they started down the porch steps, Loraine turned to Katie and said, "I forgot to mention that I attached one of my poems to the loaf of friendship bread Ella made. Did you see it on the wrapping paper when you opened the bread?"

Katie nodded. "I didn't take time to read it, but I left it on the counter, so I'll read it later when I'm done with my weeding."

"Say, with your folks gone, maybe one evening this week we can do some stamping like we'd talked about," Ella said.

"I'll have to see how it goes," Katie replied. "If I'm real busy in the stamp shop, I may be too tired to do any stamping at the end of the day."

"Well, let us know," Loraine said.

"I will."

As Loraine and Ella headed for their buggy, Katie returned to her job in the garden. By the time she'd finished weeding, she was more than ready for a walk to the pond. She gathered up her gardening tools, put them in the shed, and headed across the field behind their house.

Soon she saw the water from the pond glistening in the sunlight, offering her a welcome relief.

Katie flopped onto the ground, leaned her head against the trunk of a tree, and closed her eyes. A cool breeze caressed her face, and she was soon asleep.

~⁂~

Katie sat up with a start and looked around. It was almost dark. The sun had spread its palette of warm hues across the darkening sky, and one by one, the fireflies were beginning to appear.

Katie's stomach growled, and she realized that it was past time to fix supper. She scrambled to her feet and hurried across the field.

By the time she reached the house, the sky had darkened. She paused on the porch and peered up at the twinkling stars, enjoying a sense of calm. She hadn't felt this peaceful since she'd come home from Florida. Maybe all she'd needed was a little time alone, away from Mom's constant hovering.

When Katie's stomach rumbled again, she scurried into the

kitchen and lit the gas lantern hanging above the table. She'd just put some leftover soup in a kettle and was about to set it on the stove when she spotted the poem Loraine had written. She picked it up and read it out loud:

> "Pleasant thoughts are being sent your way;
> I know that God is with you every day.
> Remember to thank Him for being by your side;
> No matter the circumstance, in Him you can abide."

The words blurred as Katie blinked against a film of tears. Oh, how she wanted to believe that God was by her side. She felt alone and frightened much of the time.

Thump! Thump!

Katie jerked her head.

Thump! Thump! There it was again. It sounded like footsteps on the front porch.

Dad's dog howled from his dog run outside. Katie's heart pounded, and her palms grew sweaty. She hadn't heard a car or a horse and buggy come into the yard. Maybe someone had ridden in on a bike or come on foot.

She left the kitchen and headed for the living room. *Maybe it's someone wanting something from the stamp shop.*

"Who's there?" Katie called through the closed door.

No response. Nothing but the whisper of the wind.

She grasped the doorknob and slowly opened the door.

Waaa! Waaa!

Katie sucked in a startled breath and gasped. On the porch sat a wicker basket with a baby inside!

When Katie bent down, she spotted a note attached to the baby's blanket. She plucked it off and silently read it: *I can't take care of my baby, so I'm giving her to you. Her name is Susan. Please take good care of her.*

"It's a miracle," Katie murmured as she carried the baby into the house. "God's given me the thing I long for the most."

She soon discovered that whoever had put the baby in the

basket had included a few diapers, a baby bottle, and a can of formula.

Katie picked up the baby and took a seat in the rocking chair. She stroked the baby's pale, dewy skin as she rocked and hummed. Katie knew she should notify someone, but holding the precious baby girl felt so right, she couldn't even think about notifying anyone right now.

She kissed the top of the baby's downy, dark head and whispered, "I'll take care of you, baby Susan."

CHAPTER 19

As Katie lay in her bed that night, she heard the downstairs clock chime twelve times and realized it was midnight. She was tired and needed to sleep but kept getting up to check on the baby, who was asleep in her basket at the foot of Katie's bed. Little Susan had only been there a few hours, but already Katie had grown attached and didn't know if she could bring herself to part with her.

The diapers and formula that had been left with the baby wouldn't last long. If Katie kept the baby awhile, she would need to get more formula, as well as some diapers and a clean set of clothes for Susan to wear.

But how am I going to go shopping? Katie wondered. *I'm scared to drive the buggy alone. Even if I were brave enough to take it out, I'd have to take the baby along, which would bring all sorts of questions from anyone I might know.* She grimaced. *I sure can't leave the baby alone by herself.*

Katie heard the crickets singing through her open window. She drew in a deep breath and tried to relax. *I'll deal with all this in the morning. Maybe by then I'll be able to think more clearly.*

❧ ❧

Freeman flexed his shoulders and reached around to rub a kink in his back. He'd been working all morning on the broken gears of a bike and still didn't have it fixed. He didn't know if it was because the gears were harder to fix than some he'd worked on or if it was simply because he couldn't stay focused. He'd been thinking about Eunice and the way she'd looked at him last night when they'd sat on her porch before supper.

She was attracted to him; he was sure of it. He was attracted to her, too. But was attraction enough to build a relationship on? Was he even ready for a relationship with Eunice?

Freeman thought about the chicken and dumplings Eunice had made, and his mouth watered just thinking about how good they had tasted. The chocolate cream pie she'd served for dessert had been equally good.

Eunice not only looks good in the face, but she's a fine cook, he told himself. *But is that reason enough to start courting her?*

Woof! Woof! Woof!

Freeman groaned. "There goes that mutt again." Ever since he'd put Penny in her dog run, all she'd done was whine and bark.

The shop door opened just then, and Wayne stepped in. "How's it going?" he asked. "Are you keeping busy enough?"

Freeman nodded. "I'm keepin' plenty busy, but things aren't goin' so well."

"What's the problem?"

Woof! Woof!

"That pup's the problem." Freeman pointed to the window. "Guess she doesn't like her dog run so well."

"You had her in here when Fern first got her, so why not bring her back in?"

"Because she's nothing but a pescht." Freeman grimaced. "She wouldn't leave me alone—kept following me around, lickin' my hand and whimpering when I didn't stop to pet her often enough."

"She's probably just lonely and needs some attention. It's hard for a pup to be taken from its mamm."

"I realize that." Freeman pulled his fingers through the ends of his hair. "Maybe I'll bring her in after you leave. No point in her making a nuisance of herself while you're here. What brings you into the shop this morning, anyway? Do you need a new bike, or are you needing an old one fixed?"

Wayne shook his head. "Neither. I'm heading to the hardware store and figured I'd stop by and share some good news with you."

"What's the good news?"

"Loraine's expecting a boppli at the end of February." A wide smile stretched across Wayne's face. "Six months ago I didn't think I'd even be marrying Loraine, much less that we'd become parents so soon."

Freeman smiled. "God is good, jah?"

"He sure is. God opened my eyes so I'd realize that I could marry Loraine in spite of my handicap, and He provided a way for me to support my family by giving me a job in my daed's taxidermy shop."

"Do you like working there?"

Wayne nodded and moved closer to where Freeman knelt beside the bike. "Seems to me that you like your work, too."

"You're right. I do. Wouldn't want to do anything else for a living."

Wayne smiled. "Guess most of us who have a business to run like what we're doing or we wouldn't be doing it."

"That's true enough." Freeman reached for a pair of pliers. "My grossmudder mentioned the other day that your folks are planning to move into a small rented house soon. What made them decide to do that?"

"Guess they want to give Loraine and me some space, and since their new house isn't done yet, they're renting a place and moving out on their own." Wayne glanced at the door. "Guess I'd better get going. If I have time, I might stop by the Millers' place and check on Katie after I'm done with my errands."

"How come you need to check on Katie? Is she feeling sick again?"

"I don't think so, but she's alone at the house this week. Her folks went to Ohio for JoAnn's cousin's funeral and left Katie behind."

"I didn't know that."

"Guess Katie didn't want to go." Wayne turned and headed for the door. "I'd better head out or I'll never get to the hardware store. See you later, Freeman."

As the door clicked shut behind Wayne, Freeman made a decision. He'd close his shop at noon and go check on Katie.

~≈ ≈~

Eunice opened the door to Freeman's shop and stepped inside. It was dark, and she detected no sign of Freeman.

That's strange, she thought. *It's past one, and if he'd gone to lunch, I would think he would have put the* CLOSED *sign in his window.*

She glanced up at the house, thinking Freeman might have gone there to eat lunch. That made sense since the door to his shop wasn't locked.

She debated about waiting for him in the shop but decided to go up to the house instead.

When Eunice knocked on the door a few minutes later, she was greeted by Fern.

"This is a pleasant surprise." Fern motioned Eunice into the house. "Would you like a glass of lemonade or some iced tea?"

"That'd be nice." Eunice wiped the perspiration from her forehead. "It's such a warm day. A cool drink would sure hit the spot."

"What would you like—iced tea or lemonade?" Fern asked, leading the way to the kitchen.

"Whatever you're having is fine for me." Eunice glanced around the kitchen and was disappointed when she saw Fern's grandmother sitting at the table. There was no sign of Freeman.

"How are you, Sara?" Eunice asked, taking a seat beside the elderly woman.

"Doing okay. Just trying to stay cool in this hot weather we've been having." Sara fanned her face with her hand. "It's too warm for this early in the summer." She yawned. "When it's hot and sticky like this, I have a hard time sleeping at night."

"I set one of our reclining lawn chairs under the maple tree awhile ago," Fern said, placing a pitcher of iced tea on the table. "Why don't you go out there and try to take a nap, Grandma?"

"Jah, I think I will." Sara poured herself a glass of iced tea and stood. "Don't let me sleep too long, though. I need to be awake in time to help you with supper."

"If you sleep that long, I'll be sure to wake you," Fern said with a grin.

Sara shuffled out the door, and Fern took a seat at the table.

"I heard the supper you fixed for Freeman last night was real tasty." Fern bumped Eunice's arm. "I think my bruder likes you."

"Maybe it's my chocolate cream pie Freeman likes. He ate two pieces."

Fern snickered. "Well, you know what they say about the way to a man's heart."

"Guess I'll have to keep inviting Freeman over for supper. I was hoping to see if he'd be free to eat with us again one night next week." Eunice frowned. "But when I stopped at his shop to ask, he wasn't there. I figured he must have come here to have lunch."

Fern shook her head. "He told me he had an errand to run and would grab a bite to eat along the way."

"Did he say where he was going?"

"No. Just said he'd be back around one."

Eunice motioned to the clock on the far wall. "It's almost one thirty now."

"Guess his errand must have taken longer than he expected. I'm sure he'll be back soon if you want to wait."

"I'd like to, but I need to pick up some material for my mamm at the fabric shop in Shipshe. Then I may stop by the Millers' stamp shop on my way home to buy some cardstock." Eunice pushed away from the table and stood. "Would you tell Freeman that I dropped by?"

"Of course, and if you like, I'll put in a good word for you, too."

Eunice smiled. "I'd appreciate that."

When Freeman pulled his horse and buggy up to the Millers' hitching rail, he noticed that there was a CLOSED sign on the door of the stamp shop. He figured Katie might be at the house having lunch, so after he tied his horse up, he headed that way.

He was surprised to discover that all the doors and windows on the house were shut. It was a hot, humid day—must be even hotter inside.

Freeman rapped on the door. When no one answered, he knocked again. "Katie, are you here? It's Freeman Bontrager."

Several seconds went by, and then the door opened slowly. Katie, looking rumpled and flushed, stepped onto the porch and closed the door partway. "If you need something from the stamp shop, it's closed today." Wearing an anxious expression, she glanced over her shoulder.

"Didn't come to get anything from the stamp shop," Freeman said. "I heard you were alone, so I came by to see if you needed anything."

"I'm fine. Danki for stopping." Katie turned, and was about to enter the house, when what sounded like a baby's cry floated out the door.

Katie's face flamed, and she quickly shut the door.

Freeman took a step forward. "Are you watching someone's boppli today?"

"Uh. . .jah." Katie dropped her gaze to the porch floor.

"Who's baby are you watching?"

Katie cleared her throat a couple of times. "It's. . .uh. . .no one you know."

"How do you know that? Does the boppli belong to someone who lives close by?"

"Uh, maybe."

"I don't get it, Katie. What's the big secret? Why won't you tell me whose boppli you're watching?"

Tears pooled in Katie's eyes, and her chin quivered slightly. "Can you keep a secret?"

He shrugged. "Depends on what it is."

"I've gotta go." Katie whirled around and stepped into the house. Freeman quickly followed.

"Listen, Katie," he said, "if you've got a secret—" Freeman halted when Katie bent down and picked up a baby from the basket. Most people he knew didn't keep their babies in baskets.

Katie turned to face him. "Please don't tell anyone about the boppli."

He squinted at her. "Tell 'em what? Whose baby is that, anyway?"

"She was left on our front porch last night. A note was attached to her blanket, and—" The words poured out of Katie like a leaky bucket. Her lips trembled, and she stopped talking long enough to draw in a quick breath. "Are you going to tell my folks?"

Freeman scratched the side of his head. "What are you talking about? Your folks will be home in a few days, and then you'll have to tell 'em yourself." He pointed to the baby, who was now fussing and squirming in Katie's arms. "A squalling boppli isn't something you can hide for very long."

"I. . .I know that." Katie took a seat in the rocking chair, cradling the baby in her arms.

"Have you let the sheriff know about this yet?"

"No."

"Why not?"

"The phone in our shed's not working right now."

"Then why didn't you drive over to one of your neighbors and phone him from there?"

"I don't know."

"Why don't you know?"

"I feel anxious, and I—" A shadow of fear covered Katie's words, and she looked at him with a painful openness, as though she wanted to say more but couldn't.

"Why do you feel anxious?"

Katie tensed but gave no response.

Freeman moved closer and took a seat on the sofa. "You don't have to be afraid to talk to me. I'd like to be your friend."

Katie looked at him like a frightened child. "I get so jittery whenever I ride in any vehicle, and the thought of driving the buggy myself scares me real bad."

"I'd be happy to drive you and the boppli to the sheriff's office, or even over to your neighbor's house so you can use their phone."

Katie shook her head. "I'm not ready to notify the sheriff yet. Besides, whoever left the boppli on our porch must have wanted us to have her, because they left a note asking us to take care of her."

"You can't keep what isn't yours. You've got to let the sheriff know about the boppli."

Tears welled in Katie's eyes. "I just want to keep her awhile— until right before my folks come home." She stroked the top of the baby's head. "Please don't tell anyone about the boppli."

Freeman drummed his fingers along the arm of the sofa as he mulled things over. Finally, he gave a nod. "I'll keep your secret, but only if you promise to let me take you to the sheriff before your folks get home."

"I promise."

"Now that we've got that settled, is there anything I can do for you while I'm here?"

"I don't think so. Well, maybe there is."

"What?"

"I need formula, diapers, and at least one outfit for the boppli. Would you mind going to the store to get them for me?"

Freeman's eyebrows shot up. "What kind of reaction do you think I'll get if I walk into the Kuntry Store and ask for baby things?"

Katie shook her head. "I thought you could go to one of the stores where the English mostly shop. Maybe pick one that's out of our district. That way you'll be less apt to run into anyone you know."

Freeman glanced at the clock across the room. If he took time to go the store for Katie, he'd be late getting back to his shop. If he didn't go, she'd be here alone trying to care for a baby without the things she needed.

"Okay," he said, rising to his feet. "Make me a list, and I'll get whatever you need."

"Danki. You don't know how much this means to me."

The look of gratitude Freeman saw on Katie's face was all the thanks he needed.

CHAPTER 20

There's no way I can work today and take care of the baby, Katie thought as she peered out the kitchen window at the CLOSED sign she'd put on the door of the stamp shop early that morning. So far only Wayne had come by, and since the baby had been sleeping, she'd stepped onto the porch to speak with him. She hoped no one else would show up and worried that, if they did come to the shop and saw the CLOSED sign in the window, they might stop at the house. She couldn't risk anyone else knowing about the baby.

Katie moved back to the stove, where she'd started heating some soup for lunch. She dipped the ladle into the kettle and stirred it around, then held her hand beneath the ladle and took a sip. It wasn't quite warm enough, so she turned the gas burner up a bit. Freeman should be back from the store soon, and she figured he might want something to eat, since he'd given up his lunch hour to check on her.

The sound of a buggy approaching pulled Katie's thoughts aside.

She peered out the window, but the sun's glare prevented her from seeing who it was. She wiped her hands on her apron and moved over to the door. When she opened it, she was surprised to see Loraine getting out of her buggy.

Katie quickly shut and locked the door; then she rushed to the living room, where the baby lay in her basket. The last thing Katie needed was for Loraine to find out about the baby. She'd probably insist that Katie call the sheriff.

Katie stiffened when the doorknob rattled and Loraine called, "Katie, are you here?"

Tap! Tap! Tap!

The baby stirred restlessly and gave a pathetic whimper.

Please, don't start crying. Katie bent down and scooped the baby into her arms. *Shh. . . Shh. . .* She gently patted the baby's back.

Loraine called Katie's name once more; then Katie heard footsteps tromping down the steps.

She listened until she heard the whinny of a horse followed by hoofbeats.

Whew! She's gone!

Katie placed the baby back in the basket and hurried to the kitchen. She peeked out the window and saw Loraine's buggy moving down the driveway. Just then another buggy turned in.

Katie froze. *What if it's Freeman? Can I trust him not to tell Loraine that I'm here and that there's a baby with me?*

Keeping to the right of the window so she wouldn't be seen, Katie watched Eunice get out of her buggy and go around to Loraine's buggy. They visited for several minutes; then Eunice got back in her buggy and drove off. Loraine's rig pulled out behind her.

Katie gulped in some air. She hadn't realized that she'd been holding her breath until her chest started to burn. Feeling the need for a cool drink, she grabbed a glass from the cupboard and turned on the faucet at the kitchen sink. She took a couple sips of water then held the glass against her hot cheek, wondering how much longer she could keep little Susan a secret.

~❧ ❧~

Just before Loraine pulled onto the road, she turned in her seat and glanced over her shoulder. It seemed odd that Katie wasn't at the stamp shop or in the house. She knew from what Katie's mother had told her mamm that Katie hardly went anywhere by herself. With Katie's folks gone, Loraine figured Katie would be working in the stamp shop most of the day.

Maybe Katie needed some things from one of our local Amish-run stores. Or maybe she hired a driver to take her shopping in Goshen.

Loraine flicked the reins to get the horse moving in the direction of home as she made a decision. Since tomorrow was an off-Sunday from church in their district, rather than visiting a neighboring church, as they often did, she would stop by and check on Katie again.

❧ ❧

Freeman glanced at the sack full of baby things sitting on the floor of his buggy. He wondered if he was doing the right thing by keeping Katie's secret. He knew they should notify the sheriff, but Katie had been extremely upset when he'd mentioned it earlier and he didn't want to upset her any more. Maybe a day or two with the baby wouldn't hurt. Katie had seemed calmer when she was holding the baby than he'd seen her in a good long while. Maybe what Katie needed was to find herself a man, get married, and have some babies of her own. There was no way she could keep the baby she'd found. The infant belonged to someone else and wasn't Katie's to keep.

As Freeman approached the Millers' place, he spotted Eunice's buggy on the other side of the road. When his buggy passed hers, she waved and motioned for him to pull over.

"Oh great," Freeman mumbled. "I don't need this right now." He hoped whatever Eunice had to say wouldn't take too long, because he needed to be on his way.

Freeman turned his horse and buggy around and stopped behind Eunice's rig, which she'd pulled onto the shoulder of the road. Then he climbed down, tied his horse to a nearby post, and went around to see what she wanted.

"I stopped by your bike shop earlier, but you weren't there," Eunice said.

"I had some errands to run."

"Are you on your way home now?"

"Uh—jah." It wasn't exactly a lie. He would be on his way home as soon as he delivered the baby things to Katie. Of course, he wasn't about to tell Eunice that.

Eunice offered Freeman one of her most pleasant smiles. "I was wondering if you'd be free to come over to our place for supper again next week."

He scratched the side of his head. "Uh, I'm not sure. Maybe."

"Is there any particular night that would work best for you?"

"I don't know. It'll depend on how much work I have in the shop. Can I let you know?"

She nodded slowly. "I hope you can make it. I really enjoy spending time with you, Freeman."

Freeman figured she was waiting for him to say that he enjoyed spending time with her, too, so he gave a quick nod and mumbled, "Same here."

"Guess I'd better let you go so you can get back to your shop." Eunice gathered up the reins. "See you soon."

As she drove away, sweat beaded on Freeman's forehead. Despite his feelings of attraction to Eunice, he didn't care for her pushy ways. If he accepted her invitation to have supper with her again, he hoped she wouldn't expect to make it a weekly event. If he did decide to start courting her, he wanted it to be his idea, not hers.

❧ ❧

Katie swallowed down the last of her soup and put her bowl in the sink. She glanced out the window, hoping that Freeman would pull in soon, but there wasn't a buggy in sight.

What could be taking him so long? she fretted. *Did he change his mind about helping me?* She clutched the edge of the counter and frowned. *If Freeman doesn't bring the things I need for the baby, it won't be long before I'll run out of formula and diapers. Then what'll I do?*

The baby started crying, and Katie hurried from the kitchen. She was halfway there when she heard hoofbeats coming up the driveway. She halted and tensed. How long could she keep hiding here in the house whenever a customer showed up at the stamp shop?

She rushed back to the kitchen and took a peek out the window.

A feeling of relief washed over her when she saw Freeman climb down from his buggy.

She hurried back to the living room, picked up the crying baby, and opened the door for Freeman.

"Sorry it took me so long. I got waylaid talking to Eunice not far from here." He held out a paper sack. "Where would you like me to put this?"

Katie motioned to the kitchen. "You can set it on the counter. As soon as I put the boppli down, I'll get my purse and pay you for the things you bought."

Freeman shook his head. "That's okay. I'm not worried about it."

"I had some soup earlier, and there's still some on the stove," she said. "At least let me feed you some lunch before you go."

"I appreciate the offer, but I've been gone from my shop much longer than I planned to be, so I'd better go." Freeman hurried into the kitchen to drop off the sack and returned a few seconds later. "Is it all right if I come back this evening to see how you're doing?"

Katie gave a nod, already looking forward to his return.

CHAPTER 21

As Freeman drove in his open buggy toward Katie's that evening, a warm breeze blew against his face. He was awed by the way the rim of the sun spread rosy color across the sky like a drop of dye. Whenever he saw a pretty sunset like this, he felt closer to God. Not tonight, though. Because of the promise he'd made to keep Katie's secret about the baby she'd found, he felt as if he'd erected a wall between him and God. He knew what he and Katie were doing was wrong, and he didn't like being deceitful. Yet he didn't feel that he could renege on the promise he'd made to her.

Maybe I can talk Katie into notifying the sheriff this evening, Freeman thought as the Millers' place came into view. *I need to convince her that it's the best thing to do.*

Freeman guided his horse up the driveway. As he pulled his rig up close to the Millers' barn and climbed down, their old hound dog howled from his pen. Not knowing how long he'd be staying, Freeman led his horse to the corral and put him inside. After he'd shut the gate, he sprinted for the house.

He knocked several times before Katie answered the door.

"I—I wasn't sure you'd come." She nibbled on her lower lip. "You haven't told anyone about the boppli, I hope."

Freeman shook his head. He was about to suggest that Katie should call the sheriff, but the painful expression he saw on her face clutched at his heart and kept him from telling her what he thought. *Maybe later,* he thought.

"How's the boppli?" he asked.

"Fine. She's sleeping peacefully right now." Katie pointed to a couple of wicker chairs on the other end of the porch. "Would you like to have a seat?"

He nodded and sat down. Katie took the seat beside him.

Freeman leaned forward and rested his elbows on his knees. "Can you tell me about the anxiety you feel whenever you think about traveling in a car or a horse and buggy?"

Katie's hands shook as she fanned her flushed cheeks. "I don't know how to put this into words, but I get these strange sensations sometimes. They come out of nowhere when I least expect them." Her eyes glistened with tears. "I get so scared when I can't make them stop."

Freeman listened as Katie gave a detailed account of the sensations she experienced.

"The thing that scares me the most is when everything feels unreal and I have no control over what's happening to me." She dabbed at her tears.

"Have you told your folks about these feelings of unreality?" he asked.

Katie shook her head, discouragement and frustration clearly written on her face. "They know I've felt light-headed and shaky, but I haven't told them about my other symptoms." She sniffed. "I'm afraid if I tell Mom and Dad, they'll think I'm going crazy."

"Is that what you think, Katie?"

"I. . .I'm not sure. Maybe."

"You're not crazy."

"How do you know?"

"I believe what you've been having are anxiety attacks." He shifted in his chair, trying to find a comfortable position. "Some people call 'em panic attacks."

"What's that?"

"It's when a person gets a sudden attack of fear and nervousness, followed by some physical symptoms that could include sweating, a racing heart, nausea, trembling, dizziness, and a sensation of feeling as though nothing is real."

A look of surprise flashed across Katie's face, and she blinked a couple of times. "I've been having several of those symptoms."

"Panic disorders affect more people than you might realize, and everyone's symptoms aren't always the same," Freeman went on to say.

"Do...do you know what causes a panic attack?"

Freeman nodded. "Stressful events and major changes in a person's life are usually the cause, and panic attacks can hit a person at any time, anywhere." He tapped his fingers along the arm of the chair. "Once a panic attack strikes, the person becomes afraid and often tries to avoid situations that they think might bring on another attack."

Katie pursed her lips. "You sound like a doctor, Freeman. How do you know all that?"

Freeman drew in a breath and released it slowly. "Because I used to suffer from panic attacks."

Katie's face registered confusion as her eyebrows squeezed together. "Are you serious?"

He nodded. "When I was seven years old, I went to our cellar to get something for my mamm, and I got trapped down there because the door wouldn't open." Freeman gave his earlobe a tug. It wasn't easy to talk about this, but if it might help Katie to know that someone else had gone through something similar to what she was going through now, he would bare his soul. He wanted her to know that he understood her symptoms. "It wasn't long after I got trapped that I started having some weird symptoms that really scared me."

"What kind of symptoms?"

"Shortness of breath, pounding heart, a choking sensation. I felt like I was losing control and was gonna die."

"Did you tell anyone about it?"

"Not at first. Later—soon after we moved to Ohio—the horrible symptoms got worse, so I finally told my folks."

"What'd they say?"

"They were concerned and took me to the doctor. He ran all kinds of tests, but he couldn't find anything physically wrong with me, so he told my folks that he thought I was having anxiety attacks and suggested that I see a counselor." Freeman pulled his fingers through the back of his hair as memories from the past flooded over him. "At first Mom couldn't accept the idea that I was having emotional problems, but then she went to the library and got a book on the subject of panic attacks, which helped us understand things better."

"Did anything in the book tell how to make the panic attacks stop?" she asked.

Freeman nodded. "I tried some of the things suggested, but then my daed decided that I should see a Christian counselor someone had told him about."

"I hope you're not suggesting that I see a counselor, because I don't think I could do that."

"Why not?"

"He might expect me to talk about things I don't want to discuss." Tears trickled down Katie's cheeks. "He might put me on medication."

"Sometimes medication can help, and it's nothing to be ashamed of if you have to take it for a while." Freeman shrugged. "Then again, you may not need medication. Everyone's different, and one thing might work for one person, while something else works for another. It'll all depend on what works best for you."

"Did you take medication?"

Freeman shook his head. "Since my aunt runs a health food store in Ohio, she suggested I try a homeopathic remedy first. If that hadn't helped, my counselor probably would have suggested medication."

"Did the remedy work for you?"

He nodded. "It helped me feel calmer, and I took it until I learned how to manage the attacks."

"How'd you manage them?"

"I did some relaxation and deep-breathing exercises, and I learned how to face my fears without letting them control me."

Waaa! Waaa! Waaa!

Katie jumped up. "I'd better tend to the baby. If you're still here when I get back, we can talk about this some more."

"I'll be right here."

❦ ❦

While Katie changed the baby's diaper, she thought about the things Freeman had said to her. It felt good to talk to someone about the weird sensations she'd been having. It was a relief to know that what she'd been experiencing actually had a name. If Freeman had gotten over his attacks, maybe she could, too.

When Katie finished diapering little Susan, she returned to the porch with the baby in her arms. She was relieved to see that Freeman was still there.

"I made some banana nut cake earlier today," she said. "Would you like to try some?"

"Sure, that sounds good."

"Would you mind holding the boppli while I go inside and get the cake?" Katie asked.

Freeman's eyebrows shot up. "You. . .you want me to hold that tiny little thing?"

She gave a nod. "I'll only be gone a few minutes."

"I'm not sure me holding the boppli's such a good idea. I may be able to fix bikes, but I know little or nothing about *bopplin*."

"I'm sure you'll do okay. All you have to do is hold her." Katie placed the baby in Freeman's arms and hurried into the house.

A few minutes later, she returned with two glasses of milk and some slices of banana nut cake. "Want me to take the boppli now?" she asked.

He shook his head. "We're just starting to get acquainted. Believe it or not, I kind of like holding her."

Katie smiled. A warm breeze moved with the sound of the baby's breathing, and she relaxed in her chair. She drank some milk and ate a piece of cake, savoring the sweetness.

Freeman reached for a piece of cake and popped most of it into his mouth. "Umm. . .this is appeditlich. You're a good cook, Katie."

140

"Danki." As Katie glanced into the yard, she saw a host of fireflies rise out of the grass, twinkling like tiny diamonds. She never got tired of watching the fireflies. When she and her older brothers were children, they used to have a contest to see who could capture the most fireflies in one of Mom's empty canning jars. One time her brother Harold had been fooling around and knocked over Katie's jar. The fireflies had escaped, of course. It had taken almost an hour to get them all out of the kitchen. Harold had gotten in trouble with Mom for being so careless.

"Sure is a nice evening, isn't it?" Freeman asked, halting Katie's musings.

She nodded. "I like watching the fireflies as they flutter all over the yard."

"Me, too."

As they watched the sun go down and the fireflies disappeared, Freeman entertained Katie with a couple of jokes.

"Do you know who the most successful physician was in the Bible?" he asked.

Katie shook her head.

"It was Job, because he had the most patience." Freeman slapped his knee. "Get it—the most patients?"

Katie laughed. "I've never heard that one before."

"I've never heard you laugh like that before," Freeman said. "At least not since we were kinner."

"Laugh like what?" she asked.

"Like a rippling brook."

"There hasn't been much for me to laugh about. Not since the accident, anyhow."

"Sometimes we need to look for things to laugh about." He looked down at the baby, asleep in his arms. "Won't be long, and this little girl will be laughin' and gurglin' for no reason at all."

"I guess you're right about that." Katie sighed. "Too bad she won't be with me then so I can see her laugh and gurgle."

The baby started to fuss, and Katie reached for her. "I think she probably needs to be fed."

Freeman handed the baby to Katie. "I probably should head

for home. I told Grandma I wouldn't be gone long, and I don't want her to worry."

A ripple of fear shot through Katie. "You didn't tell her you were coming over here, I hope."

"Jah, I did," Freeman said, "but I just said I was going to check on you since your folks were gone. I didn't say a word about the boppli you found."

Katie blew out a quick breath. "Danki for keeping my secret. . .and for everything else you've done."

"You're welcome. I'll try to drop by again tomorrow and see how you're doing." Freeman hesitated a minute as if he might have more to say, but he stepped off the porch with only a wave.

As Katie watched him head for his buggy, tears slipped out of her eyes and spilled onto the baby's head. She wiped them away with the corner of her apron. It had been such a long time since she'd felt this peaceful and content. She wished she could make the feeling last forever.

CHAPTER 22

T he following morning, as Katie stepped onto the lawn, she appreciated the coolness beneath her bare feet. It had been much too warm last night, and she was glad for the chilly morning. She knew she couldn't linger outside very long. Even though it was Sunday, the animals needed to be fed, and she wanted to get that done before the baby woke up.

Katie was also glad that this was an off-Sunday from church. There was no way she could have gone to the service alone, much less with a baby she'd found on her porch. And she certainly wouldn't have left little Susan alone.

An image of Freeman popped into her head. He'd looked so natural holding the baby last night. Freeman might not realize it, but he'd make a good father. He had a gentleness about him, and Katie couldn't get over the compassion and understanding he'd shown when she'd told him about her anxiety attacks. She'd seen some of those same qualities in Timothy, although Timothy had been more spontaneous than Freeman and had always liked to tease. Freeman might not be as spontaneous, or a teaser, but he was a hard worker. A few weeks ago, Dad had stopped by Freeman's shop to buy a new headlight for his bike. When he'd gotten home, he'd mentioned how busy Freeman was and what a hard worker he seemed to be.

Katie shook herself mentally. *Why am I thinking about Freeman or comparing him to Timothy? I'm not interested in a relationship with Freeman, and I'm sure he wouldn't be interested in anyone like me.*

Determined to think about something else, Katie hurriedly fed the horses. When that was done, she tended to the dog and cats, then went to the coop to take care of the chickens. She stepped out of the chicken coop just in time to see a horse and buggy rumble up the driveway. It was too late to make a run for the house, so she waited near the barn to see who it was. When the horse came to a stop, Loraine stepped down from the buggy.

"I'm surprised to see you this morning. I figured you and Wayne would be visiting a neighboring church district today," Katie said when Loraine joined her by the barn.

"Wayne woke up with a *buckleweh,* so when he decided that we should stay home today so he could rest, I figured it'd be a good time for me to check on you."

"I'm sorry to hear Wayne has a backache. Will he see the chiropractor tomorrow?"

"If he's not feeling better, probably so." Loraine motioned to the stamp shop. "I came by to see you yesterday, but the stamp shop was closed, and when I went up to the house, you didn't answer my knock."

Katie's mouth went dry. She didn't feel right about lying to her cousin, but she didn't want to admit the truth, either.

"Where'd you go, Katie? Did you have errands to run?"

"Uh, no, I didn't go anywhere yesterday."

A deep wrinkle formed above the bridge of Loraine's nose. "Were you sleeping when I knocked?"

Katie shrugged. "I...uh...may have been."

"Were you feeling grank or just tired?"

"I was tired. Didn't sleep well the night before."

"Would you like to come over to our place and stay until your folks get home?"

"I appreciate the offer, but I'm doing fine here on my own." Katie glanced toward the stamp shop. "Besides, I'll need to be here tomorrow morning, in case anyone comes to the shop." She knew she wouldn't be opening the stamp shop tomorrow morning, but she wasn't about to tell Loraine that.

"You can stay at our place tonight and then come back here in the morning."

Katie nibbled on the inside of her cheek. She needed to come up with a better reason than the one she'd offered. "You have enough people at your house right now," she said. "You don't need one more."

"Ada and Crist moved into a rental yesterday." Loraine smiled. "So it's just me and Wayne now, and we've got plenty of room."

"I'm sure you'd like some time alone with your husband since you've only been married a few months and haven't had much time to be by yourselves."

"We really wouldn't mind the company."

"I'd better stay here."

"Are you sure you'll be okay?"

Katie nodded, glancing nervously toward the house. She hoped the baby wasn't crying.

Loraine touched Katie's arm. "Am I keeping you from something?"

"I. . .uh. . .was just getting ready to head inside and fix myself some breakfast."

"That's fine. I'll go in with you. We can visit while you eat."

A sense of urgency settled over Katie. She couldn't let Loraine come inside with her. She'd find out about the baby. "I'm not good company right now." Katie massaged her forehead. "I've got a koppweh, and I need to be alone."

"If you have a headache, I'd be happy to fix you something to eat, and you can lie down and rest while I'm making it."

"No, really, I'll be fine."

Loraine hesitated a moment then finally nodded. "Guess I'll be on my way home then." She gave Katie a hug. "If you need anything while your folks are gone, be sure to call and leave us a message."

"I will, danki."

Loraine climbed into her buggy, and Katie hurried to the house.

❦

"How's your back?" Loraine asked Wayne when she stepped onto the porch where he sat drinking a glass of orange juice.

"Doin' a little better than when I first woke up."

"That's good to hear. Do you think you'll need to see the chiropractor tomorrow morning?"

He shrugged. "Maybe so. I'll just have to wait and see how it goes. How are things with Katie?"

"I'm not sure."

"What do you mean?"

Loraine lowered herself into the chair beside him. "She turned down my offer to stay with us until her folks get home."

"How come?"

"She said she was getting along fine on her own and that she didn't want to impose." Loraine frowned. "I think she was using it as an excuse. I think something else is going on."

"Like what?"

"I don't know. Katie acted nervous and kept glancing at the house as though she was eager to get inside."

"Didn't she invite you in?"

"Huh-uh. She said she had a headache, and when I volunteered to fix her some breakfast, she said she wanted to be alone. I got the feeling that she really wanted me to go."

"Well, now that my folks have moved out, I'm enjoying the time we have to ourselves, so to tell you the truth, I'm not too upset that Katie turned down your offer."

Loraine glanced down at her stomach, which was still quite flat, and nodded. "I think that we'd better enjoy our alone time now, because once the boppli comes, things will definitely change for us."

He grinned. "Are you hoping for a *buwe* or a *maedel*?"

"I don't care whether it's a boy or a girl. I just want our boppli to be healthy."

Wayne reached for Loraine's hand and gave her fingers a gentle squeeze. "Same goes for me."

━━ ❧ ❧ ━━

Freeman thumped the arm of his chair as he stared at the Scrabble pieces lying before him. It would be hard to make a word when he had no vowels, and he couldn't use the ones already on the board because of how they'd been placed.

"Gebscht uff?" Fern asked, reaching down to pet Penny, who'd crawled under the card table they'd set up on the back porch.

"Jah, I give up. You beat me real good this time."

"You seemed like you didn't really have your mind on the game. If you'd just concentrated harder you might have won."

"I doubt that." Freeman stood up and started down the stairs.

"Where are you going?" Fern asked. "Don't you want to play another game?"

"Not right now. Think I'll go over to the Millers' and check on Katie."

"But you were just over there last night."

"I know that, but I want to see how she's doing today."

"I doubt she's even at home."

"What makes you think that?"

"She probably went to church at a neighboring district, or she could have gone to spend the day with one of her cousins."

"Maybe so, but I'm still going over to check on her." There was no way Freeman could tell Fern that he knew Katie would be home today because she was taking care of the baby she'd found. If he told her that, he'd be breaking his promise to Katie to keep quiet about the baby, and Fern would insist that he notify the sheriff. She'd always been the kind of person who wanted to do everything just the right way, and Freeman was sure she wouldn't understand why he hadn't told her about the baby.

Fern stared at Freeman with a strange expression. "Are you starting a relationship with Katie? Is that the reason you're going over there again so soon?"

Freeman shook his head forcefully. "I'm not starting anything with Katie. I only want to be her friend."

She lifted her brows with a disbelieving look. "Are you sure about that? The look I saw on your face when you got home from Katie's last night made me think you might be falling for her."

"I'm not falling for her, and I don't have a *look*."

Fern frowned. "I'd appreciate it if you didn't speak to me in that tone of voice. I'm older than you, and I think you should show me a little respect."

"Sorry," he mumbled, "but you shouldn't worry about what I do. I'm a grown man, not a little buwe you can boss around."

"I'm not trying to boss you, but I can't help but worry when I see you hanging around someone who's bound to break your heart."

"What's that supposed to mean?"

"Everyone with eyes and ears knows that Katie has some kind of emotional problems. She hasn't been acting right since she came back from Florida."

"So Katie has a few problems. As you well know, I had some problems of my own a few years back, but I came through them okay."

"That was different. You got help for your problems."

"Katie's getting help, too."

"How do you know?"

"Because I'm trying to help her."

"How?"

"Just listening and letting her talk things through."

"What about Eunice?"

"What about her?"

"I thought you liked Eunice. When you came home after eating supper at her place the other night, you said you enjoyed being with her and might ask her out sometime soon."

"I do like Eunice, and I might ask her out, but that's got nothing to do with me helping Katie."

Deep wrinkles formed across Fern's forehead. "How do you think Eunice would feel if she knew you were going over to see Katie so often?"

"I'm sure she wouldn't have a problem with it. Besides, I've made no commitment to Eunice, so it doesn't matter what she thinks." Freeman tromped down the steps and sprinted for the buggy shed, glad to be away from Fern and all of her questions.

Woof! Woof! Woof! Penny raced after him, nipping at his heels.

Freeman halted, scooped the pup into his arms, and headed to the dog run. "Why do you have to hang around me all the time?" he mumbled. "You're supposed to be Fern's dog, not mine!"

Slurp! Slurp! Penny swiped her pink tongue across Freeman's chin.

"Yuk!" Freeman put the dog inside the run and shut the gate. "Starting tomorrow, I'm gonna start teaching you some manners!"

CHAPTER 23

Since there wasn't much traffic on the road, Freeman gave his horse the freedom to trot. It was a nice day to be out for a ride, and if he wasn't in such a hurry to get to Katie's house, he'd have taken it slower, like the open buggy up ahead was doing.

Impatient to pass, Freeman pulled his horse into the opposite lane. When he came alongside of the other rig, he realized that it belonged to Eunice.

"Seems like we've done this before," she hollered, motioning for him to pull over.

Freeman pulled his buggy in behind hers and brought the horse to a stop. Then he climbed down and tied the horse to a nearby tree. Some well-trained, docile horses might stay put, but not his.

"Where are you headed?" Eunice asked when he came around to the driver's side of her open buggy.

"I'm goin' over to Jeremy Miller's place."

"How come you're going there?"

"Katie's folks are gone, and I thought I ought to check and see how she's doing."

A look of disappointment flashed across Eunice's face, but she quickly replaced it with a hopeful smile. "Mind if I go along?"

"Huh?"

"I can follow you there, and after we've checked on Katie, we can go over to my house for a piece of pie. I made two coconut cream pies the other day, and I think you ought to try a piece."

Freeman sucked in a deep breath. He knew he'd better think of a good excuse, and real quick. He couldn't have Eunice going over to Katie's with him. The last thing Katie needed was Eunice finding out about the baby she'd found. "I. . .uh. . .shouldn't be at Katie's too long." He rubbed his chin as he mulled things over. "Tell you what—after I leave Katie's place, I'll come over to your house for a piece of pie. How's that sound?"

"Is that a promise?"

"Sure. See you soon." Freeman untied his horse and climbed back in his buggy.

Eunice looked over her shoulder and waved; then she snapped the reins and went on her way.

~❧ ❧~

As the day wore on, it had become hot and stuffy in the house. Katie was tempted to take the baby outside until the sun went down and it had cooled off some, but that might be too risky. Loraine had showed up unannounced, and someone else might come by.

A horse whinnied, and Arnold, their hound dog, let out a howl. Katie hurried to the kitchen window and glanced outside. She was relieved to see Freeman climbing down from his open buggy.

She opened the door and stepped out onto the porch. *"Hoscht du schunn gesse?"* she asked as he came up the steps.

He nodded. "Jah, I ate lunch a short time ago, but if you haven't eaten yet, don't let me stop you. I just came by to see how you're doing."

"I'm doing okay." Katie opened the door wider. "Why don't you come inside? You can keep me company while I feed Susan and fix myself a sandwich."

"Guess I will." Freeman entered the house and followed Katie to the kitchen. "How's the boppli doing today?" he asked.

"Just fine. She's eating well and doesn't cry much at all."

"Have you thought any more about notifying the sheriff?"

Katie shifted uneasily as she struggled to put her thoughts into words. "I know I'll have to eventually, but I want a few more days with the boppli. I promise I'll do it before my folks get home, though."

"When will that be?"

"Friday. At least that's what they said when they called to let me know they'd gotten there okay."

"Should I come by on Thursday and take you to the sheriff's?"

Katie nodded and sank into a chair at the table. She hated the thought of giving up the baby, but she'd definitely have to do it before Mom and Dad came home. In the meantime, though, she planned to enjoy every minute she had to care for little Susan.

❧ ❧

Eunice paced from the porch swing to the steps and back again, stopping every once in a while to scan the road out front. The air was so hot and humid she could smell the musty odor coming from the garden. She'd spent most of the afternoon waiting for Freeman and was worried that he'd changed his mind and wouldn't come at all.

The screen door squeaked, and Eunice's mother stepped out. "I set some lunch meat and cheese on the table," she said. "Why don't you come in and fix yourself a sandwich?"

Eunice shook her head. "I'm not hungry."

Mama stepped up to Eunice and placed both hands on her shoulders. "Pacing the porch and watching the road won't bring Freeman here any quicker."

"I know that." Eunice sighed. "When I met up with him earlier, he acted kind of strange."

"In what way?"

"Like he might be keeping something from me." Eunice glanced at the road again. "I wonder if he knows that Katie's pregnant and is keeping her secret."

"Now, Eunice, you don't know for sure that she's pregnant."

"Why else would she be feeling sick to her stomach and passing out in church like she did?"

"I don't know. It does seem rather odd." Mama's lips compressed. "If Katie is pregnant, do you think Freeman might be the father?"

Eunice gasped. "There's no way, Mama! Freeman's not the kind of man who would—" She sank to the porch swing with a moan. "Ach, Mama, if Freeman is the father of Katie's baby, what am I going to do?"

"Do about what?" Eunice's little brother asked, poking his head out the screen door.

"Never mind!" Eunice shook her finger at Richard. "You're too nosy for your own good, and you shouldn't be listening in on other's people's conversations."

"I was just gettin' ready to ask Mama where the mustard is, and I heard you say that you didn't know what you was gonna do." He tipped his head and looked at her with a curious expression. "Do about what, Eunice?"

"It was nothing important." Eunice flapped her hand at him. "Now go get the mustard."

"I just told ya—I don't know where it is."

"It's in the pantry," Mama said.

"I looked there already." Richard wrinkled his nose. "I think someone must've hid it."

Eunice rolled her eyes. "Don't be *lecherich*! No one hid the mustard!"

"Your sister's right," Mama said. "It's ridiculous to think that anyone would hide the mustard."

"Did you look in the refrigerator?" Eunice asked.

He bobbed his head. "It ain't there."

"Isn't," Eunice corrected. "Haven't you learned anything in school?"

"I've learned plenty!" Richard darted into the house and returned a few minutes later with a jar of mustard. "Found it!" He marched up to Eunice, opened the jar, and stuck it under her nose. "Want some?"

"No, I don't want any mustard!" Eunice's jaw clenched as she pointed to the door. "Now go fix your sandwich and quit bothering me!"

"Aw, you're no fun!" Richard snickered, passed the mustard under Eunice's nose one more time, and scurried into the house.

Mama sighed. "Is it any wonder that my hair's turning so gray? That buwe can be such a challenge sometimes."

Eunice grimaced. Poor Mama. Just when she'd thought she was done having children, Richard had come along. He could be a little pill at times, but Eunice knew her folks loved him just the same.

Eunice glanced anxiously toward the road. "If Freeman doesn't stop by like he promised, then I think I'll just go over to his shop tomorrow and find out what happened."

Mama's eyebrows furrowed. "Are you planning to ask if he's the father of Katie's boppli?"

Eunice sucked in her breath. "Do you think I should?"

Mama shook her head. "I wouldn't if I were you. You don't know for sure if Katie's in a family way, and if you wrongly accuse Freeman of fathering Katie's boppli, it could ruin your relationship with him."

"Hmm. . . Maybe you're right." Eunice tapped her chin a couple of times. "I don't want to lose Freeman to Katie, the way I lost Sam to my so-called friend Amanda."

"Just be nice to Freeman, and I'm sure you won't lose him." Mama gave Eunice's arm a squeeze. "I'm going inside to see if your daed wants a sandwich. If you get tired of waiting for Freeman, come join us."

"I'm already tired of waiting, so I think I'll join you now." Eunice left the swing and followed her mother inside.

~ぁ ぁ～

For the last hour, Katie and Freeman had been sitting on the back porch enjoying the cool breeze as the sun went down. The silence between them was as comfortable as an old pair of shoes, and Katie felt more relaxed than she had in months.

She leaned her head back and sighed. Being with Freeman lifted her spirits and gave her a sense of hope. Maybe if she learned what to do, she could overcome her panic attacks and feel normal again. Truth was, she hadn't felt normal since Timothy died.

"Sure is a peaceful evening." A single dimple showed in Freeman's left cheek as he reached over and laid his hand on Katie's arm.

His unexpected touch gave Katie goose bumps, and she shivered.

"Are you cold?" he asked, pulling his hand aside. "Should we go back inside?"

"No, I'm fine." There was no way Katie could tell Freeman how she'd felt when he'd touched her arm. He might misread what she said and think she was interested in him.

Am I? She mentally shook her head. *Of course not. I'm still in love with Timothy. I'll never love anyone else. Besides, Freeman could never love someone like me.*

"Are you hungry?" she asked, needing to get her mind on something else. "I can fix us a sandwich or heat up some leftover soup."

"That sounds good." Freeman stood. "I'll come inside and make the sandwiches while you heat the soup."

Katie smiled. Even Timothy hadn't been that kind and helpful.

⋘ ⋙

By the time Freeman left Katie's, it was dark outside. He hadn't meant to stay so long, but the time seemed to fly by as he got to know Katie a little better. He knew she had some serious issues she needed to deal with, which were probably the root cause of her anxiety attacks. Maybe he could do something to help Katie deal with the attacks. She had a sweet, gentle spirit; he'd seen that when he'd watched her care for the baby. She deserved to be free of the anxiety attacks and free to live a happy, peaceful life again.

Freeman gave his horse the freedom to trot. As he looked up at the star-speckled sky, he thanked God for the beautiful world He'd created. Sometimes when Freeman thought about God's majesty and power, he felt overcome with emotion. The thought that God could love the people He'd created so much that He'd sent His only Son to die for them was too much to comprehend. Freeman was thankful that he'd accepted Christ as his Savior not long ago. He wondered if Katie had done the same.

As Freeman drew closer to home, he suddenly remembered his promise to stop by Eunice's for a piece of the pie she'd baked.

It's too late for that now. She's probably gone to bed already. Guess that's what I get for staying at Katie's so long. He groaned and thumped the side of his head. "Sure hope I'm not falling for two women at once."

CHAPTER 24

For the next few days, Freeman went over to check on Katie regularly. He decided not to let Grandma or Fern know where he was going so he wouldn't arouse any suspicion. He'd gone to the store for Katie again and picked up a few more things she needed for the baby. But he'd made sure he went to stores where none of their Amish friends shopped.

The previous night when Freeman had gone to check on Katie, he'd given her a book about anxiety attacks. She hadn't seemed that interested, though. Her focus had been on the baby. He guessed he couldn't blame her for that. She'd grown attached to little Susan. Maybe after Katie turned the baby over to the sheriff, she'd be more receptive to reading the book.

Freeman grabbed the handlebars of the bike that had been brought in for repairs earlier that morning and rolled it across the room, knowing he needed to quit thinking about Katie and get back to work.

As he set the bike into position to begin working on it, Fern's puppy zipped across the room and leaped on his foot. *Woof! Woof!*

"Not now, Penny. I've got work to do, and I don't have time to be playin' with you."

Penny grabbed his shoelace in her mouth and gave it a shake.

"Knock it off!" Freeman pushed the puppy aside. "Go lay down, or I'll put you back in your dog run!"

Freeman had started working with Penny a few days earlier, but he hadn't made much progress. He figured he had his work cut out for him if he was going to get the pup fully trained, but he didn't have time to bother with her now.

Penny slunk away with her tail between her legs, and Freeman got busy on the bike. He'd just taken the tires off when the shop door opened and Eunice stepped in. Her pinched lips and deep frown let him know she was unhappy about something.

"I came by on Monday morning, but there was a CLOSED sign on your door!" She stomped up to him with her hands on her hips. He'd never seen her look so disgruntled before.

"I was away from the shop for a while."

"Where'd you go?"

"Had some errands to run."

"What kind of errands?"

"Just errands." Freeman squeezed the rim of the tire. He didn't like being quizzed like this. The look on Eunice's face reminded him of Fern whenever she found something to scold him about.

"I need to talk to you about something," Eunice said.

"Go ahead, but I'll have to keep working." Freeman gestured to the bike. "I need to have this done by two o'clock."

"That's fine." Eunice knelt on the floor beside Freeman.

Woof! Woof! Penny jumped up, zipped across the room, and leaped into Eunice's lap.

Eunice frowned and pushed the dog away. "Get away from me! You're getting dog hair on my dress!"

Penny crept back to the place where she'd been sleeping.

"I'm surprised by your reaction to the pup," Freeman said. "The last time you were here, you acted like Penny was your best friend."

Eunice's cheeks turned pink. "I like the dog well enough; I just don't want to be bothered with her now. I came here to ask you a question, not to play with your hundli."

"What do you want to know?" Freeman asked.

"The reason I came by on Monday was to ask why you didn't stop by my place on Sunday like you promised," Eunice said in a little softer tone.

A surge of heat cascaded up Freeman's neck. "Sorry," he mumbled. "Katie and I started talking, and I lost track of time. I meant to swing by your place yesterday and apologize for not showing up on Sunday, but I got busy here and forgot."

"Are you interested in Katie?"

"I'm interested in helping her."

"I think it's more than that. I think you're falling for her."

"Huh?"

"If you didn't have more than a passing interest in Katie, you wouldn't be going over there so much or staying so long." Eunice pursed her lips. "That tells me you must have an interest."

Freeman shook his head. "Katie and I are just friends."

"Is it because she's pregnant? Is that why you've been going over there so often?"

"What?" The heat on Freeman's neck spread quickly to his face. "Where'd you get the notion that Katie's expecting a boppli?"

Eunice folded her arms and glared at him. "It's not hard to figure out. She's been sick to her stomach, and she even fainted during church a few weeks ago."

"That's because she's been having—" Freeman clamped his mouth shut. If he told Eunice about Katie's anxiety attacks, she might blab that around. But if he didn't tell her, she might think Katie really was pregnant and start a rumor about that. It was a no-win situation.

"Katie's having what?" Eunice asked.

"Nothing."

Eunice's eyes flashed angrily. "I wasn't going to ask you this question, but I've changed my mind."

"Ask me what?"

"Are you the father of Katie's boppli?"

Another jolt of heat shot up Freeman's neck, and sweat broke out on his forehead. "You think I got Katie pregnant?"

"I don't know; I'm just asking is all."

"As I said before, Katie and I are friends, but I've never touched her in an inappropriate way, and I'm sure she's not pregnant!"

Eunice leaned away from him. "You don't have to yell."

"I can't believe you'd accuse me of such a thing. I thought we were beginning to build a relationship." He slowly shook his head. "If you really believe Katie's pregnant and that I'm the father, then there's no chance of you and me ever having a relationship!"

Eunice's face softened, and she touched his arm. "I'm sorry. If you say you're not the father, then I believe you, Freeman."

"Do you still believe Katie's in a family way?"

Eunice shrugged. "I don't know. The symptoms she has sure makes me believe she is, and today I heard someone at the health food store talking about a young woman who's pregnant, so I'm thinking it's Katie."

"I don't see how she could be. I mean, her boyfriend died eight months ago, and Katie's skinny as a twig. If she did get pregnant before Timothy died, then she'd be eight months along. Don't you think she'd be way out to here by now?" Freeman clasped his fingers together and held his hands about a foot from his stomach.

Eunice nodded. "She's obviously not that far along. I suppose she could have gotten pregnant when she was living in Florida."

"I don't think so."

"How can you be sure?"

"Because Katie's—" Freeman blew out his breath. "Can we just drop this subject? It's lecherich."

"I don't think it's ridiculous at all!" Eunice scrambled to her feet. "I can see that you're busy, so I'll leave you alone to do your work!" She hesitated a minute, then started across the room, her shoulders drooping.

Freeman knew she was upset and probably still thought he had an interest in Katie. He needed to convince her that she was wrong about that so she wouldn't spread any rumors about Katie.

"I hope you're not gonna say anything to anyone else about your suspicions that Katie's pregnant," he called after her.

She shrugged her shoulders and kept moving toward the door.

"Would you like to go out to supper with me on Friday night," he called, feeling a sense of desperation.

She halted and turned back around. "You mean it?"

"Wouldn't have asked if I didn't."

"Which restaurant?"

"Which one's your favorite?"

"I like eating at the Blue Gate, but then Das Dutchman's really good, too."

Freeman shrugged. "Either one is fine with me, so you can choose if you like."

"Let's go to the Blue Gate."

"Okay. I'll come by your place around five and pick you up."

"I'll see you on Friday then." Eunice flashed him a smile and went out the door.

Penny left her spot on the rug and ambled over to Freeman. He reached out and stroked the pup's silky ears. "Sure hope Eunice is wrong about Katie. It'd be a real shock to everyone, especially me, if she really is pregnant."

            ❦

Like all the other days since Mom and Dad had been gone to Ohio, Katie kept the stamp shop closed and stayed in the house with the baby. Twice that morning someone had stopped at the stamp shop and then come to the house and knocked on the door. Katie hadn't answered, even though the baby was asleep. It was too risky to answer the door to anyone but Freeman.

Katie took a seat in the rocking chair and placed the sleeping baby in her lap. She nuzzled the top of the infant's head, wishing she could keep her, but knowing it was an impossible dream. There was no way Mom and Dad would let her keep the baby; they'd notify the sheriff for sure.

Tears welled in Katie's eyes as she was overcome with a sense of guilt. The precious little girl in her arms wasn't hers to keep. She'd been wrong to keep Susan this long.

I won't wait until Wednesday to notify the sheriff, she decided. *The next time Freeman comes by, I'll ask him to take me there.*

            ❦

Eunice knocked on Sara Bontrager's door. When no one came, she peered in through the screen. "Is anybody here?"

No response.

Maybe they're upstairs or somewhere out back.

Eunice turned and was about to step off the porch when the screen door swung open and Sara stepped out. "Fern's not in the house. She's working out back," she said.

"Oh, okay. I'll go there now."

Eunice found Fern bent over a row of peas in the garden. *"Guder mariye,"* she said, stepping carefully between the rows.

Fern looked up and smiled. "Good morning, Eunice."

"Are you weeding or picking?"

"A little of both." Fern motioned to the plastic pail nearby, "I should have a nice mess of peas we can have with our supper this evening."

"The peas in our garden have all shriveled up from the hot weather we've been having," Eunice said with a shake of her head. "Keeping the garden watered is nearly a full-time job."

"I know what you mean. I usually water every other day, and sometimes that doesn't seem to be enough." Fern stopped picking and wiped her forehead with the corner of her choring apron. "Should we go up to the house and have something cold to drink? I'm more than ready for a little break."

"A cold drink sounds good to me."

Fern picked up the bucket of peas, and she and Eunice headed for the house.

"If you'd like to have a seat on the porch swing, I'll go inside and get us some iced meadow tea. Or would you rather have a glass of lemonade?"

"Meadow tea's fine for me. I like the minty taste." Eunice lowered herself to the swing.

Fern disappeared into the house and returned a few minutes later with two glasses of iced tea and a plate of oatmeal cookies. She set the cookies on the small table nearby, handed one of the glasses to Eunice, and took a seat beside her. "What brings you by this morning? Have you been out to the bike shop to see Freeman?"

Eunice nodded. "I went there to ask why he didn't come by to see me on Sunday like he promised."

Fern's brows lifted slightly. "I thought he went to see Katie. At least that's where he said he'd gone."

"Freeman passed my buggy Sunday afternoon, and we stopped and talked for a few minutes. He said he was going over to check on Katie but that he'd stop by my place for a piece of pie on his way home." Eunice frowned. "Of course, he never showed up." She took a sip of tea and held the cool glass against her forehead. "Freeman's sudden interest in Katie has me worried. One minute he acts as if he likes me, and the next minute he's running off to check on her."

Fern patted Eunice's arm in a motherly fashion. "I don't think you have anything to worry about. My bruder has always liked to fix broken things, and I believe he thinks Katie needs fixing."

"Why would he think Katie needs fixing?"

"She's been carrying around a lot of emotional baggage since the accident that took her boyfriend's life. I'm sure Freeman sees Katie as someone who needs his help, but certainly not as his aldi."

"I hope you're right, but with her being pregnant—" Eunice covered her mouth. "Oops! Guess I shouldn't have mentioned it."

Fern's eyes widened. "Are you serious?"

Eunice nodded.

"Where'd you ever get an idea like that?"

Eunice told Fern about the conversation she'd heard at the health food store awhile back and then mentioned the symptoms Katie had been having.

Fern's lips compressed into a thin, straight line. "Have you said anything to Freeman about this?"

Eunice nodded. "I mentioned it to him when I was in the bike shop awhile ago. We almost ended up in an argument when I asked if he was the father of Katie's boppli."

Fern blinked a couple of times and jerked her head. "You accused my bruder of that?"

"I did, but Freeman denied it."

Fern's head moved slowly from side to side. "If Katie's pregnant, which I'm not convinced that she is, there's no way that Freeman could be the father."

"How can you be so sure?"

"Think about it, Eunice. The only time Freeman's been alone with Katie is the few times he's stopped to check on her since her folks left for Ohio."

Eunice tapped her chin as she thought things through. "Maybe the father is someone Katie met while she was living in Florida. It's the only logical conclusion."

⁓ ✥ ⁓

Shortly after noon, Katie glanced out the kitchen window and spotted Freeman getting out of his buggy. She wiped her wet hands on a dish towel and hurried to the door.

"How are you doing?" Freeman asked when he entered the house a short time later. "Do you need anything else for the boppli?"

"I've still got plenty of everything." She motioned to the counter where she'd begun making a sandwich. "I was about to fix myself some lunch. If you haven't eaten yet, maybe you'd like to join me."

Freeman smiled. "I haven't eaten, so I'd be glad to join you."

Katie buttered the bread and was getting ready to cut some ham slices when she heard the baby crying in the other room. "I'll be right back. I need to see about the boppli."

Freeman stepped up to the counter. "I'll take over the sandwich making."

Katie smiled as she left the room. She couldn't get over how helpful Freeman seemed to be. Each time she was with him, she found herself longing for the one thing she wanted most but was sure she'd never have—a husband and children.

When Katie returned to the kitchen, she found two ham and cheese sandwiches sitting on the table.

"Is the boppli doing okay? I don't hear her crying anymore," Freeman said.

"She's fine. I changed her *windle*, and she went right back to sleep." Katie pulled out a chair and sat down. After they'd said their silent prayers, she looked over at Freeman and said, "I did some serious thinking this morning, and I've decided that it's time

164

to take Susan to the sheriff."

"But you said before that your folks won't be back until the end of the week. What made you decide to see the sheriff today?"

"I'm growing attached to the boppli. It's only making me feel worse because I know I can't keep her." Katie groaned. "I should have notified the sheriff right away. Keeping the baby wasn't right, and I feel guilty about it."

"When do you want to go?"

"As soon as we're done eating, if you have the time."

"I'll make the time." Freeman looked away and dropped his gaze to the floor.

"Is something wrong? You look kind of thoughtful."

He pulled his fingers through the back of his hair and grimaced. "Something's bothering me, Katie, and I'd like to talk to you about it, but I'm not sure how."

"What is it?"

"Well, someone mentioned. . ." He cleared his throat a couple of times. "This is so hard for me to say."

"Did someone mention something about me?"

He nodded.

"Is it about the boppli?"

"Jah."

"Does someone else know that I found little Susan on the porch?"

"Uh, no. . ." Freeman blew out his breath in a puff of air that sent the napkin on his knees floating to the floor. He lifted his gaze and looked at her. "Are you in a family way, Katie?"

She sucked in her breath, and her face heated up. "Who—who told you that?"

"I'd rather not say." He looked at her with such intensity that her heart started to pound. "Is it true?"

She shook her head so hard that the ties on her covering whipped around her face. "I've never been intimate with any man, and I can't believe someone would spread such a rumor about me." Tears stung her eyes, and she nearly choked on the sob rising in her throat.

"I didn't want to believe it, Katie, but I had to ask so I could put a stop to any rumors that might be going around."

"Who told you that I'm pregnant? I need to know."

"It doesn't matter who told."

"It matters to me!"

"I shouldn't have said anything. I'm sorry I've upset you."

"So you're not going to tell me who told you I'm pregnant?"

He shook his head.

Bitter disappointment weighed Katie down. She couldn't believe Freeman wouldn't tell. With a sense of irritation, she pushed her chair aside and jumped up. "I'll get the boppli ready now. As soon as you're done with your sandwich, we can head to the sheriff's."

Freeman blinked a couple of times. "Are you sure you want to do this right now? Your face is awfully pale, and you look kind of shaky. Maybe you should eat something before we go."

"I'm not hungry!" Katie's legs wobbled as she raced from the room.

When she returned with the baby several minutes later, Freeman had finished eating and was washing the dishes.

"We're ready to go," she said in a voice barely above a whisper.

Freeman dried his hands and reached for the diaper bag Katie held under one arm. Then he opened the door and waited for Katie to go out first.

She hesitated a minute, drew in a quick breath, and plodded down the stairs.

As they were headed to Freeman's buggy, a car came up the driveway. When the back door opened, two people got out.

Katie gulped. "Oh no. It's Mom and Dad!"

CHAPTER 25

Katie, whose boppli is that you're holding?" Mom asked as their driver pulled his car away.

Katie's mouth felt so dry she could barely swallow. She glanced over at Freeman, hoping he might say something, but he stood beside her with a blank expression.

"Katie, answer your mudder's question," Dad said sternly. "Whose boppli are you holding?"

Katie moistened her lips with the tip of her tongue. "I. . . uh. . .found her on our front porch the night you left for Ohio."

"What?" Mom's eyes widened, and Dad looked like he'd been hit over the head with a hammer.

Katie quickly explained about the note that had been attached to the baby's blanket and how she'd taken care of little Susan for the past several days.

"Did you notify the sheriff?" Dad asked.

She shook her head. "Freeman and I were—"

"I can't believe you kept the boppli all this time and didn't let the sheriff know about it!" Mom's shrill voice sent shivers up Katie's spine. "What on earth possessed you to do such a thing?"

"I was afraid to drive the buggy, and I—well, I became attached to the boppli and didn't want to give her up."

Mom glared at Katie. "What an upheaval you've caused by your immature actions!"

"Calm down, JoAnn. You're gettin' yourself all worked up." Dad touched Mom's arm. "We just need to take the boppli to the sheriff, and that'll be the end of it."

Mom shook her head forcefully. "No, it won't. What if the sheriff puts Katie in jail?"

Katie's heart pounded, and her throat constricted. The thought that she might be put in jail for keeping the baby had never entered her mind.

As if sensing her fears, Freeman touched her arm and said, "It's gonna be okay, Katie. I'm sure once we explain things to the sheriff and he sees that the boppli's unharmed, he won't—"

Dad moved closer to Freeman. "How long have you known about the boppli?"

"Since the morning after Katie found her," Freeman replied. "I came over to see if Katie was doing all right, and she told me about the boppli."

"So you've kept Katie's secret the whole time we've been gone?"

Freeman's face flamed as he nodded.

"Didn't you even think to suggest that she take the baby to the sheriff?"

"I did. Even said I'd take her myself, but she didn't feel ready to go there until now." Freeman gestured to his horse and buggy tied to the hitching rail. "We were getting ready to go to the sheriff's office in Middlebury when you and JoAnn showed up."

Dad gave his beard a tug. "You can go home now, Freeman. Katie's mamm and I will see that the baby is taken to the sheriff."

"I'd like to go along," Freeman said.

Dad shook his head. "No need for that. I'm sure you've got things you need to do at your shop."

"Besides," Mom put in, "this is *our* problem, not *yours*."

"Okay." Freeman offered Katie a sympathetic smile. "I'll be praying for you."

※ ※

As Freeman drove away from Katie's house, he couldn't help but feel concerned. She was not only upset with him for asking if she was pregnant, but now she was faced with going to the sheriff's, fearful that she might be arrested. She'd looked so pathetic trying to explain things to her folks. Seeing the way her eyes glistened with tears had tugged at his heartstrings.

I should have insisted that she notify the sheriff right away, Freeman berated himself. *The longer she kept the baby, the more attached she became. Now she's in trouble with her folks and could be in trouble with the sheriff.*

Freeman thumped his head a couple of times. "I'm as much to blame for all this as she is." He knew that keeping quiet about the baby was wrong, but he'd gone along with it in order to appease Katie.

Maybe I'm too softhearted for my own good. Maybe Fern's right. I might need someone to tell me what to do.

Freeman thought about the look of agony he'd seen on Katie's face when he'd asked if she was pregnant, and he wondered if she'd ever trust him again.

By the time Freeman turned onto his driveway, he'd gotten himself all worked up.

Pray for Katie. Pray for Katie.

Freeman halted his horse in front of the buggy shed and bowed his head. *Heavenly Father, please be with Katie when she goes to the sheriff's. Give the sheriff an understanding heart, and may Your will be done for Katie and the boppli she found.*

～❧ ❧～

Katie sank to her bed with a moan. They'd returned from the sheriff's office a short time ago, and she'd gone straight to her room. She could still see the shocked expression on the sheriff's face when she and her folks had walked into his office with little Susan. After Katie had told him the story of how she'd found the baby, he'd told them an equally surprising story. Three days ago, he'd gotten a call from an English woman who'd said that their teenage daughter had told them she'd given birth to a baby the week before while she was staying with a friend. The young woman knew she couldn't care for the baby, so she'd left it on an

169

Amish family's front porch. When her parents asked where the house was, she'd said it was dark outside and she couldn't remember exactly where she'd gone. She just knew it was an Amish home because she'd seen a buggy parked outside by the barn.

Katie let her head fall forward into her hands and gave in to the tears she'd been holding back all day. She was relieved that she hadn't been accused of any crime, but it had hurt to see the compassion in the sheriff's eyes when Mom said, "Our daughter suffered a tragic loss several months ago and hasn't been the same since, so she wasn't thinking clearly."

Katie squeezed her eyes tightly shut as tears trickled down her cheeks. It seemed as if every time she opened her heart to someone, she lost that person. She'd not only lost little Susan, but thanks to Freeman's accusations, she'd lost him as a friend, too. After all, why have a friend who wouldn't tell her who'd been saying she was pregnant? Who was Freeman protecting, anyway?

A knock sounded on Katie's bedroom door, pulling her thoughts aside.

"Supper's ready," Mom called.

"I'm not hungry."

"You need to eat."

"I don't want any supper. Please leave me alone."

Katie felt relieved when she heard Mom's footsteps clomping down the stairs.

She stretched out on her back, staring at the ceiling and searching for a ray of hope that would offer comfort yet finding none. Sometime later the shadows in Katie's room faded into darkness, and she fell asleep.

CHAPTER 26

As Katie hung a towel on the clothesline the following morning, a pang of regret shot through her like a knife. It was the same towel she'd used when she'd bathed little Susan. It seemed like everything she did caused her to think about the baby.

I need to keep busy and try not to think about the boppli. It'll only make me sadder if I think about how awful I felt having to give Susan up to the sheriff. Katie swallowed past the lump in her throat. *How could any mother leave her little girl on the porch of a complete stranger like that? If I had a boppli, I'd never give it up.*

Forcing her thoughts to come to a halt, Katie hurried through the process of hanging the clothes and was getting ready to head back to the stamp shop when Dad came out of the house and motioned to her.

"I was wondering if you'd do me a favor," he said when Katie joined him near the porch.

"What do you need?"

"I'd like you to go to the Kuntry Store and pick up the clock I ordered for your mamm. Since tomorrow's her birthday and we've made plans to eat supper out, I want to be sure I get the gift on time."

"Can't you pick it up?"

He shook his head. "I don't have the time for that today. I've got several customers coming to pick up windows they ordered, and I need to get out to my shop right away."

"Can't your helper take care of the shop while you're gone?"

Dad shook his head. "Alvin's sick, so he won't be in today."

Katie shuffled her feet a few times and stared at the ground. The thought of driving the buggy anywhere made her feel sick to her stomach. "I. . .I don't have the time, either," she mumbled. "Mom needs my help in the stamp shop."

"You haven't been that busy all week. I'm sure your mamm can manage fine on her own for an hour or so."

"But what am I supposed to tell her? I mean, you don't want her to know about the clock you ordered, right?"

"Just tell her you're running an errand for me. She doesn't have to know where you'll be going or what you're getting."

Katie kicked at a clump of dirt with the toe of her sneaker as she mulled things over. She didn't want to go anywhere in the buggy alone. Just the thought of it made her face feel hot and her stomach churn.

Dad nudged her arm. "What's it going to be? Will you pick up the clock for me or not?"

Katie didn't want to disappoint Dad, and she wanted Mom to have her birthday present on time, so she gave a slow nod and said, "I'll go right after lunch."

Dad smiled and patted Katie's shoulder. "Danki, I appreciate it very much."

⚜

Katie's arms ached as she guided her horse, Dixie, to pull the buggy slowly down the road. She clung to the reins so tightly that her fingers felt numb, but she wouldn't relax her grip. She had to keep the horse from going too fast; she had to stay focused on the road.

Things went along fairly well for a while—until they came to a bend in the road. A car whipped around them, blasting its horn. The horse whinnied, reared up, and then bolted down the road.

A shrill scream tore from Katie's throat, and she jerked on the reins.

Dixie kept running, full speed ahead.

Katie's face flooded with heat, and her heart thumped furiously; then she was hit with a wave of nausea. The dreaded feeling of unreality converged on her like a dark cloud, ready to snuff out her life. Everything seemed to be moving in slow motion. She could see things around her, but they didn't seem real. She gulped in a quick breath of air and looked around frantically, searching for something that would help her gain some control.

Katie grabbed the lever on the windshield wipers and pushed it back and forth. Anything to bring her back to reality. *Squeak! Squeak! Squeak!* The wipers scraped noisily against the front window.

She could see Dixie's rear end, but the horse seemed far away, as though Katie was seeing her in a dream. She gulped in a few more breaths and started counting. *One. . .two. . .three. . .four. . .* There, that was a little better. She could see things clearly again, although her heart still pounded and her hands felt so clammy she could barely hold on to the reins.

"*Sachde!*" Katie shouted as her senses returned. "Slowly, Dixie! Go slower, now!"

Dixie finally slowed to a trot, and then she continued with a normal walk.

Katie was tempted to turn around and head straight for home but knew she'd have to answer to Dad if she showed up without Mom's gift.

"I have to go on," she told herself. "I need to get to the store and get back home."

By the time Katie arrived at the Kuntry Store, she was shaking so badly she could hardly walk. Gritting her teeth, she tied the horse to the hitching rail and forced herself to go into the store.

"Do you have the clock my daed ordered?" Katie asked Laura Petersheim, the middle-aged Amish woman behind the counter.

"Got it right here." Laura bent down, picked up a cardboard box, and placed it on the counter.

Katie reached into her purse and handed Laura the money Dad had given her.

Laura's forehead wrinkled. "Are you all right, Katie? Your hands are shaking."

"My horse spooked on the way here, and it. . .it upset me real bad." Katie picked up the package, and was almost to the door when she bumped into Ella, who was just coming in.

Ella's forehead wrinkled as she stared at Katie. "Are you okay? Your face is nearly as pale as goat's milk."

"I'm fine." Katie pushed past Ella and hurried out the door. She'd just placed the box in the back of the buggy when Ella stepped up to her.

"Are you feeling grank?"

"No. I said I'm fine."

"I don't believe you. Tell me what's wrong."

Katie knew she would never get away from Ella if she didn't offer some sort of explanation, so she told her about the horn honking and Dixie getting spooked, but she left out the part about her panicking and the strange sensation of things being unreal that had followed.

"That must have been frightening. I wish folks wouldn't honk their horns when they pass." Ella grimaced. "I think some people get impatient with our buggies."

"You're probably right." Katie shifted uneasily, thinking about the trip home. She dreaded getting back into the buggy. What if she had another panic attack? What if she couldn't control the horse? What if the buggy flipped over or ran into a car? What if she were killed?

Ella bumped Katie's arm. "Did you hear what I said?"

"Uh, jah. You said some people get impatient with our buggies."

"That wasn't the last thing I said."

"What'd you say?"

"I was telling you about an article I read in today's newspaper. I wondered if you'd read it, too."

"What article?"

"It was about a teenage English girl who'd given birth to a boppli, kept it for a week, and then left it on some Amish family's porch." Ella slowly shook her head. "Can you imagine such a thing?"

Katie swallowed hard. Did Ella know that she was the one who'd found the baby? Should she say anything?

"Did you read the article?" Ella asked.

Tears welled in Katie's eyes. She figured she may as well own up to it, because the newspaper might have given her name. "I'm the one who found the boppli," she murmured.

Ella gasped. "Seriously?"

Katie nodded.

"Tell me about it."

Katie quickly related the story of how she'd found little Susan and had taken care of her for several days.

"Why'd you keep the boppli so long?"

"I was lonely with my folks gone, and the boppli kept me company. Besides, she was so sweet, and it was hard to let her go."

Ella's disapproving frown made Katie cringe. "If you were lonely, you should have let me know. You could've come over to our place to stay, or I could've stayed with you. Didn't you realize that the sheriff needed to be told about the boppli right away?"

Katie sniffed, trying to hold back her tears. "You don't have to be so judgmental. Freeman understood why I kept the baby so long. He didn't try to make me feel guilty."

Ella's eyes opened wide. "Freeman knew you had the boppli, and he kept quiet about it?"

Katie nodded once more. "He went to the store to get me some things for the boppli, and then the day Mom and Dad got home, he was going to—"

"I can't believe you'd do something like that, Katie. I'm really disappointed in you."

Katie's throat clogged, and her eyes stung with tears. "I—I need to go." She stepped up into the buggy, gathered the reins, and clucked to the horse. She wished she'd never run into Ella. She wished she hadn't agreed to pick up the clock for Dad. She wished she'd told him she had a headache, because she had one now!

⤙ ⤚

JoAnn glanced out the window of the stamp shop and frowned.

Katie had been gone a long time, and she was beginning to worry. What if something had happened to her as she was out running the errand for Jeremy? Ever since the accident Katie and her cousins had been involved in last fall, JoAnn had worried about Katie.

But for the grace of God, it could have been Katie's life that was taken that day, she thought ruefully. But the Lord had spared Katie, and even though she'd suffered from the emotional effects, she hadn't been physically hurt. At first JoAnn had thought Katie just needed some time to get over the shock of losing Timothy. But when she'd tried to get Katie to visit Timothy's grave and seen her reaction, she'd realized that Katie had a long way to go in overcoming her grief over losing Timothy. Now, with Katie having all sorts of physical and emotional problems, JoAnn was even more concerned. What if Katie never snapped out of it? What if she got worse instead of better?

The *clip-clop* of horse's hooves drew JoAnn's attention to the window again. She was relieved to see Katie climb down from her buggy. Now she could stop worrying and get back to work.

When Katie entered the stamp shop a few minutes later, JoAnn said, "That errand your daed sent you on must have taken some time."

"Jah, it did," Katie said with a nod.

"Wouldn't have anything to do with my birthday, would it?"

Katie grimaced as she rubbed her forehead. "I really can't say."

"What's wrong? Aren't you feeling well?"

"I have a koppweh. Seems like I've been getting a lot of them lately."

"I'm sorry to hear that. Why don't you go up to the house and lie down for a while?"

"Don't you need my help this afternoon?"

"Things have been slow here today, so I'm sure I can manage on my own." JoAnn smiled and patted Katie's arm. "Run along now, and take a couple of white willow bark capsules before you lie down."

Katie nodded and hurried out the door.

When Freeman looked up from the bike he'd been working on and saw Ella enter his bicycle shop with a pinched expression on her face, he knew she must be upset about something.

"What's wrong? Is there a problem with your bike?" he asked, picking up the wrench lying beside the bike's back wheel.

She shook her head.

"Do you need some part or new reflective tape?"

"No."

"What'd you come in for then?"

"I just came from the Kuntry Store, and while I was there, I saw Katie. She told me about the boppli."

Ella's word pierced Freeman like a knife, and he dropped the wrench on his toe. A shooting pain zinged up his foot, causing him to grimace. A cloud of doubt settled over him. Could Katie really be pregnant?

"What boppli are you talking about?" he rasped.

"The boppli Katie found on her porch." Ella leaned against Freeman's desk. "She said you knew about the boppli but kept quiet about it."

Freeman nodded, feeling a sense of relief. At least Ella wasn't saying that Katie was pregnant. "Katie asked me not to tell anyone about the boppli she found."

"And you agreed to that?"

"Jah, I did."

Ella's face flamed. "What in all the world were you thinking?"

"I wanted to help her, and I figured—"

"What you did was wrong! You didn't help Katie one little bit by protecting her, either." Ella eyed him critically. "I hope you're not leading Katie on."

"What's that supposed to mean?"

"Katie might think the interest you've taken in her goes deeper than friendship, and I don't want her to get hurt." Ella shook her head. "She's already been hurt enough, and I hate to see how naerfich she's become."

Freeman tapped his foot, feeling more frustrated by the minute. "I'm not leading Katie on. I just want to help her deal with her panic attacks."

Ella drew back like she'd been stung by a bee. "Katie's having panic attacks?"

A burst of heat shot up Freeman's neck and spread quickly to his cheeks. "I—I figured from what you said about Katie being nervous that she must have told you she was having panic attacks."

"I knew she was nervous and had been struggling with some health issues, but I had no idea she was having panic attacks."

Freeman groaned. "Guess I shouldn't have opened my big mouth."

"I'm glad you told me. Now that I know, maybe I can help Katie."

"Have you ever had a panic attack?"

"No."

"Then what makes you think you can help her?"

Ella blinked in rapid succession. "Well, I—"

"Unless you've had panic attacks and have been treated for them, I doubt you could help her at all."

"I care about Katie, so as soon as I have the chance, I'm going over to see her, and if there's any way I can help, I surely will."

Freeman knew he had to talk to Katie before Ella did. "Sorry, Ella, but I can't talk anymore. I've got an errand to run." He grabbed his hat and rushed out the door.

⊰ ⊱

As Freeman headed over to Katie's on his bike, he rehearsed what he was going to say. He'd been wanting to see how she was doing since she'd turned the baby over to the sheriff, and now he needed to let her know that he'd blabbed to Ella about her panic attacks. It seemed that he'd been messing up a lot lately where Katie was concerned, and he needed to make things right.

When Freeman entered the Millers' stamp shop a short time later, he spotted JoAnn stacking some scrapbook paper on one of the shelves, but he didn't see Katie anywhere.

"Is Katie here?" he asked.

"She has a headache and is up at the house resting." JoAnn frowned deeply. "With all the problems Katie's been having, it doesn't surprise me that she's been getting so many headaches lately."

Freeman nodded and shuffled his feet. "Would you mind giving Katie a message?"

"Of course."

"Would you tell her that I'm sorry for blabbing to Ella about her panic attacks?"

JoAnn tipped her head. "Ella's having panic attacks?"

"No, I'm talking about Katie."

"Katie?"

"Jah. While you and Jeremy were gone, she told me about her panic attacks."

JoAnn sank into the chair at her desk. "I. . .I had no idea!"

Freeman groaned. He couldn't believe he'd blown it again.

CHAPTER 27

The following day while Katie emptied the trash and rearranged some of their older stamps, JoAnn sat at her desk filling out an order for some supplies they needed. She had a hard time concentrating though. Ever since Freeman had come by and said that Katie was having panic attacks, JoAnn had been thinking about things and fretting over whether she should mention it to Katie or not. She'd planned to speak to Jeremy about the situation last night, but he'd gone back to work in his shop right after supper. By the time he'd come in, she'd fallen asleep. As soon as they had the opportunity to hash things over, she wanted to discuss it with Katie. If Katie really was having panic attacks, they needed to get her some help.

As Eunice stood at the kitchen window waiting for Freeman to pick her up for their date, a sense of excitement welled in her soul. The fact that he'd invited her out for supper gave her hope that he might be looking for more than friendship. She certainly hoped so, because she really wanted to get married.

"Staring out the window isn't going to bring your date here any quicker," Mama said, joining Eunice at the window.

Eunice smiled. "I know, but I'm anxious for Freeman to get here."

"You don't want to appear too anxious." Mama gestured to the table. "Why don't you sit and try to relax? We can visit while you wait for Freeman."

Eunice took a seat. Mama was right; she was overanxious, but it was hard not to be when she wanted to be with Freeman so badly. She hadn't had any steady boyfriends since Sam had broken up with her two years ago. Freeman was the first man who'd showed an interest in her since they'd moved to Indiana. He was nice-looking, had a pleasant personality, and owned his own business. What more could she ask for in a husband?

"Would you like a glass of lemonade or something to snack on while you're waiting for Freeman?" Mama asked.

Eunice shook her head. "I'm holding out for the meal we'll be having at the restaurant."

"I guess that makes sense." Mama took a seat beside Eunice and picked up the newspaper that had been lying on the table. "Did you read the article in here about the English boppli that was left on an Amish woman's porch?"

"No, I didn't. What'd it say?"

"See for yourself." Mama handed the paper to Eunice.

Eunice read the article and frowned. "That's *baremlich*!"

"I think it's terrible, too."

"I wonder if the family who found the boppli is anyone we know."

"As a matter of fact, it was Katie Miller."

"Seriously?"

Mama nodded. "When I was outside the Kuntry Store yesterday, I overheard Ella and Katie talking. Katie said she'd found a boppli on her porch and had kept it several days before taking it to the sheriff."

Eunice sucked in her breath. "No wonder the stamp shop was closed when I went by there. Katie must have been in the house with the boppli."

"That's not all," Mama said. "Katie said that Freeman knew about it and had bought some baby items for her."

Anger boiled up in Eunice. "Now I know why Freeman's been

181

acting so secretive lately. He told me he'd gone over to check on Katie once, but I'll bet he was going over there all the time so he could play with the boppli and hold Katie's hand."

"Now you don't know that for sure."

"I know he was over at Katie's last Sunday." Eunice ground her teeth together. "At least he admitted that much."

"If I were you, I wouldn't say anything to Freeman about this," Mama cautioned.

"Why not?"

"It might make him angry if he thinks you don't trust him."

"Well, I don't trust him. Not anymore."

"Even so, if you're hoping for a relationship with Freeman, you ought to tread lightly, don't you think?"

Eunice shrugged.

"A man doesn't like it when a woman pushes too hard or becomes demanding. If you want to have a meaningful relationship with Freeman, you need to be careful about what you say and do."

"You may be right, but if I'm given the opportunity this evening, I'm going to tell Freeman that I know about the boppli Katie kept hidden." Eunice stood and rushed to the window. "I think I hear a horse and buggy coming up the driveway. I hope it's Freeman."

~≈ ≈~

"Are you hungry?" Freeman asked as he and Eunice were ushered to their seats at the restaurant.

She nodded. She'd been quiet on the way to the restaurant, trying to think of how to broach the subject of Katie. She knew she'd have to handle it tactfully so that Freeman didn't get upset.

"I think I'll have the baked chicken." Freeman licked his lips and pointed to the menu. "Maybe I'll have some ham to go with it. What appeals to you, Eunice?"

She studied her menu a few minutes. There were so many choices that it was hard to decide. "Guess I'll have the turkey dinner."

They placed their orders with the waitress then bowed their heads for silent prayer.

When Eunice opened her eyes, she found Freeman staring at her.

"What's wrong? Why are you looking at me like that?" she asked.

"I was just thinking what pretty blue eyes you have."

"Danki." Eunice smiled as her face warmed. Freeman had never given her such a nice compliment before. She felt like she was floating on a cloud. *Maybe he does care for me,* she thought. *He might have been helping Katie with the baby only because he felt sorry for her.*

"The weather was much cooler today than it has been lately." Eunice continued to smile at Freeman. "Maybe we'll get some rain."

He nodded. "We could probably use some, all right."

While they waited for their food, they talked about the weather, Freeman's bike shop, and Eunice's inability to find a job.

"I'm thinking I might try selling candles and scented soaps," she said. "Maybe I can get some of the women in our community to host some parties in their homes."

"That might be a good idea," he said. "Guess it's worth a try at least."

"That's what I think, too."

Soon after the waitress brought their meal, Eunice noticed Freeman staring across the room. Her gaze followed his, and heat flushed her cheeks. Katie and her folks sat at a table on the other side of the room, and Freeman was looking at Katie!

～✢ ✢～

Katie reached for her glass of water and glanced across the room. Her hand froze in midair when she spotted Freeman sitting at a table with Eunice. A wave of envy washed over her. Freeman and Eunice were obviously on a date.

Katie knew she had no reason to be jealous, because she had no claim on Freeman. He had every right to date Eunice or anyone else he chose, so it was useless to think about her having a relationship with Freeman. *Then why does it make me feel sad to see him with her?*

"Aren't you hungry?" Mom pointed to Katie's plate. "You've hardly touched your chicken."

"I'll eat it. I just need a drink of water right now." Katie gulped down some water and set her glass on the table. Then she cut a piece of chicken and popped it into her mouth.

"Are you enjoying your birthday supper?" Dad asked Mom.

She nodded. "Everything's real *gut*."

Katie glanced across the room again and was surprised when she saw Freeman heading their way. Eunice remained at their table with a glum expression on her face.

"How are you doing, Katie?" Freeman asked as he strode up to her side of the table.

"Okay."

"I came by the stamp shop to see you yesterday, but your mamm said you had a headache and were in the house resting. Are you feeling better now?"

"I'm fine."

"How'd things go with the sheriff?"

"He was very understanding after we explained things to him," Mom said before Katie could respond.

Dad nodded in agreement.

Freeman pulled out the empty chair next to Katie and took a seat. "I also wanted to apologize to you."

"For what?"

"For blurting out to your mamm that you've been having panic attacks. I thought your folks probably both knew by now."

Dad's face turned bright red, and he looked at Katie in disbelief. "Is this true?"

Tears sprang to Katie's eyes as she slowly nodded.

"Why didn't you tell us?"

"I. . .I was afraid to."

"Afraid of what?"

"Afraid you wouldn't understand. Afraid you might think I was crazy."

Freeman's face turned bright red. "I'm real sorry, Katie," he said. "I assumed that your folks both knew by now, and after all the things you and I discussed about your panic attacks, I'm surprised you didn't tell 'em."

Katie looked away. She felt betrayed by Freeman. She'd thought he was her friend, but he'd been saying and doing things lately to prove that he was anything but.

"Will you accept my apology?" Freeman asked.

She gave a noncommittal shrug.

Dad cleared his throat and looked at Freeman. "I think my fraa and I need to talk to Katie alone."

"Oh, okay."

Katie felt Freeman's eyes on her, but she refused to look at him. She didn't want him to see the tears burning her eyes, and she didn't want his pity. She felt relief when Freeman pushed his chair aside and stood. "I'm really sorry, Katie," he said once more. Then he walked back to the table where Eunice waited for him.

∽≪ ≫∽

On the drive home, Freeman kept berating himself. He felt like a heel for hurting Katie. If he'd known she hadn't told her folks about her panic attacks, he never would have said anything. Maybe in some ways it was good that the truth had come out. Katie's folks might insist that she get some help. Freeman wished he'd been able to help her, but they hadn't spent enough time together for that. Besides, he wasn't a trained counselor. The only thing that made him qualified to discuss Katie's panic attacks was that he'd suffered from them, too.

"What's wrong?" Eunice asked, giving Freeman's arm a light tap. "You've been awfully quiet ever since you went over to the Millers' table at the restaurant."

Freeman shrugged.

"Did Katie say something to upset you?"

"No."

"Do you wish you'd been having supper with her instead of me?"

Freeman turned to face her. "'Course not. I just went over there

185

to find out how Katie was doing and to apologize for something I said."

"What'd you say?"

"I'd rather not talk about it."

"Does it have anything to do with the boppli she kidnapped?"

"She didn't *kidnap* the boppli; she found it on her porch." Freeman glared at Eunice. "How'd you find out about it, anyhow?"

"It was in the newspaper. I'm sure everyone in our community knows about it by now."

Freeman gripped the reins a little tighter. "I read the article in the paper, too, and it didn't give the name of the woman who found the boppli."

"Well, my mamm overheard Katie and Ella talking about it yesterday. Katie came right out and said that she was the one who found the boppli. She also said that you were in on it the whole time."

"I wasn't *in* on it. I just helped Katie out by buying some things she needed for the boppli."

"Humph! At least now I know why you've been acting so secretive and why you stayed at Katie's so late last Sunday. Are you in *lieb* with Katie?"

"No, I'm not in love with her! Now, can we just drop the subject?" Freeman's face heated up, and a trickle of sweat rolled down his forehead. He didn't like being grilled like this. It made him feel like he was a little boy.

They rode in silence the rest of the way home, and when Freeman pulled into Eunice's yard, she hopped down from the buggy and sprinted for her house without saying good-bye.

"Wish I'd never asked her out for supper," Freeman mumbled as he drove away. "Wish I'd never gone over to the Millers' table tonight and shot off my big mouth!"

By the time Freeman arrived at his house, he was quite worked up. Instead of having a pleasant evening with Eunice, he'd upset both her and Katie, and now he was upset as well.

He hurried to get the horse and buggy put away and then headed for the house.

When Freeman stepped into the living room, he halted. Fern knelt on the floor sobbing like a child.

"What's wrong?" He moved quickly toward her.

With a shaky finger, she pointed across the room to where Grandma lay on the sofa. "I. . .I think she's dead!"

CHAPTER 28

Katie groaned and shielded her eyes from the ray of sun streaming through the curtain in her bedroom window. It was time to get up and help Mom with breakfast, but she didn't want to leave her bed. On Sunday they'd gotten word that Sara Bontrager had died from a heart attack. Today was Sara's funeral. Even the thought of going sent shivers up Katie's spine. She hated funerals. Hated anything that reminded her of death.

With a weary sigh, she climbed out of bed, plodded over to the window, and stared out at the cloudless sky. *I wish I had a good excuse not to go to Sara's funeral.* She dug her nails into the soft wood of the windowsill. *Mom and Dad will expect me to go, and I don't think they'll let me stay home no matter what I say.*

Katie thought about Freeman and Fern and wondered how they were dealing with the loss of their grandmother. She thought about how horrible she'd feel if either of her grandparents died, and she remembered the agony she'd felt when Timothy died. Even though she was still angry with Freeman for telling Mom and Dad about her panic attacks, her heart went out to him today.

On the way home from Mom's birthday supper last night, Dad had quizzed Katie about the panic attacks and said he thought they needed to get her some help. Katie had responded by saying that it wasn't as bad as Freeman made it seem, and she was sure she could handle the panicky feelings on her own. Dad's response to that was, *"We'll talk about it later."*

With the news of Sara's death, Mom and Dad had other things on their minds. At least, Katie figured, they wouldn't bring up the subject of her panic attacks for a while.

～❧ ❧～

Freeman stood with his family in front of Grandma's coffin, gazing at her softly wrinkled face. They'd had a short service that morning for their closest relatives. Soon the main service would begin, with everyone else in their community invited.

"I'll miss you, Grandma," Freeman whispered, swallowing around the lump in his throat.

Freeman's mother placed her hand on his shoulder. "We'll all miss her, but we can take comfort in knowing she's in a better place."

He nodded slowly. "I. . .I still can't believe she's gone."

"Me neither." Tears ran down Fern's face, and she swiped them away with a trembling hand. "It was a shock to find her lying dead on the sofa." She sniffed and blew her nose on her hanky. "Grandma hardly ever got sick, and she rarely complained about anything. I had no idea she had a weak heart."

"None of us did," Dad said with a shake of his head.

Freeman moved away from the coffin, leaving Mom, Dad, and his brothers and sisters who'd come from Ohio and several other states to say good-bye to Grandma. Some of their church members had begun to arrive, and he knew it would soon be time to close the casket before the main service began.

～❧ ❧～

A few minutes past nine o'clock, Katie and her folks arrived at the Bontragers' place for Sara's funeral. Katie took a seat beside Ella and prayed for the strength to make it through the day.

Ella reached for Katie's hand and gave it a gentle squeeze. "Are you okay?" she whispered.

Katie nodded and forced a smile. She couldn't let on how uneasy she felt. She needed to keep her emotions under control and stay as relaxed as she could.

She glanced around the room at the people who'd come to this somber occasion—men and women dressed in black—young children and teens, all sitting quietly on their backless wooden benches.

The service began at nine thirty, with one of the ministers speaking about creation. He quoted from John 5:20–30 and from the latter portion of 1 Corinthians 15. Both passages dealt with the resurrection of the dead.

Then another minister preached for twenty minutes more, and the final message was delivered by the bishop, followed by some scriptures and a prayer.

Katie closed her eyes, determined to focus on something else. She thought about the baby she'd found on her porch. She thought about Florida and warm sunny beaches. She thought about the pond out behind their house, wishing she could be there instead of here.

Katie heard someone sobbing, and her eyes snapped open. Fern and Freeman were sitting with their family, and Fern's shoulders shook as the bishop read Sara's obituary. Then the casket was opened, and the viewing began. The home church men went into the room where Sara's body lay. The home church women followed so they could help the men sing a few songs while the people filed through.

As Katie approached Sara's casket, she choked back a sob. Sara, lying still and pale inside her plain, simple coffin, wore a peaceful look. Did that mean crossing from this life to the next had been a joyful occasion for her? Had Sara gone to heaven to be with Jesus, or had her spirit merely vanished into nothingness when it left her body?

That's how I feel whenever I'm having a panic attack, Katie thought as she made her way out of the room. *It's like I'm floating away into nothingness.* Just thinking about the experience made her tremble.

She stepped quickly out the door and drew in a couple of deep breaths.

"Are you okay?" Ella asked, coming up behind Katie. "You

look like you might pass out."

"I. . .I'm fine. Just need to breathe in some fresh air."

"It was quite stuffy in there," Ella said. "When you get that many bodies in one place, it's bound to be warm." She touched Katie's arm. "When I saw how pale and shaky you looked, I was worried that you might be having a panic attack."

Katie gulped. "Where'd you get that idea?"

"Well, after what Freeman said to me the other day—" Ella's face flamed. "Did you know he spoke to me about you?"

Katie's fingers clenched as she shook her head. "What did he say?"

"Said you've been having panic attacks, and I said I wanted to help you." Ella frowned. "But between my job helping Dad, and Mom not feeling well again, I haven't been able to speak to you until now."

Irritation welled in Katie's soul. "Freeman had no right to tell you that. I wouldn't have told him about my panic attacks if I'd known he was going to blab it all over the place."

"I'm sure he wasn't trying to be malicious. He's concerned about you, and he thought I knew."

"I never told anyone until the night I admitted it to Freeman, and now he's told you, Mom, and Dad." Katie grimaced. "Who knows who else he's told about my panic attacks?"

"Who's having panic attacks?" Loraine asked as she joined them on the lawn.

Katie dropped her gaze to the ground. "Apparently Freeman's been telling everyone, so I guess you may as well know that I've been having panic attacks."

Loraine touched Katie's arm. "Ach, I'm so sorry. Do your folks know about this?"

Katie nodded. "Freeman blabbed to them, too."

"What are you going to do?" Loraine asked.

Katie opened her mouth to reply, but Ella bumped her arm and motioned to the long line of buggies in the yard. "Looks like we're getting ready to head to the cemetery for the graveside service, so we'd better go."

❧ ❧

Katie had been holding things together fairly well until they gathered at the cemetery. When the men set the casket in place over the freshly dug hole, she struggled to keep her composure. She felt shaky and hot, as if she might pass out, and her legs felt like two sticks of rubber.

Could this be the beginning of another panic attack? Help me, Lord. Help me to stay calm and in control.

As several men who were related to Sara began to fill in her grave, Katie swayed unsteadily. With every clump of dirt that hit the coffin, she thought of Timothy and the horrible feeling she'd had in the pit of her stomach the day he was buried.

Katie gulped in a quick breath of air and squeezed her eyes shut. *Think about something else. Breathe in. Breathe out.*

When the graveside service was finally over, Katie relaxed a bit. Now they could go back to the Bontragers', eat the simple meal that had been prepared, and head for home.

❧ ❧

After the funeral dinner was over, Loraine decided to have a talk with Ella. She was worried about Katie and hoped Ella might have some idea as to what they could do to help her. She'd been watching Katie throughout the graveside service and had noticed how nervous and wobbly she seemed to be. No doubt she'd been remembering the day Timothy was buried.

Loraine didn't know much about panic attacks, other than the little bit she'd read in a magazine one day. What she'd read had made her realize that anyone dealing with panic attacks needed some kind of help.

Loraine spotted Ella talking with her sister Charlene near the barn.

"How are you feeling?" Charlene asked when Loraine walked up to them. "I hear you've been having some morning sickness."

Loraine nodded. "Some days it's worse than others, but today it hasn't been so bad."

"I hate feeling sick to my stomach." Charlene wrinkled her nose. "If I ever get married and am expecting a boppli, morning sickness is the one thing I won't like."

Ella tapped her sister's shoulder. "That's a ways off for you, and maybe by then you'll have gotten used to the idea."

Charlene shook her head. "I doubt that very much."

They engaged in small talk for a while; then Charlene left to visit some of her friends.

Loraine moved closer to Ella and lowered her voice. "I'm really worried about Katie."

"Me, too. She made it through the funeral okay, but at the graveside service, she looked so shaky I was afraid she might pass out." Ella's expression was full of compassion. "I was thinking about my bruder Raymond's funeral, so I'm sure Katie was thinking about Timothy's funeral, too."

"Can you think of anything we can do to help with her emotional problems?" Loraine asked.

Ella shrugged. "I don't know much about panic attacks, so I'm not sure we can help her get over them, but maybe we can help in some other way."

"Like what?"

"Let's think of something fun we could do. Maybe if her mind's off herself, she'll learn to relax and won't have so many panic attacks."

"We still haven't gotten together to do any stamping," Loraine said. "Let's try to do that with Katie soon."

Ella nodded. "It'll be like old times."

"Except Jolene won't be with us." Loraine sighed. "I sure do miss her."

"So do I."

"Do you think she'll ever come home?"

"Maybe for a visit, but now that she's deaf and can't teach school, I doubt she'd stay for good."

"You're probably right. Jolene was very happy being a teacher, and I'm sure she still misses her students." Ella glanced across the yard. "I haven't seen Katie in a while. Do you know if she's still here?"

Loraine shrugged. "I'm not sure."

"Let's go see if we can find her," Ella suggested. "I want to see when she might be free to do some stamping."

~❧ ❧~

As soon as Katie finished eating, she headed for the creek behind Sara's house. She needed to be alone for a while to think and calm down. During the meal, she'd noticed a few people staring at her. She wondered if they knew about her panic attacks. Worse yet, what if they thought she was pregnant? Oh, how she wanted to know who'd told Freeman such a thing. She wished she could have made an announcement—tell everyone she wasn't pregnant and that she wasn't the only person in the world suffering from panic attacks.

When the water finally came into view, Katie was relieved that no one else was around. She took a seat on the grass, removed her shoes, and dangled her feet in the water. Then she closed her eyes and lifted her face to the sun. She sat like that for several minutes until a twig snapped from behind.

Katie jumped.

"Sorry, I didn't mean to startle you," Freeman said, taking a seat beside her. "Are you all right?"

"I'm fine." Katie shifted uneasily. She was still upset with Freeman for revealing her secret, but the sympathy she felt for him losing his grandma overruled her anger. "I'm sorry about your grandma. She was a kind woman, and she'll be missed by everyone."

He nodded. "The house will sure seem empty with her gone."

"Will you and Fern continue to live there?"

"Jah. She left the place in both of our names."

"That's good." Katie wondered what would happen if either Freeman or Fern got married. Would one of them move out? But she didn't voice the question.

Freeman rubbed the bridge of his nose and squinted. "I hope you're not still mad at me, Katie."

"You mean for telling Ella and my folks about my panic attacks?"

He nodded. "I never would have said anything if I'd known you hadn't told 'em."

Tears burned Katie's eyes and trickled down her cheeks.

Freeman touched her arm. "Will you forgive me?"

"The truth's out now, and I guess it wouldn't be right if I didn't forgive you." She sniffed and swiped at her tears. "I. . .I'm really scared."

"Of what?"

"I'm scared that I'll never get over my panic attacks. I'm scared that people will think I'm crazy, or worse, that I'm pregnant." Katie choked on a sob.

"Don't cry, Katie. It's gonna be okay. No one else has mentioned it to me, and if they do say anything, I'll nip it right in the bud." Freeman touched her arm. "You can find things to help overcome the panic attacks, and I'll help in any way I can." He slipped his arms around her waist, and she clung to him as if her life depended on it. "It'll be okay. Just give it some time," he whispered in her ear.

～※ ※～

Eunice had seen Freeman heading for the creek, so a bit later she decided to follow. She was almost there when she caught sight of him sitting on the grass, hugging Katie.

Eunice ground her teeth together. *He takes me out for supper and says nice things about my pretty eyes, and now he's hugging her! How could he do this to me? Is Freeman planning to drop me for Katie the way Sam did when Amanda started hanging around?*

She tapped her foot and continued to watch Freeman and Katie. *Maybe it was Katie who initiated the hug. I'll bet that's exactly what happened.*

Eunice whirled around and started back toward the house. *I should find a way to get even with Katie Miller. I ought to tell everyone I know about the baby Katie found, and how I'm almost sure that Katie's pregnant.*

CHAPTER 29

Did you see how sullen Katie was on the way home from the Bontragers'?" JoAnn asked Jeremy as they sat on the porch swing together that evening.

He nodded soberly. "When I helped her into the buggy, I noticed that her eyes were red and swollen. She seemed kind of shaky, too."

"Katie didn't know Sara that well, but she seemed to take her death pretty hard."

"She takes everything hard these days. Makes me sad to see her acting so naerfich all the time." Jeremy's nose crinkled when he frowned. "Do you really think she's suffering from panic attacks?"

JoAnn shrugged. "Freeman said so, and Katie admitted it, too."

"If that's the case, don't you think we oughta get her some help?"

"What kind of help?"

"I think we should talk to the bishop about Katie's problem."

"When did you want to speak with him?"

"How about now? Since Katie went to bed soon after we got home, she's probably asleep by now and won't even know we're gone."

JoAnn nodded slowly. "I suppose you're right; we shouldn't put this off."

~≈ ≈~

Katie had just slipped into her nightgown when she heard the sound of buggy wheels rolling along the driveway. She figured either they had some late evening company or Dad had decided to go someplace.

She yawned and stretched her arms over her head. The events of the day had left her feeling exhausted. She glanced at the clock on her nightstand and realized it was only eight o'clock. Even so, she was more than ready for bed.

She stood in front of the dresser and removed the pins from her hair. She was about to pick up her hairbrush when she caught sight of a pink baby bootie sticking out from under her bed.

Katie bent to pick it up, slipped it in the bottom drawer of her dresser, and sank to the edge of her bed with a moan. One more reminder of the baby she'd had to give up.

Her thoughts shifted gears as she remembered the way Freeman had hugged her today. Was it possible that he had feelings for her that went beyond friendship?

She shook her head. *I'm being stupid for even thinking he might be interested in me. What man would want to marry a woman who can't go anywhere on her own without having a panic attack? He needs someone strong and stable like Eunice, not an immature woman who's afraid of her own shadow. As long as I'm trapped in my fears, I can't live a normal life.*

It was probably for the best, Katie decided. The thought of falling in love again frightened her. If she were to love another man and lost him the way she's lost Timothy, it would be too much to bear.

~≈ ≈~

"What's that hundlin got under her head?" Freeman's dad asked when he took a seat on the porch beside Freeman.

"It's one of Grandma's slippers." Freeman grunted. "Come here, Penny. Get your head off that slipper."

The puppy just lay there, staring up at him.

197

He reached over and pulled the slipper out from under the pup's head. "Give that to me now!" So much for trying to train the mutt to do what he said.

Penny whimpered and stared longingly at the slipper.

"I don't think she was hurtin' it any," Dad said. "She's still a pup and doesn't understand. Maybe she misses my mamm the way we all do and the slipper brings her comfort."

"Guess you're right. I might be expecting too much from the hundli." Freeman tossed the slipper back on the porch.

Penny flopped her head down on Grandma's slipper and let out a grunt.

Freeman rolled his eyes and shook his head.

The screen door creaked open just then, and Fern, Mom, and two of Freeman's other sisters stepped onto the porch.

"Mind if we join you?" Mom asked, taking a seat in the chair on the other side of Dad.

" 'Course not." Freeman motioned to the remaining folding chairs on the porch. "You'll be leaving for home soon, so we need to take every opportunity we have to visit."

They began sharing their memories about Grandma and some of the things she'd said or done over the years that had been special to them.

When the women started singing "Glory Gates," which had been one of Grandma's favorite songs from the *Heartland Hymns* book, Freeman leaned his head against the wall and closed his eyes. He thought about Grandma for a while, until an image of Katie popped into his mind. He could still see the pathetic way she'd looked at him when they'd visited at the creek. He thought about how he'd impulsively hugged her and wondered if he'd been too forward. She hadn't pulled away, and the gesture had seemed to help calm her down. Truth be told, the hug had made Freeman feel comforted, too. He hoped Katie hadn't misread his intentions, though.

Woof! Woof!

Penny leaped into Freeman's lap, and he jumped.

"What do you want, girl?" He patted the dog's head. "Are you feeling lonely without Grandma to rub your belly and stroke your ears?"

Penny whined and nuzzled Freeman's hand with her nose.

"I think that pup really likes you," Mom said with a smile.

Freeman nodded. "I've finally accepted that fact."

~≪ ≫~

The following morning as Katie and her mother worked together in the stamp shop, Katie decided to try making some cards using one of their new paper punches.

Katie felt safe here among the stamping supplies, but she wished she could work here alone without having to wait on customers.

"How's that punch working out for you?" Mom asked.

Katie sighed. "It keeps slipping, and I'm having a hard time getting it set straight on the paper."

"Just keep on trying," Mom said. "Everyone feels better when they know they've done their best."

Katie frowned. "Are you saying I'm not trying to do my best?"

"That's not what I'm saying at all." Mom stepped up to the table where Katie sat and put her hands on Katie's shoulders. "You feel so tense. If you're having that much trouble with the punch, then you ought to set it aside and do something else."

Katie pushed her chair away from the table and stood.

"Where are you going?"

"I need a drink of water." Katie hurried to the bathroom, grabbed a paper cup, and filled it with water from the sink. As she took a drink, she made the mistake of looking in the mirror. Her eyes looked bloodshot, and there were dark circles beneath them. She obviously needed to get more sleep.

When Katie stepped out of the bathroom a few minutes later, she discovered Mom standing just outside the door with her arms folded.

"Since we have no customers at the moment, I'd like to talk to you about something," Mom said.

"What about?" Katie moved back to the table and took a seat.

Mom sat in the chair on the other side of her. "Your daed and I went to see the bishop last night after you'd gone to bed."

"How come?"

"We went there to talk to him about the panic attacks you've been having."

Katie's spine stiffened. "You told the bishop about that?"

Mom nodded. "He said we should take you to see one of the counselors in the place dedicated to us Amish at the mental health clinic in Goshen."

"You want to send me away because you think I'm going crazy, don't you?"

Mom shook her head. "Of course not! We just want you to get help. You wouldn't have to stay there. You could be seen as an outpatient."

"I don't want to go. Freeman gave me a book about panic attacks, and I think I can get better on my own by reading that."

"Your daed thinks it's a good idea for you to go to the clinic, and he plans to talk to you about it this evening. I just thought it would help if I explained things to you first."

Katie leaped out of her chair, sending it crashing to the floor. "I'm not going to the clinic! And he won't talk me into it!"

CHAPTER 30

Katie raced from the stamp shop, tears streaming down her cheeks. She needed to be alone. Needed time to think. The best place to do that was at the pond, so she tore off in that direction.

It was another warm day, and the unrelenting grip of the summer heat wave made her feel as if she couldn't breathe. Farm fields had been baked brown, and everyone's gardens were withering badly. They needed some rain, and they needed it soon.

When Katie reached the pond, she removed her shoes and waded into the water, letting it cool her feet. She plodded back and forth along the shallow edge, kicking and splashing the way she'd done as a child. If only her life could be as simple and happy as it had been back then. She still couldn't believe Mom and Dad were trying to force her to go for counseling. Didn't they realize how frightening it would be for her to talk about her problems with a stranger, not to mention the stress of having to hire a driver for getting to and from the clinic?

She flopped onto the grass with a weary sigh. The sun glinted off the water, and she looked up, shielding her eyes from the glare. She tried to pray, but words wouldn't come. What was the use of praying, anyhow? It seemed that God answered so few of Katie's prayers.

I wish there was someone I could talk to about this, she thought. *Maybe I should have begged Grandma and Grandpa to let me move to*

Wisconsin with them. At least they didn't try to make me do things I didn't want to do. I was much happier living in Florida with them.

The more Katie mulled things over, the more agitated she became. It made no sense that the panic attacks came at certain times and not others. It made no sense that the symptoms she'd been experiencing were so weird and left her feeling weak and confused.

Freeman had told Katie that he'd gotten over his panic attacks, so there must be a way. *Oh Lord, please let there be a way.*

Katie thought about the book Freeman had given her about panic attacks. She'd stuck it away in her dresser and hadn't even looked at it, but since she'd mentioned it to Mom, she guessed she'd better start reading it right away. Maybe there was something in the book that would help her. If she could get over the horrible attacks on her own, maybe Mom and Dad wouldn't insist on her seeing a counselor.

Katie scrambled to her feet and started walking toward the house. She was halfway there when she spotted Loraine heading in her direction.

"I stopped by the stamp shop to see you," Loraine said when she caught up to Katie. "Your mamm said you'd gotten upset about something and had run out of the shop. I checked the house first, and when I didn't find you there, I figured you might have gone to the pond."

Katie nodded. "I needed some time alone."

"If you'd like to talk about whatever's bothering you, I'm willing to listen. In fact, that's why I'm here—so we can talk about some things."

Katie hesitated a minute then nodded. "Let's go back to the pond where we can sit and visit."

"Sounds good to me. I might even decide to go wading."

When they reached the pond, they took seats under the shade of a maple tree.

Katie leaned back on her elbows and sighed. "I envy you, Loraine."

"Why's that?"

"You're married to the man you love, and—"

"Your time will come. Someday you'll find the right man and get married."

Katie shook her head. "I found the right man once, but he was taken from me. Besides, I can't even think about getting married as long as I'm having panic attacks."

"There must be something you can do to get over them."

Katie shrugged. "Mom and Dad want me to go for counseling, but I don't want to go."

"How come?"

"The thought of riding in a car makes me naerfich enough, but the idea of having to share my innermost thoughts with a total stranger makes me feel like I could throw up." Katie groaned as she touched her cheeks. "Do you know how embarrassed I feel because of my panic attacks? I'm afraid people are looking at me, thinking what a crazy person I am."

Loraine shook her head. "No one thinks you're crazy. And you might feel like you stand out or that people are looking at you, but don't let that give you an excuse to hide your embarrassment."

"I do look for excuses," Katie admitted. "Sometimes I look for reasons not to go places or do certain things. I feel safer when I'm at home."

"I hope you don't mind, but I discussed your panic attacks with Wayne, and he gave me some information to give you."

"What kind of information?"

"Wayne's chiropractor taught him to use a tapping method on certain acupressure points to help his phantom pains after his leg was removed."

"Did it work?"

Loraine nodded. "The chiropractor told Wayne that some people have used the tapping method as a way to relax and deal with their panic attacks."

Katie nibbled on the inside of her cheek. Between the book Freeman had given her and the information about tapping, maybe she could get on top of her anxiety attacks. "Do you have the tapping information with you?" she asked.

"Jah. It's in my buggy. I'll get it for you before I leave." Loraine touched Katie's arm. "There are a couple more things I wanted to talk to you about."

"Like what?"

"Ella and I want to get together with you to do some stamping. Can we do it one evening this week after the stamp shop is closed?"

"I guess that would be okay. How about Friday?"

"Friday should work." Loraine smiled. "It's been a long time since the three of us did anything fun together. It'll be like old times."

"Uh-huh." Katie shifted her legs to a more comfortable position. "How are you feeling these days? Is your morning sickness any better?"

"Some. The tea I got at the health food store has helped."

"Maybe I should try some of that, too."

"What for?"

"I get waves of nausea sometimes."

Loraine fidgeted with the ends of her head covering ties and sucked in her lower lip. "I'm, uh, not quite sure how to say this, but when I was at the health food store today, I heard someone say something I just couldn't believe."

"What was it?"

"They said you'd planned to keep the boppli you found on your porch, and that you only gave it up because your folks came home and made you take it to the sheriff."

Katie's face felt like it was on fire. "That's not true! Freeman and I were getting ready to go to the sheriff's when Mom and Dad showed up." Her eyes narrowed. "Who said that, anyhow?"

Loraine pulled on a piece of grass and twirled it around her fingers. "I'd rather not say."

"I think I have the right to know who's spreading rumors about me, don't you?"

"Maybe you're right." Loraine sighed. "It was Eunice."

"How would she know anything about what I'd planned to do with the boppli?" Katie clenched her teeth so hard that her jaw ached.

"Maybe Freeman said something to Eunice. From what I've been told, he and Eunice are pretty good friends."

Katie knew that Freeman and Eunice were good friends, although she couldn't understand what Freeman saw in Eunice. She seemed pushy and spoiled, used to having her own way.

"Did Eunice say anything else about me?" Katie asked.

Loraine nodded slowly. "She said that you're expecting a boppli."

Katie balled her fingers into the palms of her hands. "Awhile back, Freeman told me that he'd heard the same thing, only he never said who'd been spreading that rumor." Tears welled in Katie's eyes. "I don't know what I'll do if Mom and Dad get wind of this."

Loraine clasped Katie's hand. "Please tell me it's not true."

Katie shook her head real hard. "It's a lie, plain and simple!"

"Then why were you asking me about raspberry tea, and how come you're suffering from bouts of nausea?"

"It's one of the symptoms I've been having with my panic attacks." Katie frowned. "Sometimes I feel lightheaded and like I'm not really here."

"That sounds strange. What exactly do you mean?"

"It's a strange sensation—like things aren't real."

"Ach, that's baremlich, and it must be very frightening!"

Katie nodded. "It's the most terrible, scary feeling I've ever had, and it makes me feel like I'm losing control."

"I can only imagine."

Katie leaned closer to Loraine. "You don't believe I'm pregnant, I hope."

Loraine shook her head. "I never really thought you were, but I felt that I should let you know what's being said so you didn't hear it from someone else."

"I'm glad you did."

"If I hear any more such talk, I'll make sure they know it's not true."

"Danki, I appreciate that."

The more Katie thought about things, the more agitated she

became. She jumped up and started pacing. If Freeman had told Eunice that she'd planned to keep the baby, then he wasn't her friend at all! And if Eunice was telling folks that she thought Katie was pregnant, she needed to be stopped!

CHAPTER 31

As long as you're living in this house, you'll do as I say!"

Katie cringed as Dad's fist came down hard on the table. Ever since they'd finished supper, he and Mom had been talking about the need for Katie to get help for her panic attacks. She'd tried to explain to her folks that she planned to read the article on tapping from Wayne, as well as the book Freeman had given her, but Dad said he thought it was all a bunch of hooey and insisted that she needed to go for counseling.

"You were very depressed after Timothy died," Dad said. "Now that you're having these panic attacks, your mamm and I feel that it's time for you to get some professional help."

Katie wasn't ready to accept that. She was afraid to speak with a counselor, and she was afraid to ride in a car to the clinic. It seemed as if her whole world was falling apart and she was powerless to stop it. "I. . .I don't know why you're making me do this," she said sniffling.

"It's because we love you and want to see you happy and well adjusted again." Mom slid her chair a little closer and draped her arm across Katie's shoulders. "I know you're feeling naerfich about riding in a car, so I've decided to close the stamp shop and go with you on Friday."

Katie grabbed a napkin from the basket in the center of the table and wiped her tears. Short of moving out of Mom and Dad's house, there was no way she could get out of seeing the counselor, so she may as well resign herself to the fact.

Dad pushed away from the table. "Now that we have everything settled, I'm going out to the barn."

"I guess we'd better get these dishes cleared off the table." Mom grabbed their plates and took them over to the sink.

"Do you want me to wash or dry? Katie asked, picking up the silverware and glasses.

"Whatever you prefer."

"Guess I'll wash." Katie placed the dishes into the sink and turned on the water. *At least I'm still allowed to make some choices of my own,* she thought bitterly. *I wish I'd never come home for Loraine's wedding. If I could have stayed in Florida. . .*

A knock sounded on the back door.

"I'll see who that is." Mom hurried from the room and returned with Freeman.

Katie stiffened and looked away. "What are you doing here?" she mumbled.

Mom frowned. "Is that any way to speak to your friend?"

"He isn't my friend." Katie grabbed a glass and poked the sponge inside. "Not anymore."

~ ≈ ~

Freeman glanced at JoAnn, wishing she'd leave so he could speak to Katie in private.

As if sensing his need, JoAnn gave Freeman a nod and quietly left the room.

"What'd you mean when you said I'm not your friend?" Freeman asked, moving closer to the sink.

Katie shrugged and kept washing the dishes.

Freeman grimaced. Something wasn't right. Katie had been friendly enough when they'd visited at the creek yesterday, even letting him hug her. Maybe that was the problem. Katie might have misunderstood his intentions and thought he was being too forward.

"I owe you an apology," he said.

Katie glanced over her shoulder. "I know you do."

"I'm sorry for hugging you yesterday. It wasn't right for me to—"

"Is that all you're sorry for?" She whirled around to face him. Her face had turned red, and her eyes held no sparkle. "Eunice has been spreading rumors about me. She told my cousin Loraine that I'd planned to keep the boppli I found, and she even told someone that she thinks I'm pregnant."

Freeman's jaw dropped. "I can't believe she would spread rumors like that."

Katie dropped the sponge into the soapy water, sending bubbles up to the ceiling. "Eunice is the one who told you I was pregnant, isn't she?"

He nodded slowly. "I didn't think any good could come from me telling you that, Katie. Figured it would only make things worse if you knew who'd told."

"You're not my friend, and neither is Eunice!" Katie's chin trembled, and her eyes filled with tears. "The next time I see her, I'm going to tell her what I think about the lies she's been telling."

"Let me talk to Eunice," Freeman was quick to say. "I'm sure I can get her to listen to reason and stop spreading such rumors."

"You can do whatever you want, but I doubt it'll do any good." Katie turned and fled the room.

Freeman froze. Then he rushed out the door. He planned to stop by Eunice's place on the way home and have a little talk with her!

~❧ ❧~

For the last twenty minutes, Eunice had been sitting on the front porch watching the sun go down and thinking about Freeman. When she spotted his horse and buggy pull into the yard, her heart lurched. She hadn't expected to see him this soon, so this was a pleasant surprise.

She resisted the urge to run out to his buggy but remained where she was so she wouldn't appear too eager.

Freeman stepped onto the porch, scowling.

"What's wrong?" she asked. "You look *uffriehrisch*."

"I am agitated." He flopped into the chair beside her and tapped his foot. "I just came from seeing Katie. She told me something I didn't like at all."

"What was that?"

"She said you told Loraine that Katie was planning to keep the baby she found, and worse than that, you said you thought Katie might be pregnant." He frowned deeply. "You shouldn't start rumors like that—especially when they're not true."

"I wasn't trying to start a rumor. I was only repeating something I'd heard someone else say." Eunice flapped her hand like she was shooing away a pesky fly. "As I said before, Katie's symptoms make me think she's definitely pregnant."

Freeman shook his head. "I'm sure she's not, but I'm really worried about her."

"How come?"

"She's going through a rough time right now and doesn't need anything more to feel stressed about."

"What about me?" Eunice's throat constricted. "Doesn't it matter if I feel stressed out when I see Katie in your arms?"

"What?"

"I saw the two of you at the creek the day of your grossmudder's funeral, and you were hugging her." Tears welled in Eunice's eyes.

"It's not what you think. I need you to understand how things are with me and Katie."

"How are things, Freeman?"

"Katie and I are just good friends. I didn't mean anything by the hug; I was only comforting her."

"Why would she need comforting? It was you who lost your grossmudder, not Katie."

A muscle in Freeman's jaw quivered. "Katie's going through some emotional problems right now, and since I've been through something similar, I think I can help her."

Eunice tipped her head and squinted at him. "What are you talking about?"

"I used to have anxiety attacks."

Her eyebrows shot up. "Huh-uh!"

"It's true. When I was a buwe I had panic attacks just like Katie's having now."

"Katie's having panic attacks?"

He nodded. "I figured you probably knew, since you seem to know everything else."

Eunice shook her head. "How would I know that? It's not like Katie and I are best friends or anything. She doesn't confide in me the way she does you."

Freeman's face turned red, and he looked at Eunice with a pleading expression. "Maybe I shouldn't have said anything, but I wanted you to realize that Katie's not pregnant. I'm sure her symptoms are caused by the panic attacks she's been having. Please don't tell anyone what I told you about Katie."

She gave a noncommittal shrug.

"I mean it, Eunice. Katie's had enough gossip spread about her."

"What about you, Freeman?" she asked. "You wouldn't want anyone knowing you used to have panic attacks, would you?"

"It's no big secret, and there's no shame in admitting you've had some emotional problems, so if you feel the need to tell others about me, then go right ahead."

Eunice knew she'd never have Freeman for herself if she did that, so she smiled sweetly and said, "Don't worry, I won't say a word about you or Katie."

CHAPTER 32

Katie's heart pounded as she sat beside Mom in the counselor's office on Friday morning. She'd done okay on the drive here, but now, faced with talking about things she'd rather not talk about, to a man she didn't know, she felt on the verge of another panic attack.

She glanced around the room, which was decorated in a western theme. It was neat and orderly, and the leather furniture had a strong odor. She felt uncomfortable.

To make matters worse, ever since they'd come into the room, Mom had interrupted several times and kept answering most of the questions Dr. Coleman, the counselor, had asked Katie. Only a few times had Katie been able to respond herself, and that made her feel even more on edge.

"What are you feeling right now?" Dr. Coleman asked Katie.

"I...I'm nervous, and I hope that I'm able to get over my panic attacks, but I feel that—"

"Hope isn't a feeling, Katie. Hope is something you do." Mom looked over at the counselor and smiled. "Isn't that right, Dr. Coleman?"

"Yes, of course, but I think we should hear what your daughter has to say." He nodded at Katie. "Go ahead."

Katie twisted her fingers around the narrow ribbon ties on her head covering. It wasn't easy to talk about her feelings, especially to someone she'd just met.

Mom nudged Katie's arm. "You were saying that you hope you can get over the panic attacks."

Katie nodded. "But I have this feeling that I never will."

"Why do you think that?" Dr. Coleman asked.

"Because the strange sensation I get when I have an attack seems to be getting worse, and—and it is happening more often."

"Maybe that's because you're thinking about the panic attacks so much," Mom said. "You might be bringing the attacks on by doing that. Don't you agree, Dr. Coleman?"

"It's possible." He looked back at Katie. "Could you describe the feelings you get when you have an attack?"

Katie explained about the feelings of unreality, and how she often felt dizzy, nauseous, shaky, and like she couldn't get her breath. "I just don't understand why these feelings come on so quickly and with no warning." She sighed as she shrugged her shoulders. "Then they disappear as quickly as they came. Whenever I'm expected to go anywhere, I get scared because I'm afraid it'll happen again."

Dr. Coleman explained that everyone's symptoms are different, and that Katie's symptoms were fairly common among those who experienced panic attacks. "One of the strange things about a panic attack is that it usually subsides as quickly as it started." He tapped his pen against the edge of his desk a few times. "Feeling short of breath is a common symptom of panic attacks, but it's not dangerous."

"What causes that to happen?" Mom wanted to know.

"It happens when a person breathes from the chest and not the diaphragm." He looked at Katie again. "What is the worst thing a panic attack ever did to you, Katie?"

She shrugged. "I guess it was when I passed out in church."

"That could have been because it was such a warm day," Mom put in. "You've never fainted before, so I'm sure the heat we had that day was the cause."

"Jah, maybe so," Katie mumbled. Why did Mom think she had all the answers?

Dr. Coleman looked at Katie. "Is there anything else you'd like to tell me about your panic attacks?"

"I. . .I don't think so."

"I mentioned that panic attacks can trick a person's mind into thinking there's danger. Do you have any questions about that?" he asked.

Katie opened her mouth to respond, but Mom cut in again. "I read a little in a book about panic attacks that Katie got from one of her friends. It said that a person's supposed to decide whether the feelings they have during a panic attack are dangerous or just uncomfortable."

Dr. Coleman nodded. "That's true. Most of the feelings a person might encounter during a panic attack are uncomfortable but not dangerous. So asking yourself that question is a good way to gauge whether you should be concerned about the feelings you're having."

"That makes sense to me," Mom said. She asked Dr. Coleman a few more questions and gave her opinion on several more things.

Katie frowned. *Why is Mom talking so much and answering questions that are meant for me? It's as though Mom thinks she's the patient instead of me.*

Katie leaned her head back and let her mind wander as Mom went on and on about some other things she'd read in the book on panic attacks. *I wonder if Freeman talked to Eunice about the lies she's been telling about me. Should I say something to Mom about this, or would it be better to wait until I talk to Freeman again to find out how things went? If I tell Mom, she'll probably say more on the subject than I want her to say, and she might want to talk to Eunice herself. That would really be embarrassing.*

Dr. Coleman cleared his throat loudly and looked at his watch. "We're almost out of time for this session, but I'd like to see Katie again next Friday, and then we'll delve deeper into the mystery of panic attacks." He handed Katie a notebook. "I'd like you to make a list of the fears you have during a panic attack, and it's also a good idea if you keep a panic journal and record every panic attack you have and how you feel during the attack."

"We'll be here next Friday, and I'll make sure Katie does her homework," Mom said before Katie could respond. She rose from her chair and motioned for Katie to do the same.

Katie stood and started for the door, more than anxious to go. Today had gone even worse than she'd expected.

"Why don't you wait out in the waiting room, Katie?" Dr. Coleman said. "I'd like to speak with your mother for a few minutes."

Katie gave a quick nod and hurried from the room. She was glad the session was over and wished she could talk Mom into staying home next week. But that would mean she'd have to come alone, and that thought caused her stomach to plummet like a roller coaster ride.

~≈ ✦~

JoAnn seated herself and waited for Dr. Coleman to speak.

He folded his hands on his desk and leaned slightly forward. "When you bring Katie here next week, I think it would be best if you stay in the waiting room while she's in talking to me."

JoAnn bristled, and she clenched her fingers so hard that they turned numb. "How come?"

"I know you're concerned about your daughter, but if Katie's going to make any kind of progress, she needs to feel free to say what's on her mind without interruptions or distractions."

"Did I talk too much today? Is that the problem?"

"You did tend to monopolize the conversation quite a bit." He picked up his pen and tapped it against the edge of his desk. "Katie needs the freedom to express herself without fearing that you might disapprove. She needs to know that—"

"I don't disapprove! I'm just concerned about my daughter and want her to get better."

"So do I," he said with a nod. "However, I think we'll make more headway if I'm able to speak with Katie alone."

"I. . .I see. I'll do as you wish." JoAnn stood and hurried from the room. Maybe she'd made a mistake in bringing Katie here!

When she entered the waiting room, she found Katie standing

in front of the window with her head bowed and her hands folded as if she was praying.

JoAnn touched Katie's shoulder. "I'm ready to go. Our driver should be waiting for us."

Katie turned around. "What'd Dr. Coleman say to you?"

JoAnn tucked a stray hair under the side of Katie's head covering. Katie had obviously not done a good enough job with her hair this morning. "He asked if I'd wait out here during your next counseling session," she said with a huff. "I'm not the least bit happy about it, either. I'm your mudder, and it's my place to be with you when you're talking to him."

"I think you should stay home next week, Mom."

"What?"

"It made me feel naerfich having you here today. I felt like I couldn't really say what was on my mind."

"I'll do as Dr. Coleman suggested and wait out here so you'll be free to say whatever you want to him, but I won't stay home."

Katie dropped her gaze to the floor. "You need to take care of the store."

"That's not as important as being with you. I'm sure our customers will understand if the stamp shop is closed for a few hours. Besides, we haven't been that busy lately."

Katie's jaw clenched, and a muscle in her cheek quivered. "I. . .I'd rather come here alone."

JoAnn was tempted to argue further, but she didn't want to make a scene in front of the other people waiting in the room. She slipped her arm around Katie's waist and whispered, "We can talk about this later."

～≈ ≈～

When Katie opened the door to the stamp shop that afternoon, she discovered an envelope with her name on it.

"Who's that from?" Mom asked, following Katie into the shop.

"I don't know." Katie tore open the envelope, slipped behind the counter, and silently read the note:

Dear Katie,

I spoke with Eunice the other day, and she said she wasn't trying to start a rumor about you and that she won't tell anyone else. I hope you believe that I didn't betray your trust. I'm really sorry if I said anything to upset you. Seems like I've been opening my big mouth a lot lately, saying things that get me in trouble.

Freeman

Mom stepped up to Katie and nudged her arm. "Well, who's it from?"

"Freeman Bontrager."

"What'd he have to say?"

"He. . .uh. . .just wanted to explain something to me." Katie quickly slipped the note into her purse, hoping Mom wouldn't press for details. She was relieved when Mom said she had some things to do in the house and left the shop.

Katie leaned against the counter and folded her arms. *Guess I'd better accept Freeman's apology. He did sound sorry, and it's the right thing to do. I just hope Eunice stops gossiping about me.*

The bell on the shop door jingled, and Ella and Loraine stepped in. "We came a little early to look around before we do our stamping together," Ella said.

Katie's face warmed. Thanks to the stress of the day, she'd forgotten about their plans.

"I invited Eunice to join us this evening, but she's selling candles and scented soaps now, and she said she has a party to do somewhere out of our district," Ella explained.

"Ada's hosting one of Eunice's candle parties next week," Loraine said. "Would either of you like to go?"

Ella smiled. "I might go and buy a few candles. How about you, Katie?"

Katie shook her head. "I'm not that interested in candles or scented soaps." She motioned to the worktable. "Since I have no customers at the moment and Mom's up at the house, I guess we could start stamping now." Katie was glad Eunice hadn't been able to come, and she sure didn't want to go to one of her parties.

"I've been looking forward to this all day." Ella pulled out a chair and sat down. "We have several birthdays coming up in our family, so it'll be fun to make a few cards."

Loraine reached for the stack of cardstock in the center of the table. "I think I'll make Ada and Crist a card to go with the gift Wayne and I are giving them for their new house. I might include one of my poems on the inside of the card."

"What'd you get them?" Katie asked.

"Wayne made a coffee table. He says he's not an expert carpenter, but I think he did a good job. I'm sure his folks will be real pleased."

"Due to our current economic situation, a lot of people are making more things rather than buying store-bought items," Ella said. "My folks have decided to stay home for more meals instead of eating out so often."

"Guess everyone needs to do their part to help out when money's tight," Loraine said.

"That's true," Ella agreed. "Charlene and I have been helping our mamm put up a lot more produce this summer. It'll save us a lot of money at the grocery store come winter." She looked over at Loraine. "Changing the subject, I've been wondering how Wayne's three-legged sheep is getting along."

"Tripod's doing real well. The critter still follows Wayne all over the place like she's his pet."

"I guess she is," Ella said with a nod.

"Listen to us going on and on about so many unimportant things." Loraine leaned closer to Katie and tapped her arm. "Didn't you have a counseling session today?"

Katie nodded.

"How'd it go?"

"Okay." Katie hoped Loraine wouldn't question her about what had been said during her session with Dr. Coleman. She didn't want to talk about it. She just wanted to spend a few hours having some fun.

For the next half hour, Katie worked quietly on some cards

while she listened to Ella and Loraine visit. Every once in a while, she left the table to wait on a customer.

Soon after Katie took her seat again, she noticed Loraine clenching her teeth as she clutched her stomach.

"Are you okay?" Ella asked.

"I've been having a few stomach cramps off and on all day. They weren't too bad at first, but they seem to be getting worse." Loraine grimaced as she pushed away from the table and stood. "I think I'd better use the bathroom."

When Loraine left the room, Katie looked over at Ella and said, "Sure hope it's nothing serious."

"It's probably indigestion. My mamm had that a lot when she was carrying Charlene."

A few minutes later, Loraine returned, looking pale and shaken. "I. . .I need to go home. I'm bleeding!"

CHAPTER 33

Katie's chair squeaked as she took a seat at the kitchen table. She had no appetite for food. How could she think about eating supper when she was worried about Loraine? They hadn't heard anything for several hours—not since Loraine had been taken to the hospital.

"Let's pray," Dad said after he'd taken his seat at the head of the table.

Katie bowed her head and closed her eyes. Searching for the right words, she silently prayed, *Please, God, don't let Loraine lose her boppli. She and Wayne have been through a lot, and they deserve to be happy. Take away my fears, and help me with my panic attacks. And please bring all the gossiping about me to an end.*

Dad rustled his napkin, and Katie's eyes snapped open. Mom took a spoonful of potato salad and handed the bowl to Katie. Katie stared at it a few seconds then handed it to Dad.

Mom nudged Katie's arm. "Aren't you having any potato salad? I made it with plenty of mustard, just the way you like."

Katie passed the plate of ham to Dad as she shook her head. "I'm too worried about Loraine to think about food."

"You don't have to *think* about food; just eat it." The lines running across Dad's forehead deepened. "You eat like a bird, and you're way too skinny."

"Your daed's right," Mom agreed. "You'll end up sick if you

don't start eating more."

Katie's skin prickled. She was tired of Mom and Dad badgering her all the time.

"Have some of this." Mom plopped a huge spoonful of coleslaw in the middle of Katie's plate.

"I'm not hungry!" Katie leaped out of her chair and was almost to the stairs leading to the second floor when a knock sounded on the back door. She opened the door. The bishop stood on the porch, and he wasn't smiling.

"Mom and Dad are in the kitchen," Katie said.

He shook his head. "Didn't come to see them. Came to see you."

"Oh? What about?"

"There's a rumor going around that you're expecting a boppli. Is it true?"

"Is what true?" Dad questioned as he came to the door. "What's this all about?"

"Can I come in?" asked the bishop.

Dad nodded and led the way to the kitchen. Katie followed, her legs trembling like a newborn colt. Eunice had obviously taken her story to the bishop, probably hoping to make Katie look bad for trying to hide her pregnancy from everyone.

"Now what's this all about?" Dad asked again.

The bishop pulled out a chair at the table and sat down. "I'm not here to be judgmental, but there's a rumor going around that your daughter's in a family way. I came to find out whether it's true or not."

"Of course it's not true," Mom said with a quick shake of her head. "I don't know why anyone would think Katie's pregnant."

Dad touched Mom's shoulder. "Now don't get yourself all worked up, JoAnn. As the bishop said, it's only a rumor." He turned to face Katie. "Tell the bishop what he needs to hear."

"It's not true," Katie said, slowly shaking her head. "Eunice made it up, but Freeman said she wasn't going to keep the rumor going. I guess he was wrong about that."

Mom rubbed the bridge of her nose as she stared at Katie. "How long have you known about this rumor?"

Katie shrugged. "Awhile."

"And you never said a word to us? Why, Katie?" Dad asked.

"I didn't want you to be upset or think that I might be—"

"We know you're not pregnant, Katie." Mom looked at the bishop. "As you know, Katie's dealing with some emotional issues."

He gave a nod.

"One of her anxiety symptoms is nausea, and another one's feeling lightheaded and shaky. Maybe Eunice assumed Katie was pregnant because of her symptoms."

"That could be." The bishop pushed his chair back and stood. "Well, I won't take up any more of your time." He smiled at Katie. "If I hear any more rumors about you, I'll put an end to them real quick."

"We appreciate that," Mom said before Katie could respond.

After the bishop left, Katie decided that she needed to be alone by herself for a while, and some fresh air might help clear her head. "I'm going outside," she said.

"Please come finish your supper first," Mom said, motioning to Katie's plate.

Katie shook her head. "I told you before, I'm not hungry." She turned and rushed out the door.

~ ❧ ~

JoAnn looked over at Jeremy and frowned. "I don't know what we're going to do about Katie."

"Surely you don't think she's lying about not being pregnant."

She shook her head. "I wasn't talking about that. I was talking about the symptoms she's been having. Some might be related to her panic attacks all right, but being nauseous and shaky could be because she doesn't eat enough."

Jeremy lifted his broad shoulders. "Not much we can do about that. It's not like it was when she was a maedel and we could take away her desert if she didn't eat supper."

"I'm hoping Katie's counseling sessions will bring her back to us." JoAnn sighed deeply. "I won't be there to hear what Dr. Coleman has to say when Katie goes next week."

"How come?"

"He asked me to wait outside, and even though I wasn't thrilled about the idea, I agreed." She frowned. "But then Katie said she wants me to stay home next week, and if I agree to that, she'll be all alone."

Jeremy drank some of his water. "Might be for the best. Katie needs to learn to go places by herself and do things on her own. She'll never be able to function as a woman if she doesn't."

"Jah, well, Katie might be able to do that once she's feeling better emotionally. Right now, though, I feel she needs someone to go with her to offer moral support and to ask Dr. Coleman questions she might not think of."

He set his glass down and frowned at her. "You're overprotective where Katie's concerned, and you have been ever since she was a boppli. I don't know if it's because she's our only maedel or because she's the youngest of our kinner, but it's gotten worse since she came back from Florida. You hover over her all the time and offer way too many suggestions."

Irritation welled in JoAnn's soul. "I'm not overprotective, and I don't hover! I care about our daughter and want what's best for her."

"Then let her stand on her own two feet, and offer support through your love and prayers instead of pushing so hard. If Katie needs something, I'm sure she'll ask. If Katie's hungry, I'm sure she'll eat." Jeremy slid his chair away from the table. "I'm goin' outside on the porch to read the newspaper!"

"But you haven't finished your supper."

"I ate as much as I want, and I'm not a little buwe, so stop tellin' me what to do!" Jeremy strode across the room and jerked open the back door.

JoAnn cringed when the door slammed shut. Was she the only one who cared about Katie?

～❧ ❧～

As soon as Freeman pulled his bike into the Millers' yard, he spotted Katie's dad sitting on the porch.

"Is that an English or Amish newspaper you're reading?"

Freeman asked as he stepped onto the porch.

"English. This one's out of Goshen." Jeremy motioned to the chair beside him. "Take a seat if you like."

"Anything interesting in there?" Freeman asked as he sat down.

"Lots of bad news, including more about our depressed economy and how it's affecting us here." Jeremy frowned. "Seems to be gettin' worse all the time."

Freeman nodded slowly. "I know. With so many of the RV factories either shut down or having cut way back, a lot of men in our area have lost their jobs or have had their hours cut back."

Jeremy crossed his legs. "A man can't support a family when he has no work. Some may have to move if things don't improve. I don't know an Amish man who won't do whatever it takes to provide for his family."

"Guess some might need to look at other options for making money," Freeman said.

"Like what?"

"Maybe making birdhouses, wooden plaques, baked goods, or anything handcrafted that could be sold at the Shipshewana flea market or in some of our local shops. The Amish probably won't buy 'em, but maybe the tourists would."

Jeremy nodded. "It doesn't help the economy any when our property taxes keep going up, either." He pointed to the newspaper. "Yet it looks like they're planning to raise 'em again."

"It amazes me that some people think we Amish don't pay any kind of taxes, when we pay most of the same taxes as the Englishers."

"That's true, and besides paying taxes, we fund our own schools." Jeremy heaved a sigh. "All that said, if we Amish stick together, I'm sure we'll survive any crisis that comes our way. Always have; always will."

"Guess you're right about that." Freeman glanced over his shoulder. "Is Katie in the house? I'd like to know if she got the note I left her at the stamp shop."

Jeremy gestured toward the barn. "She was wandering around out in the yard when I came out here awhile ago, but then she went in there. Think she was lookin' for a place to be alone."

"Maybe I shouldn't bother her then."

Jeremy shook his head. "I'm pretty sure it was her mamm she was trying to get away from. Don't think she'd object to seein' you, though."

Freeman wasn't sure if he should comment on that, so he stared at the barn, trying to decide whether he should bother Katie.

"JoAnn took Katie to see one of the counselors at the mental health facility today." Jeremy sighed loudly. "It didn't go so well with JoAnn bein' in there while the counselor was trying to talk to Katie. She said he asked her to wait outside the next time they come."

"Guess it makes sense that he'd want to speak with Katie alone."

"She'll be alone all right. Told her mamm she didn't want her going to the next session with her at all." Jeremy gestured to the barn again. "Feel free to visit with Katie if you like. I'm sure she'll be glad to see you."

Freeman wasn't so sure about that, but he said good-bye to Jeremy and headed for the barn. He found Katie inside, sitting on a bale of hay with a fluffy gray cat curled in her lap.

"How are you doing?" Freeman asked, taking a seat beside her.

"Okay," she mumbled without looking up.

Freeman cringed. Was she still mad at him?

"I. . .uh. . .was wondering if you got the note I left for you."

She nodded and stroked the cat's head. It began to purr and nestled deeper into her lap.

"Are you still angry with me, Katie?"

"I guess not."

"Then what's wrong? I can see that you're unhappy about something."

"I'm upset about several things."

"Like what?"

"For one thing, our bishop was here awhile ago, asking if I was in a family way."

"Are you kidding?"

"No, I'm not. He said he'd heard a rumor that I was pregnant, and he wanted to find out whether it was true or not." Katie frowned. "It was Eunice who started the rumor, of course."

"I'm really sorry, Katie. Were you able to convince him that the rumor's not true?"

She nodded. "He said if he hears any more gossip about me, he'll put a stop to it."

"That's good."

"Then to make my day even worse, Loraine's at the hospital, and she may lose her boppli."

"I'm sorry to hear that. I know how excited she and Wayne were about becoming parents, so I hope and pray it'll go okay for her."

"Me, too."

Freeman reached over and stroked the cat's head. "Before I came in here, I was talking to your daed, and he said you went to see the counselor today."

"Uh-huh. I saw Dr. Coleman."

"How'd it go?"

"Okay, I guess, but he didn't really say much to help me."

"It's gonna take time, Katie. It took awhile for your panic attacks to start, and it'll take awhile for you to learn how to deal with 'em."

"I hope you're right. I have another appointment with Dr. Coleman next week, and I asked my mamm not to go with me again."

"How come?"

"She kept answering all the questions Dr. Coleman asked me, and when she wasn't answering questions, she was asking them. I could hardly get in a word." Katie shuddered and sighed. "I'm already feeling naerfich about going there alone, but I don't want Mom to go with me again."

"Would you like me to go with you? I'd stay in the waiting room while you're in with the counselor, of course."

"You. . .you'd be willing to do that?"

"If it'd make you feel more comfortable, I'd be glad to ride along."

"What about your work? I wouldn't want you to get behind on

things at the bike shop because of me."

"I'm pretty well caught up right now, so it shouldn't be a problem if I'm gone for a few hours once a week."

Katie smiled. "Danki, Freeman. I would like you to ride along with me."

Just then Katie's dad stepped into the barn, shaking his head and wearing a frown. "I just checked the answering machine, and we got some bad news. Loraine lost the boppli."

Katie pushed the cat aside, jumped off the bale of hay, and stormed out of the barn. "That's it!" she shouted. "I'm done praying for things!"

CHAPTER 34

Are you sure you're feeling up to doing that?"

Loraine turned from the stove where she'd been heating some soup, as well as some water for tea. "I'm fine," she said, smiling at her mother.

"But it's only been a few days since you miscarried, and I don't want you overdoing it."

"I'm not. Besides, cooking a meal gives me something to do. It's better than sitting around feeling sorry for myself."

The teakettle whistled, and Loraine removed it from the stove and dropped in a couple of tea bags.

Mom opened the cupboard door and started setting the table. "I know how disappointed you must feel, because I felt the same way when I miscarried."

Loraine's eyes widened. "When was that? I never knew you had a miscarriage."

"It was before you were born, and I never saw a need to mention it until now." Mom stared out the window.

"Was it your first pregnancy?"

"Jah." Mom sighed. "Have you ever had the feeling that something in your life was too good to be true?"

Loraine nodded.

"Well, that's the way I felt when I first learned I was pregnant— I was bursting with happiness. But then when I lost the boppli, your daed and I felt so disappointed I wondered if either of us would ever feel happy again." Mom smiled. "But God was good, and within a year, I got pregnant again. I finally came to realize that the boppli I'd lost might have been born with serious problems and that losing it might have been God's will for me."

Loraine turned down the gas on the stove and took a seat at the table. "I've been telling myself that, too. As Wayne said last night, 'God knows our needs, and for whatever the reason, He chose to take our boppli to heaven.'"

Mom placed the rest of the dishes on the table and sat across from Loraine. "No one ever said life would be easy, but if we keep God in the center of our lives, with His help, we can make it through."

Loraine nodded. "That's the only way for me."

A knock sounded on the back door, and moments later Ella stepped into the kitchen.

"Sorry I didn't get over here sooner, but Mama came down with a bad cold, so Charlene and I have had to take over all the household chores." Ella handed Loraine a paper sack. "I baked you a loaf of friendship bread, and there's a scripture verse attached to the plastic wrap."

"Danki, I appreciate that." Loraine opened the sack and removed the bread. Then she read the verse out loud. " 'And we know that all things work together for good to them that love God, to them who are the called according to his purpose.' Romans 8:28."

Tears welled in her eyes. "Mom and I were just talking about how God knows our needs. This scripture verse goes along with that."

Mom gestured to a chair. "We won't be eating for another half hour or so. If you have the time, why don't you sit and visit with us awhile?"

"Sure, I've got a few minutes to spare." Ella offered Loraine a sympathetic smile. "How are you feeling physically?"

"I'm doing okay. Since I came home from the hospital, Mom's been coming over every day to fix our meals. She's also done the laundry and some cleaning, so I've been able to rest a lot."

"That's good. Rest is what you need right now." Ella gave Loraine a hug. "I'm real sorry you lost the boppli. It must be very disappointing."

Loraine swallowed around the lump in her throat. "It is, but Wayne and I are trusting that God will allow us to have other bopplin in the future."

※ ※

"Are you feeling naerfich?" Freeman asked as he helped Katie out of the van.

She shook her head. "Not so much. I appreciate your riding with me, though. I was trying to be brave when I asked Mom to stay home, but I don't think I could have gone to my counseling session alone today."

"I'm glad to do it." Freeman stuck his head into the van. "Can you pick us up in an hour and a half?" he asked Mary Hertz, their driver. "I think we should be ready to go by then."

Mary nodded. "I'll be waiting right here when you come out."

As Katie walked to the building, she noticed that she felt a bit more confident than she had last week. Something about being with Freeman made her feel a sense of calm.

She was surprised when Freeman held the door and let her walk in first. No one had done that for her since Timothy died.

They took seats in the waiting room, and Freeman found a magazine to read. A few minutes later, Katie was called into the counselor's office. She glanced at Freeman, and he gave her a reassuring smile. Drawing in a quick breath, she stepped into Dr. Coleman's office.

He motioned to the chair on the other side of his desk, and she took a seat.

"How did your week go, Katie? Did you have any anxiety attacks?"

She shook her head. "I don't understand why I have them at certain times and not others. Or for that matter, why I started having them in the first place."

"There's no set time for an anxiety attack to occur, but they do seem to happen more often when a person's under a lot of stress. Panic onset can be caused by many things, such as the death of a loved one or trying too hard to please someone."

Katie nodded. "I felt depressed after my boyfriend died, but the panic attacks didn't start until I left Florida and came home."

"Is there someone you're trying too hard to please?"

"I...I don't think so. Well, maybe my folks, but it's always been that way."

"You'll need to work on that, Katie. We can't always please other people, and you can stress out if you try too hard."

Katie sat staring at her folded hands as she mulled things over.

"Where do your panic attacks seem to happen the most often?" he asked.

"When I'm riding in a car or our buggy. They've also happened when I'm in a stuffy room with a lot of people." Katie smoothed the wrinkles in her dress, a nervous gesture she'd had since she was a young girl. "Do you think I'll have panic attacks for the rest of my life?"

He rested his elbows on his desk and smiled at her. "Take heart, Katie. You *can* recover from panic attacks; it's just going to take some time and a lot of patience on your part. There are several things you can try, and it may take awhile before you find one that works best for you."

Katie gripped the edge of her chair. "Another thing I don't understand is how come the panicky feelings make me feel like everything's unreal."

"You mentioned that in our last session. Is it sort of like you're dreaming?"

"Kind of. It's hard to describe. I get this warm prickly sensation, and then it's as though nothing seems real anymore." She shivered, remembering the fear she'd felt the last time she'd had an attack. It had left her feeling confused and shaky for nearly an hour.

"Have you made any changes in your daily routine in order to avoid having another panic attack?" Dr. Coleman asked.

She nodded. "I look for excuses not to go places, and the thought of driving the buggy by myself makes me feel like I'm going to throw up or even faint. After passing out in church not long ago, I'm afraid to go there, too."

"Do you force yourself to go places?"

"Sometimes. Church is one of the places where I make myself go, but it's getting harder all the time. I have trouble concentrating on the service because I'm so afraid that I'm going to feel panicky again."

"Fear of a potential attack can almost paralyze a person," Dr. Coleman said. "Struggling against the fear is like trying to put out a fire with a can of gas."

Katie reached into the canvas tote bag she'd brought along. "One of my friends gave me this." She placed the book Freeman had given her about panic attacks on the counselor's desk. "It's the book my mother was telling you about last week. And my cousin gave me this." She handed him the article on tapping that Loraine had given her.

Dr. Coleman read the article and scanned through the book. "I'm familiar with the things mentioned in this book. It has many good points that we'll be talking about here, and you can put them into practice right away. I'm not that familiar with the tapping method, but you're welcome to try it. Before you leave today, I'll give you a few other things you can try, as well." He folded his hands. "Of course, you also need to trust God and ask Him to calm your heart and give you a sense of peace as you practice the things I'm going to suggest."

Katie frowned. "It's my feeling of fear that keeps me from trusting God."

"It's your choice to trust in God that will change your feelings of fear," he said, motioning to the Bible on his desk. "Remember this: The beginning of anxiety is the end of faith, and the end of anxiety if the beginning of faith."

Katie nibbled on her lower lip as she fought against the urge to chew her nails.

"Is there something else bothering you?"

"I think one of the reasons I feel so anxious is because I can't forgive myself for causing the accident that killed my boyfriend."

"What makes you think you're to blame?"

"A bee got in the van, and I freaked out. Our driver turned around to see what the commotion was about, and he lost control of the van." Katie blinked against the tears stinging her eyes. It was hard to talk about that day.

"You're not to blame for the accident, and you shouldn't let yesterday's regrets or tomorrow's anxieties get the best of you. You need to give them over to God."

Katie wasn't sure she could give anything to God, because ever since the accident, she'd been mad at Him for letting Timothy die.

Dr. Coleman picked up the Bible. "Before I give you some breathing exercises to do this week, I'd like to read you a verse of scripture found in 2 Timothy 1:7." He opened the Bible and read the verse out loud. " 'For God hath not given us the spirit of fear; but of power, and of love, and of a sound mind.' " Then he wrote the verse on a slip of paper and handed it to Katie. "If you memorize this, you'll be reminded that God doesn't want you to be fearful. He wants you to get well, Katie."

Katie swallowed around the lump in her throat. "I. . .I want that, too."

~ ✤ ~

Freeman glanced at the clock above the receptionist's desk. Katie had been in with the counselor almost an hour, so he figured she should be out soon. He hoped the counselor would be able to help Katie get her panic attacks under control soon. On the other hand, if she recovered quickly, then she wouldn't need him anymore. He didn't know why that thought bothered him so much. Was it because, like Fern often said, he liked to fix broken things? Or was he drawn to Katie for some other reason? He had been interested in Katie when they were children, but that was a long time ago, and she'd been a different girl back then.

Guess it really doesn't matter, he thought as he turned to look out the window. *Katie's still pining for Timothy and has no interest in me. Besides, I'm supposed to be courting Eunice. Despite my irritation with her at times, I must admit that I'm physically attracted to her.*

~·✺·~

As Eunice pedaled her bike up to Freeman's shop, excitement welled in her soul. She knew she probably shouldn't come over here so often, but she couldn't seem to help herself. From the way Freeman often looked at her, she was sure he was interested in her. She definitely liked him.

Eunice found the CLOSED sign on the shop door. Disappointed, she glanced at her watch. It was nearly three o'clock, so Freeman wasn't out for lunch. Maybe he'd had an errand to run or had gone to pick up some parts.

Guess I may as well stop at the house and see if Fern's at home. Eunice climbed back on her bike and pedaled up the driveway. She found Fern sitting under a maple tree in the front yard with a basket of mending in her lap.

"Are you too busy to visit?" Eunice asked as she rolled her bike across the lawn.

"I'm never too busy for you." Fern smiled and motioned to the house. "Grab a chair from the porch and bring it over."

Eunice parked the bike near the porch, picked up a chair, and hauled it over to the tree. "Whew, it's another warm day, isn't it?"

Fern nodded. "That's why I'm doing my mending out here. It's too warm in the house, and I'm sure not looking forward to cooking supper this evening."

"Maybe Freeman will take you out to eat," Eunice said as she took a seat.

Fern shook her head. "I don't think so. Thanks to Katie Miller, my bruder will be working late tonight."

Eunice puckered her lips. "What's Katie got to do with Freeman working late?"

"She had an appointment with one of the counselors at the mental health facility in Goshen, and Freeman went along as moral support." The tiny lines in Fern's forehead deepened when she frowned. "Seems like fixing bikes isn't good enough for my bruder these days. He's got it in his head that he can help Katie get over her panic attacks."

"Do you think he can?" Eunice asked.

Fern shrugged. "I don't know, but I think he'll keep trying as long as he thinks Katie needs his help."

Eunice bit her bottom lip until she tasted blood. Every time she turned around, Freeman was with Katie. It had to be more than him just trying to fix her problems. Katie was probably trying to win Freeman's heart.

If I don't do something about this soon, it might be too late, she thought. *I need to come up with some way to make Freeman spend more time with me and less time with Katie.*

CHAPTER 35

June quickly slipped into the more humid days of July and August. Katie was still plagued by panic attacks, but as Freeman continued to accompany her to the counseling sessions, she found herself drawn to him and wishing that he might see her as more than a friend. He'd dropped by the stamp shop several times and had come over to the house some evenings just to visit. Katie kept reminding herself that Freeman was going out with Eunice. He'd given no indication that he felt anything for Katie other than friendship, and if he ended up marrying Eunice, then the friendship he and Katie had now would be over.

Katie wondered if Freeman might see her as more than a friend if she were prettier and more outgoing like Eunice. Or maybe he'd be attracted to her if she was emotionally stable and didn't have panic attacks.

As Katie sat in Dr. Coleman's office one afternoon, she told him that she was getting impatient in her search for something that would put an end to her panic attacks and that she was about to give up.

"We've talked about this before, Katie," he said. "Impatience shows a lack of faith. You must be willing to tell God that you surrender your will to His and that you'll trust Him and not lose heart. When we ask God to do something, we often want to tell Him how and when to do it. We want it to be done our way. In the end, though, it must be God's will, not ours."

It sounded so easy, but Katie had never felt close enough to God to surrender her will to Him. She didn't tell Dr. Coleman that, though. Instead, she sat with her hands folded, staring at the floor.

Dr. Coleman handed her a slip of paper. "Here's another verse for you to memorize and use whenever you start to doubt. 'What time I am afraid, I will trust in thee.' Psalm 56:3." He smiled. "As you practice some of the suggestions I've given you, trust the Lord and visualize Him helping you."

Katie swallowed hard, hoping she wouldn't break down and cry. If only it were that simple.

"Have you been keeping a panic journal like I suggested?" he asked.

She shook her head. "I've written down a few things, but I usually forget."

"I believe it will help if you write down where you were and what was happening during an attack, then record your level of discomfort, the thoughts you had, and your behavior during the attack."

"I'll try to do better with that."

"What about the breathing techniques I asked you to try? Are you practicing them regularly?"

She nodded. "I have been doing those, and I've been trying to relax the parts of my body that are the tensest during a panic attack."

"Are you making yourself do things that frighten you, or are you still avoiding them?"

"I. . .I'm avoiding them whenever I can, and I get nervous just thinking about going anywhere alone."

"The goal of exposing yourself to the things that frighten you is to bring on an attack so you can practice responding to it in a more comfortable way."

"That sounds hard."

"It won't be easy at first, but it's important for you to acknowledge your urge to flee, yet stay in place and work through the panic attack."

Katie clenched and unclenched her fingers. Just thinking

about an attack made her feel as if she could have one right now.

"Have you tried getting angry at the attacks—talking back to them, telling them to do their best?"

"No, I haven't tried that yet."

"Have you taken the horse and buggy out alone?"

"I'm too scared to try driving the buggy alone. The last time I took it out by myself, I had a very bad panic attack." Katie shuddered, and tears blurred her vision. "Now I'm afraid of losing control."

"Maybe it's time for you to try some medication to help you feel calmer."

"I don't want that."

"Why not?"

"I'm afraid I'll become dependent on it or that it'll make me feel sleepy." She blotted the tears on her cheeks and sniffed. "If at all possible, I want to do this without medication."

He stared at the notes on his desk. "What about the homeopathic remedy you said your mother got from the health food store? Have you tried taking that to see if it makes you feel calmer?"

She shook her head.

His eyebrows furrowed as he leaned forward and looked at her intently. "Do you want to get better, Katie?"

She stiffened. "Of course I do!" She couldn't believe he'd even asked her that question.

"Then you need to practice the things I've suggested, and if you're not going to let me prescribe some medication, I want you to try the homeopathic remedy." He glanced at his watch. "Our time is up for today, but when you come back next week, I'll expect a progress report."

Feeling as though she'd been thoroughly scolded, Katie gave a quick nod and hurried from the room.

❧ ❧

When Katie stepped out of the counselor's room, her head was down and her shoulders were slumped. Freeman knew immediately that she was upset. He was tempted to ask how it had gone but decided that if Katie wanted to talk about it she would. It might upset her more if he pressed for details.

Freeman opened the door for Katie, and they walked silently across the parking lot.

"How'd your appointment go, Katie?" Mary Hertz asked when they climbed into her van.

"Okay," Katie said with a shrug.

Freeman hoped Mary wouldn't question Katie further, and he decided to try to get her talking about something else. "Did you get some shopping done?" he asked.

Mary shook her head. "Decided there wasn't anything I needed right now, so I stayed in the van and got caught up on my reading." She lifted a copy of *The Budget* newspaper. "I read several of the articles written by various Amish scribes around the country. Many related to accidents that had occurred last month."

Freeman glanced at Katie, who sat staring out the window as though deep in thought.

Mary pointed to the newspaper and frowned. "In Ohio, a young Amish woman was hit by a car when she was crossing the street to get to a phone shed." She pointed to another article. "Someone's buggy in Pennsylvania was hit when a car failed to stop at a stop sign." Her finger slid down the page. "Then in Illinois, a young boy was killed when he fell from the hayloft." She shook her head slowly. "Guess one never knows when their time will be up."

Freeman glanced at Katie. Her chin quivered, and her fingers were curled tightly into the palms of her hands. She was obviously distressed. Was it the things Mary had shared from *The Budget*, or was Katie upset about whatever had been said during her counseling session?

Usually Freeman headed straight to his shop after they dropped Katie off at her house, but today he thought he'd better stick around for a while and see if she would tell him what was bothering her.

~≪ ≫~

As they headed down the road, Mary continued to comment on

the accidents she'd read about in *The Budget,* and Katie felt like she could scream. By the time they got to her house, she was on the verge of a panic attack. She paid Mary for the ride, said good-bye to Freeman, and stepped out of the van.

"Wait up, Katie!" Freeman called as Katie hurried toward the stamp shop.

Katie halted and turned around. "I need to help my mamm."

"I'd like to talk to you a few minutes, and I promise I won't keep you long." Freeman motioned to the pond beyond their barn. "Why don't we take a walk out there so we can visit in private?"

Katie glanced at the parking area on the side of the stamp shop. She saw only one car and no buggies, so she figured Mom wasn't that busy at the moment. "I guess I can take a few minutes to talk, but maybe we should sit on the porch so I can watch the stamp shop in case more customers show up and Mom gets real busy."

Freeman nodded. "That's fine with me."

They stepped onto the porch. Katie took a seat on the swing, and Freeman leaned against the porch railing.

"What'd you want to talk to me about?" Katie asked.

"I noticed when you came out of the counselor's office that you seemed upset."

Katie's face heated up, and perspiration beaded on her forehead.

"If you'd rather not talk about it, I'll understand."

"It's all right. I might feel better if I do talk about it." Katie sighed as she massaged the back of her neck. "Dr. Coleman got after me for not doing some of the things he'd suggested, and then he accused me of not wanting to get better. He also said I might need to try medication."

"Are you going to?"

She shook her head. "I think I'll try the homeopathic remedy my mamm bought at the health food store some time ago."

"That's a good idea. Remember, a remedy worked well for me."

The swing squeaked as Katie pushed it back and forth with her feet.

"Were you upset only because of what Dr. Coleman said, or did something that Mary mentioned reading about in *The Budget* upset you?"

"I. . .I don't like hearing about people dying," Katie mumbled.

"Death is part of life," Freeman said.

"I know that, but I don't have to like it."

"That's right—you don't, but you shouldn't get upset just because someone talks about dying."

She nibbled on the inside of her cheek, wondering how much she should say. Freeman might not understand the way she felt about things. "Can we please change the subject? I really don't want to talk about death."

"How come?"

"I just don't, that's all."

"You're not afraid of death, are you, Katie?"

Tears clung to her lashes, and her throat felt so clogged she could barely swallow. "Jah. To be honest, I'm afraid of dying."

"I think most everyone fears death a little, but that's because the process of dying is something we haven't experienced before. But if we know where we're going, then—"

Katie shook her head vigorously. "I don't."

"Don't what?"

"I don't know where I'm going." She drew in a shaky breath. "If I died tomorrow, I don't know if I'd go to heaven."

"You'd go there if you believe that Jesus is the Son of God and have invited Him into your heart." Freeman took a seat on the porch swing beside her. "Didn't you make that commitment and profession of faith when you joined the church?"

She shrugged. "I'm not sure. I just said what was expected of me, and I've never really understood it or felt as if I know God in a personal way."

"Have you ever read John 11:25–26, about Jesus being the resurrection and the life?"

"I don't know."

"It says: 'I am the resurrection, and the life: he that believeth in me, though he were dead, yet shall he live. And whosoever liveth and believeth in me shall never die.'"

Katie shifted on the swing. She didn't think she'd ever heard those verses before. If she had, she must not have been paying attention.

"In order to make it to heaven, we have to accept Christ as our Savior and believe that He died for our sins." Freeman touched Katie's arm. "Have you ever accepted Christ as your Savior and asked Him to forgive your sins?"

Katie shook her head.

"Would you like to do that now?"

She nodded, for she didn't trust her voice.

"All you need to do is tell Jesus that you believe in Him and acknowledge that He's the Son of God, who died for you."

"I'd like to do that right now." Katie bowed her head and silently prayed, *Heavenly Father, I believe that Jesus is Your only begotten Son, and that He died on the cross for me. I believe that He rose from the dead to give me a new life. I confess my sins and ask You to wash them away. Amen.*

When Katie opened her eyes, a gentle breeze caressed her face, and she drew in a deep breath. Her heart was raised to God in joyful adoration and thankfulness. She wanted to bask in this comfortable feeling forever. She was filled with an overwhelming sense of gratitude to Freeman for helping her finally see the truth. She wondered if her fear of death could have been the root cause of her panic attacks. She couldn't help but think that God knew all about her anxiety attacks and that He would help her find a way to overcome them. It was the first time she'd felt any real sense of hope that she might get better.

She looked over at Freeman and smiled. "Danki for being my friend."

He returned her smile. "You're welcome."

❧ ❧

That afternoon while Katie was in the stamp shop organizing some colored pens and pencils they'd recently gotten in, she thought about the time she'd spent with Freeman on the porch and how, for the first time in her life, she no longer feared death. Her only concern was the panic attacks that plagued her. Maybe she needed to force herself to do things, like Dr. Coleman had said. She would keep doing her breathing exercises for relaxation, try out the tapping method Wayne had used for his phantom pains, write down her thoughts, and face her fears head-on. She knew it would take courage to drive the buggy by herself, but with God's help, maybe she could.

"Ach, Katie, kumme. . .schnell!" Mom hollered from the back room where she'd gone to cut some cardstock.

Katie raced into the room, wondering why Mom was telling her to come quickly. When she saw Mom's hand covered with blood, her breath caught in her throat.

"What happened?"

Mom teetered unsteadily. "I cut my hand on the paper cutter, and it's bleeding really bad."

Fearful that Mom might pass out, Katie grabbed a clean towel from the bathroom and wrapped it around Mom's hand. Then she pulled out a chair so Mom could sit down.

"I think it's going to need stitches," Mom said shakily. "You'd better get your daed and tell him to call one of our drivers."

Katie slowly shook her head. "Dad's not in his shop right now. He went to Shipshe to pick up some supplies at the hardware store, and his helper went home already."

"Oh, that's right." Mom's face was as pale as a bedsheet, and blood had begun to seep through the towel wrapped around her hand.

"I'll run down to the phone shed and call for help. Just sit right there and apply pressure to the wound." Katie rushed out the door.

When she reached the phone shed a few minutes later, she was nearly out of breath. She dropped into the folding chair inside the shed, picked up the receiver, and was about to dial Mary Hertz's number when she realized that the phone was dead. The wind storm they'd had the previous night must have knocked out the power.

Katie's stomach churned, and her mind spun in circles. The only way she could get help for Mom was to go over to the Andersons', their closest English neighbors. It was too far to walk, and she knew she couldn't take the time to hitch a horse to the buggy, so she decided to ride her bike over there.

She left the phone shed and raced back to the stamp shop. Mom was slumped over the table, looking even paler and more shaken than she had before.

Katie grabbed another towel from the bathroom and wrapped it around Mom's hand. "The phone's dead, so I'm going to bike over to our neighbor's and get help."

Mom nodded. "Schnell, Katie. Schnell!"

CHAPTER 36

Katie yawned and rolled out of bed. Dark still covered the window, but she needed to get up. She'd gone to bed early last night, exhausted after the ordeal with Mom's hand. Mom's thumb had required several stitches, and she'd been given a tetanus shot, but there was no permanent damage, and Katie was grateful. She'd been so concerned about Mom that she hadn't even been nervous when she'd ridden her bike to the Andersons' place. Peggy Anderson had given Mom and Katie a ride to the hospital, and while Mom was getting her hand worked on, Katie had waited and prayed. The whole ordeal had made Katie realize all the more that she needed to practice doing the things she was afraid of, regardless of whether she had a panic attack or not.

Katie had set her alarm clock to go off at four, knowing her folks wouldn't be up until six. She figured that should give her enough time to hitch her horse to the buggy and go out on the road for half an hour or so. There wouldn't be much traffic, and she hoped that would help her not to be quite so nervous.

Katie padded across the room, pushed the curtain aside, and opened the window. Outside, everything was calm and still. Stars twinkled in the sky, crickets sang, and a gentle breeze caressed her face. God seemed very near. Surely He would see her through the coming days.

Filled with a sense of peace she hadn't known in many months,

Katie hurried to get dressed and slipped quietly from her room. She tiptoed down the stairs, being careful not to step on any that squeaked.

When she reached the first floor, she ducked into the kitchen and took one of the homeopathic tablets for calming. Then she grabbed a flashlight and opened the back door.

The sky was still dark, but the moon shone brightly, so she didn't need the flashlight until she got to the buggy shed. Being careful not to make too much noise, she opened the door and pushed one of their smaller open buggies into the yard. Then she hurried into the barn to get Dixie, their gentlest mare.

By the time Katie had the horse hitched to the buggy, her hands had begun to shake. This was going to be a lot harder than she'd thought it would be.

"*You need to face your fears,*" Dr. Coleman had said during one of her counseling sessions. "*Don't avoid situations where you've had a panic attack before.*"

Katie leaned against the buggy, closed her mouth, and inhaled slowly through her nose, pushing her stomach out like Dr. Coleman had instructed her to do. Then she opened her mouth and exhaled by pulling her stomach in. "I'm afraid, Lord," she whispered. "Help me overcome these horrible panic attacks. My future looks dark and impossible, but I know You are with me."

A verse of scripture she'd read before going to bed popped into her head. "*What time I am afraid, I will trust in thee.*"

My choice to trust God will help calm my feelings of fear, Katie told herself.

Two more verses came to mind: "*I can do all things through Christ which strengtheneth me*"—*Philippians 4:13;* and "*Peace I leave with you, my peace I give unto you: not as the world giveth, give I unto you. Let not your heart be troubled, neither let it be afraid*"—*John 14:27.*

A sense of calm stole into Katie's heart again. It was the same peaceful feeling she'd had in her bedroom. Surely God wouldn't forsake her. She needed to trust Him and keep asking for strength and courage.

Katie opened the flap on the driver's side of the buggy so she'd have plenty of fresh air, climbed inside, and took up the reins.

There's nothing to be afraid of. With God's help I can do this. I'll just go as far as I feel comfortable, she told herself. *If I start to panic, I can turn around and come back home.*

In Katie's mind's eye she pictured the Lord gathering her up in His strong arms. He loved her. He cared for her. He was here with her now.

Katie felt more confident as she guided Dixie down the driveway, but when she came to the road, her heart started to pound and her hands grew so sweaty she could barely hang on to the reins.

"Stop it! Stop it! Stop doing this to me!" she shouted.

Katie mentally shook herself. That was the wrong approach. What was it that Dr. Coleman had suggested she say and do? When she was frightened like this, it was hard to think.

Oh yes, now I remember. "Panic attack, you can't control me anymore!" she shouted. "Go ahead and do your best!"

Katie's horse whinnied and twitched her ears.

"It's all right, Dixie, I'm not hollering at you." Feeling a little more relaxed, Katie clucked gently to the horse and eased her onto the road.

They'd only got a short ways when Katie noticed a blinking light on the shoulder of the road to her right. She hadn't expected to see anyone on this stretch of the road in the wee hours of the morning. As her buggy drew closer she realized it was their English paperboy delivering the morning newspaper on his bike. She'd only met the young man once, when he'd come to the house to collect the money he was due. Katie didn't know his name but figured from his youthful appearance that he was probably in his late teens or early twenties.

"You're out early. Where are ya headed?" he called to her.

"Just taking a ride." She flicked the reins and got the horse moving faster. There was no time for idle chitchat. Especially not with someone she barely knew.

As Katie continued down the road, things went along fairly well. She felt more relaxed driving the buggy than she thought she would. Maybe there was some hope of her living a normal life without fear of panic attacks.

She relaxed against the seat, enjoying the cool, early morning breeze.

Ribet! Ribet! A chorus of frogs serenaded her.

When the sun peaked over the horizon, Katie decided it was time to head for home. Since things had gone so well, she thought she might take the buggy out early every morning this week.

She turned up their driveway, put the horse and buggy away, and entered the house just in time to see Dad step out of his and Mom's room.

"I'm surprised to see you up and dressed already," he said, passing her in the hall.

"I woke up earlier than usual this morning," Katie replied. Did Dad suspect that she'd been outside? She hoped he wouldn't question her further.

"Since you're up already, would you mind putting the coffee on?" he asked. "Your mamm's still getting dressed."

"Sure." Katie picked up the coffeepot and filled it with water from the sink.

"Guess I'll head outside to do my chores," Dad said.

"I'll have breakfast ready when you get back," Katie called as he went out the door. She breathed a sigh of relief.

❧ ❧

As Katie headed for the stamp shop later that morning, she stopped in the garden, bent down, and plucked a leaf from one of their mint plants. She rubbed the leaf between her fingers, relishing the sharp aroma. She hadn't noticed things like this in such a long time.

She turned, closed her eyes, and stood with her face lifted to the sun. It felt good to be alive.

A horse whinnied, and Katie opened her eyes just in time see Ella's buggy come up the driveway, headed toward the stamp shop.

Katie hurried to the shop and stopped just outside the door to wait for Ella.

"How are things with you?" Ella asked. "Are you still seeing the counselor at the clinic once a week?"

Katie nodded and smiled. "Freeman's been riding with me, and that's helped me feel more confident about going."

Ella's brows puckered. "Are you in love with him?"

" 'Course not. Why do you ask?"

"You got a dreamy-eyed look on your face as soon as you mentioned his name."

"I did not."

"Jah, you did." Ella poked Katie's arm. "Does he feel the same way about you?"

"He sees me as a friend, nothing more."

"That's good, because from what I've heard, Freeman's been going out with Eunice, and after talking to her the other day, I realized that she's convinced that she and Freeman are going steady."

Katie shrugged, but her skin prickled. "What's that got to do with me?"

"It could have everything to do with you if you're in love with Freeman."

"I'm not."

Ella gave Katie's arm a light tap. "You do like him, though, don't you?"

"I like him as a friend." Katie quickly opened the door to the stamp shop, needing to change the subject. "Let's go inside so you can buy whatever you came here for."

Freeman pulled out his set of tools to begin working on a bike, but he hadn't been at it long before he found himself thinking about Katie. He was pleased that she'd accepted Christ as her Savior. It had to be a relief for her to know that her heart was right with God and that if she died, she would go to heaven.

Freeman wasn't sure why, but Katie's sweet response to the things he'd shared with her yesterday had stirred up a longing in his heart for more than friendship. But it seemed like an impossible dream, because as far as he knew, she hadn't stopped loving Timothy or grieving for him. Until she did, Freeman saw no way they could be together. Besides, Katie was still struggling with her panic attacks, and that was enough for her to deal with right now.

Then there was Eunice. From the way she looked at him and the comments she made whenever they were together, Freeman knew she was getting serious about him. Probably thought he was serious about her, too. Might even be hoping for a marriage proposal. Trouble was, he wasn't sure how he felt about Eunice. She had a pretty face, cooked well enough, and had a way of flirting that made him feel like a man. But he didn't think he was in love with her. At least not like he was with—

Woof! Woof! Penny raced across the room and slurped his hand. He patted the pup's head and smiled. "What do you want, girl? Do you need to go outside for a while?"

Penny whined and raced for the door. Freeman followed.

When he opened the door, Ella stepped in. Penny darted between her legs and dashed into the yard, yipping and wagging her tail.

"What can I do for you?" Freeman asked, smiling at Ella. "Do you need something for your bike?"

She shook her head. "I'm here because I'm concerned about Katie."

"What do you mean?"

"I don't think it's a good idea for you to see Katie so much."

"I don't see her that much—just every Friday when she goes for her counseling session."

"Katie's dealing with a lot of things right now, and I don't want her to get hurt."

Freeman frowned. "How's she gonna get hurt? What exactly are you saying?"

"I'm saying that I think you're seeing too much of her, and she might begin to think you care for her."

"I do care for her; we're good friends." Freeman wasn't about to admit to Katie's cousin how he felt about Katie. She was likely to blab it to Katie.

"She might think it's more than that, and with you going steady with Eunice and all—"

The shop door opened again, and an English customer stepped in.

"I can see you're busy, so I'll just say one thing before I go. Please don't lead Katie on." Ella hurried out the door before Freeman could respond.

He turned to his customer and said, "Can I help you with something?"

CHAPTER 37

Katie clucked to her horse and turned onto the road. For the last two weeks, she'd been taking her family's open buggy out every morning to practice driving alone. In between those times, she practiced her breathing exercises and affirmations, wrote her thoughts in a journal, prayed, and read her Bible regularly. She'd had a couple of panic attacks, but they'd been mild, and she was determined to keep trying. If she didn't, she'd never get better, and if she never got better, there would be no chance for her and Freeman.

Katie thought about the way Freeman had looked at her on their way home from her counselor's appointment yesterday afternoon. Was it a look of longing she'd seen on his face, or had it just been the friendly smile of a good friend? She wished she felt free to tell Freeman how much she'd come to care for him, but that would be too bold. Besides, if he wasn't interested in her romantically, she'd be opening herself up for rejection, which she knew she couldn't handle right now. Katie wasn't really sure where things stood with Freeman and Eunice, but if they were serious about each other, it wouldn't be right to do or say anything that might come between them.

As Katie turned down County Road 13, she saw a flashing light, and as she drew closer, she realized that a bicycle was lying on its side. A young man stood beside it. When she slowed the horse, she recognized their paperboy. "Are you having a problem with your bike?" she asked, pulling the buggy alongside him.

"Yeah. I've got a flat tire." He motioned to the canvas satchel lying beside his bike. "I haven't finished delivering my papers, so this wasn't a good time for something like this to happen."

Katie thought about offering to give him a ride so he could make the rest of his deliveries, but that would take up more time than she had. The sun would be up soon, and she needed to get home before Mom and Dad got up.

"I think there's room for your bike in my buggy, so if you want to put it in the back, I can give you a ride home," she said.

"Thanks, I appreciate that." The young man lifted his bike into the back of her buggy then climbed into the passenger's seat up front. He looked over at Katie and said, "My name's Mike Olsen, and you're Katie Miller, aren't you?"

She nodded. "How'd you know my name?"

"I make it my business to know the names of every pretty girl along my route." He chuckled and bumped her arm.

Katie's face warmed. She was glad it was too dark for him to see her blushing. No one except Timothy had ever called her pretty.

"Sure will be glad when summer's over and I can head back to Florida," Mike said.

"Are you from Florida?" Katie asked with interest.

"Yeah, my folks live just outside of Sarasota."

"Then what are you doing here?"

"I got into some trouble this spring, and they sent me up here to stay with my grandparents for a while, hoping it'd straighten me out." Mike snorted. "Like a few months of mending fences and delivering papers is gonna make me a better person."

Katie wondered what kind of trouble he'd been in, but she didn't voice the question, since it was really none of her business.

"Do you like Florida better than here?" she asked.

"Sure do. I hope to be on my way back there before fall. Can't wait to say good-bye to boring Indiana and hello to Florida's white sandy beaches."

Katie had never thought of Indiana as boring, but she'd enjoyed spending time on the beach near Sarasota, looking for shells and wading near the shore. "I lived in Sarasota for seven months," she said.

"By yourself?"

"No, with my grandparents."

"Did you like it there?"

"Yes, I did."

"Then why'd you leave?"

"I came home for my cousin's wedding, and then my grandparents moved to Wisconsin, so I had to stay here."

"Who says you have to stay here?" Mike reached in his shirt pocket and pulled out a cigarette. "Want one?" He waved it in front of Katie's nose.

She shook her head. "No thanks."

"If you liked Florida so much, why don't you go back?"

"I just told you, my grandparents moved to Wisconsin."

He lit the cigarette and took a puff. "Who says you have to live with them?"

"Well, I'd need a job and a place to stay."

"You can always find a job in Sarasota, and if you need a place to crash for a while, you can stay with me." He patted his pocket. "By the end of this summer, I'll have plenty of money, so I won't have to rely on my folks anymore, and I'll get my own place."

Katie's mouth went dry. A few months ago, she'd have given most anything to go back to Florida. But with Grandma and Grandpa not there, the idea didn't have quite as much appeal. Besides, it wouldn't be proper for her to stay with Mike. "I appreciate the offer," she said, "but I'm happy staying here right now."

He blew a puff of smoke in her direction. "A lot can happen between now and fall, so if you change your mind, just let me know."

~≈ ≈~

Eunice groaned as she climbed out of bed. She'd been drifting in and out of sleep most of the night, thinking about Freeman and wondering why he seemed to be cooling off toward her lately. The last time he'd taken her out to supper, he hadn't said more than a few words, and she was worried that he might be losing interest in her.

Since I can't sleep, I may as well get up and start some coffee going, Eunice decided. She slipped off her nightgown, put on a dress, and headed outside to see if the newspaper had been delivered yet.

As Eunice walked down the driveway, her thoughts remained on Freeman. Tonight there would be a young people's gathering at Ella's, and Freeman had agreed to take her. Of course, she'd been the one to bring it up. In fact, she'd suggested several of their outings and had invited him to her house for supper at least once a week. She'd been trying to keep Freeman too busy with her to think about Katie. Eunice thought if she spent more time with Freeman, he would realize that they were meant to be together. If things went as she planned, by this time next year, they could be married.

As Eunice approached the paper box, she heard the rhythmic *clip-clop* of horse's hooves. She squinted at the flashing lights coming down the road, but as the buggy drew closer, she couldn't make out who was inside.

When Eunice heard a woman's voice, she froze. It sounded like Katie Miller, and she was talking to a man.

Eunice quickly stepped behind a bush and strained to listen as the buggy went past.

Eunice caught just a few of their words, but she was sure now that the woman speaking was Katie. She didn't recognize the man's voice, though. What she couldn't figure out was why Katie would be out on the road so early—and with a man, no less!

Maybe Katie's seeing someone and doesn't want her folks to know, Eunice thought. *She might have snuck out of bed so she could be with him. Or maybe they've been out all night together.*

Eunice was relieved that Katie wasn't with Freeman. If Katie had a boyfriend, Eunice had nothing to be concerned about. Now all she needed to do was let Freeman know that Katie had a boyfriend.

CHAPTER 38

"Aren't you going to play anymore?" Ella called to Eunice as she stepped away from the volleyball net after the last game had ended.

Eunice fanned her cheeks. "It's hot, and I'm tired! Think I'll take a break from playing for a while." She found a chair under a leafy tree and flopped down. She'd only been sitting there a few minutes when she spotted Freeman talking to Katie on the other side of the yard.

What's he doing with her? she fumed.

Eunice leaped out of her chair and rushed over to where they were standing. "I'm really thirsty, Freeman," she said, stepping between them. "Would you mind getting me something cold to drink?"

Freeman nodded. "Sure, I can do that." He looked over at Katie and smiled. "Would you like something, too?"

"Jah, that'd be nice," Katie replied.

As soon as Freeman moved away, Eunice turned to Katie and said, "Can you keep a secret?"

Katie nodded.

"Freeman plans to join the church this fall, so by next spring we'll be planning our wedding."

Katie blinked a couple of times. "Oh, I. . .didn't realize he'd asked you to marry him."

"It's not official yet, so we're keeping it quiet until we're published." Eunice smiled. "Of course, since you're one of Freeman's closest friends, I figured you'd want to know."

"I hope you'll be very happy." Katie gave a quick nod and hurried away. Eunice sighed, feeling pleased with herself. She may have lost one boyfriend, but she wouldn't lose another.

A few minutes later, Freeman returned with two paper cups. He handed one to Eunice. "I brought you both some punch."

"Danki."

He glanced around. "Where's Katie?"

Eunice shrugged. "I really couldn't say. She rushed off without a word." Freeman turned his head to the left. "Oh, there's Katie, walking toward the barn. Guess I'll head over there and see if she wants some punch."

He hurried away quickly, and Eunice followed. She'd only taken a few steps when she stumbled, spilling punch all over the front of her dress.

"Ach!" she cried. "My ankle!"

"Are you all right?" Andrew asked, catching hold of her arm as he walked by.

"I was going after Freeman, and I think I must've stumbled on a rock." Eunice grimaced.

Andrew called to Freeman, and he turned around.

"What happened?" Freeman asked, hurrying to Eunice's side.

"I. . .I tripped on a rock, and—" Eunice winced as she bent down and touched her ankle. "I don't think I can walk by myself."

"We'll help you," Andrew said.

Freeman nodded. "Jah, of course."

Eunice hung on to Freeman's arm with one hand and Andrew's arm with the other as they helped her to the nearest chair.

"I'll run into my aunt's house and get you some ice." Andrew glanced down at Eunice with a look of concern; then he sprinted across the lawn.

Freeman knelt beside Eunice. "Maybe we should call someone to take you to the hospital so you can have your ankle x-rayed."

She shook her head. "I'm sure it's just sprained. As soon

as Andrew gets back with the ice, I think you should take me home."

Freeman nodded. "Whatever you think is best."

❦

When Katie saw Andrew coming out of the house, she hurried up to him. "I'm not feeling well. Would you mind taking me home?"

"Sure, I can do that as soon as I take this out to Eunice." He lifted the bag of ice in his hand.

"Why does Eunice need ice?"

"She stumbled on a rock and twisted her ankle."

"That's too bad," Katie mumbled. It was hard to feel sorry for Eunice when she acted so superior all the time. It was especially hard now that Katie had admitted to herself that she was in love with Freeman, yet she had no chance with him because he loved Eunice.

That's what I get for letting myself fall in love again, she berated herself. *I lost Timothy to death, and now I've lost Freeman to Eunice. Guess he's better off without me as his friend. Why would he want to tie himself down with someone like me when he can have her?*

"If you'd like to wait for me in the barn, I shouldn't be long," Andrew said.

"Okay." A lump formed in Katie's throat as she moved away. It had been a shock to hear that Freeman had asked Eunice to marry him, although she should have seen it coming. After all, Freeman had been going out with Eunice all summer, and he hadn't asked Katie out even once.

Well, why would he? she asked herself. *He's only spent time with me because he's been trying to help me get over my panic attacks. He's probably been so nice only because he feels sorry for me.*

Katie stared out across the field behind Ella's house and winced as a hawk swooped down and snatched a field mouse. She felt as helpless as the poor, defenseless mouse. *If Freeman marries Eunice, the friendship we have now will be over.*

Katie pushed her shoulders back as she made a decision. *As soon as I have enough money saved up, I'm going back to Florida.*

CHAPTER 39

As Freeman drove Eunice home, he thought about the decision he'd made earlier to break up with her and wondered if this was the right time to bring up the subject. She'd hurt her ankle, and he was sorry about that, but he couldn't let that stop him from telling her the way he felt. If he kept going out with Eunice, it would be even harder to break up, and Eunice might expect a marriage proposal.

Eunice fidgeted on the seat beside him and leaned down to reposition the bag of ice Andrew had given her.

"How's your ankle?" Freeman asked. "Does it feel any better?"

"A little. I think the ice has helped some." She moved closer to him and rested her head on his shoulder. "Sure is a pretty night, isn't it?"

"Jah. Lots of stars and a bright full moon."

"It's the perfect night for a buggy ride."

"Uh-huh."

They rode in silence the rest of the way, and Freeman wondered if Eunice had fallen asleep.

Maybe I'd better not say anything about breaking up with her tonight, he decided. *I can talk to her about it another time when her ankle's feeling better.*

When Freeman guided his horse and buggy up Eunice's driveway, she sat up and looked around. "Are we here already?"

"Jah. I think you slept part of the way home."

259

She touched his arm. "Would you like to come in for a piece of pie and a glass of milk?"

"I'd better not. Tomorrow's Sunday, and we'll have to get up early."

"It's not that late. Surely you can come in for a few minutes."

"I really can't. I've got a stop to make on my way home."

Her eyebrows furrowed. "Whose house are you stopping at?"

"Just have a delivery to make."

"What kind of delivery would you have to make on a Saturday night?"

"One of my customers ordered a part for his bike, and I said I'd drop it off this afternoon, but I got busy in the shop and never made it there. Figured I could do it on my way home tonight."

"You're going over to see Katie, aren't you?" Eunice's shrill voice and pinched expression let Freeman know she was angry with him.

"I'm not going to see Katie," he insisted.

"Right."

"I said I'm not. Now can we please drop the subject?"

Eunice sat with her arms folded, staring straight ahead. "Are you still riding to the mental health clinic with Katie every week?"

"Jah. Why do you ask?"

"I don't want you to go with her anymore. She's not a boppli; she ought to be able to ride there by herself."

"I've explained this to you before, so I don't know why you're bringing it up again. Katie feels better about riding in the van if someone's with her."

"Well, it doesn't have to be you! She can find someone else to ride with her!"

Freeman knew if he didn't leave soon he'd say something he might regret. He hopped down from the buggy and held his hand out to her. "I'll help you into the house, and then I need to be on my way."

"Do you like her more than you do me?"

"Who?"

"Katie, of course. Who else were we talking about?"

Freeman grunted. "Not this again."

"Just answer me. Do you like her more than you do me?"

"I've said this before, but apparently you need me to say it again. Katie and I are just good friends."

"She has a boyfriend, you know."

Heated radiated up the back of Freeman's neck. Was Eunice trying to get a rise out of him? "Are you getting out of the buggy or what?"

"Don't you want to hear about Katie's boyfriend?"

"Her boyfriend's dead."

"Not that boyfriend. She has a new one now."

"Katie's never mentioned having a boyfriend to me."

"Maybe she doesn't want anyone to know. That could be why she's been sneaking around in the wee hours of the morning with him."

Freeman's heart pounded like a trotting horse. "What are you talking about?"

"I went out to get the newspaper early this morning, and a horse and buggy came by the front of our house. I heard talking and recognized Katie's voice. The other person was a man, but I don't know who it was." Eunice leaned close to Freeman. "I smelled smoke when the buggy went past, so I'm sure that either Katie or her boyfriend was smoking."

"Katie doesn't smoke."

"How do you know?"

"I would have smelled it on her if she did."

"Then I guess her boyfriend must have been smoking."

Freeman grimaced. Did Katie really have a boyfriend? Was it possible that she'd been out in the fellow's buggy? *Who can it be?* he wondered. *Should I come right out and ask Katie who she was with this morning?*

Eunice tugged on his arm. "I'm sorry if I upset you, but I thought you had the right to know that Katie's not the innocent girl you think her to be."

Anger boiled in Freeman's chest. He'd had enough of Eunice

261

putting Katie down! He turned to her and said, "It's over between us, Eunice."

Her chin trembled, and her eyes filled with tears. "You—you can't mean that!"

"Jah, I do."

"It's because of her, isn't it? She's made you think that she's a nice girl, but she's really—"

"That's enough!" Freeman shouted. "I won't listen to another spiteful word about Katie!"

"You'll be sorry for breaking up with me. Someday you'll be very sorry." Eunice stepped down from the buggy and ran to her house.

"Guess her ankle's not hurtin' quite as bad as she let on," Freeman mumbled as he climbed into the buggy and got the horse moving again. "Maybe I'll head over to Katie's and see what I can find out about the fellow she was out riding with this morning."

❧ ❧

Katie had just taken an aspirin for her headache and was getting ready to go upstairs to her room when a knock sounded on the back door. "I'll get it," she called to her folks, who were in the living room playing a game of Dutch Blitz.

When Katie opened the door and saw Freeman on the porch, she froze. "What are you doing here? I thought you were still at the gathering."

"I left early after Eunice twisted her ankle."

Katie peered around him, into the yard. "Is Eunice with you?"

Freeman shook his head. "I took her home." He shuffled his feet a few times. "Came here to ask you a question."

"What's that?"

"Eunice said that she'd heard a buggy coming down the road near her house early this morning and that you and some man were in it. I. . .uh. . .wondered whether that was true or not."

Katie nodded. "It was me all right. I was giving our paperboy a ride to his grandparents' house because the tire on his bike was flat."

Freeman gave his earlobe a tug. "Mind if I ask what you were doing out on the road so early?"

"I was doing what Dr. Coleman said I should do—facing my fears." Katie massaged her throbbing head. "I figured the easiest way to do that was to practice driving the buggy when there aren't so many cars on the road."

"Guess that makes sense." Freeman took a step closer. "Katie, I—"

"I don't mean to be rude, but I have a koppweh, and I'm really tired, so I need to go to bed."

"Sorry to hear you have a headache. I'll let you go then." Freeman started down the stairs but halted and turned around. "I'll see you on Sunday, and then again on Friday for your counselor's session."

"That's okay," Katie was quick to say. "I won't need you to go with me next time."

He tipped his head. "How come?"

"I need to start doing things on my own. *Gut nacht*, Freeman." Katie hurried inside and shut the door.

~⚹ ⚹~

"Calm down, Eunice, and tell me why you're crying like a wounded heifer," Mama said as she took a seat beside Eunice on the sofa.

"Freeman broke up with me!" Eunice hiccupped on a sob.

"What happened?"

"It—it's all because of Katie. He cares more about her than he does me." *Hic! Hic!*

"What makes you think that?"

"He's always talking to her when he should be talking to me." Eunice hiccuped again and wiped away her tears. "I tried telling him that Katie has a boyfriend, but he wouldn't believe me. He never believes anything I say about Katie."

Mama reached for Eunice's hand. "I know how badly you want a husband, but it was wrong for you to try to turn Freeman against Katie in order to get him for yourself." She clucked her tongue. "I hate to say this, but you're getting just what you deserve."

"What's that supposed to mean?"

"It means you set yourself up for this when you spread rumors about Katie wanting to keep that boppli she found on her porch, not to mention your telling everyone that you thought Katie was pregnant. Hopefully, you'll learn a lesson from this and will wait for your true love to come along instead of trying to force it to happen."

"You don't understand how I feel," Eunice wailed. "Don't you even care how miserable I am?"

"I do care, but I can't condone your actions. It's time for you to grow up and face the fact that you can't always have what you want."

"Jah, I can! I'll give Freeman some time to think about things, and then I'll talk to him again. Hopefully, I can get him to change his mind about us." Eunice pulled the quilt off the back of the sofa and draped it across her lap. "I sprained my ankle at the gathering, and it hurts too bad to walk up the stairs, so I'm sleeping here tonight!"

CHAPTER 40

For the next several weeks, Katie got up early every morning and took her horse and buggy out on the road. Each time, her confidence grew, and when she felt nervous or afraid, she prayed, did some deep breathing, repeated her affirmations, and talked back to the panic attacks.

One morning, as Katie was about to pull out onto the road, she spotted Mike peddling his bike up to their paper box. "I see you're up early again," he said, shining his flashlight on her.

Katie shielded her eyes from the light and nodded. "I see you got your bicycle fixed."

"Sure did." He climbed off his bike, leaned it against the wooden post, and walked to her buggy. "I'll be leaving for Florida soon. Think you might want to ride along?"

"Are you planning to take the bus there?"

"No way! I came by bus, but I'm goin' back in style. Should have the money I need to buy a car by the end of next week, and I'll leave soon after that." He pulled a package of gum from his pocket and stuck a piece in his mouth.

"I'd like to go," she said, "but like I said, I'd have no place to stay until I found a job."

"And if you'll recall, I said you could stay with me."

"I couldn't do that."

"Why not?"

"It wouldn't be proper."

His jaw moved up and down as he chomped on his gum. "Well, give it some thought. If you change your mind, you can leave me a note in your paper box." Mike slapped his hands together and grinned. "See you later, Katie!"

~❦ ❦~

"Did you see any sign of Katie outside?" JoAnn asked Jeremy when he entered the kitchen after doing his chores.

He shook his head. "She wasn't in the barn or the yard, so she's probably still in her room."

"No, she's not. I checked there already."

"Guess she could be in the bathroom."

"I looked there, too."

Jeremy reached under his hat and scratched the side of his head. "That makes no sense. She's either got to be in the house or outside somewhere. Want me to go back out and take a look around?"

"Maybe you should." JoAnn sighed. "You know, Katie's been acting kind of peculiar ever since she went to that young people's gathering at Ella's. It makes me wonder if she's keeping secrets from us again."

"What kind of secrets?"

"I don't know, but she's been very quiet, and when I mentioned the other day how nice it is to have her working in the stamp shop with me, she got all teary eyed."

"You worry too much." He gave her shoulders a squeeze. "You need to give Katie some space and stop mothering her so much. If she has something she wants to tell us, she'll say it in her own good time."

She sighed. "That remains to be seen."

He turned toward the back door and was about to open it when Katie stepped in, red-faced and looking very flustered.

"Ach, you scared me, Dad! It's still early, and I didn't think you were up yet."

"As you can see, both me and your mamm are up, and she's been lookin' for you."

Katie's face turned crimson. "I. . .I was outside."

"That's obvious, since you just came inside." JoAnn stepped up to Katie. "What were you doing outside so early?"

Katie shifted from one foot to the other and stared at the floor.

"I just came from the barn and you weren't there." Jeremy quirked an eyebrow. "Didn't see you in the yard, either."

Katie lifted her gaze and pushed her shoulders back. "Guess I can't keep it a secret any longer. For the past few weeks, I've been taking the horse and buggy out early every morning, before you and Mom got up."

"What for?" JoAnn questioned.

"So I could practice driving the buggy."

Jeremy's eyebrows furrowed. "You already know how to drive a buggy, so why would you need to practice?"

"Dr. Coleman said the best way for me to get over my panic attacks is to face my fears and force myself to do what I'm most afraid of."

"That makes sense," JoAnn said, "but why so early in the morning?"

"Because there are fewer cars on the road, and I didn't want you and Dad to know what I was doing."

"Why not?" Jeremy asked. "Didn't you think we'd approve?"

"It's not that. I wanted to be sure I was getting better before I told you, and I wanted it to be a surprise."

"If I'd known what you were doing, I'd have offered to ride along with you," JoAnn said.

Katie sank into a chair at the table. "I need to make a life of my own and stop relying on you and Dad for everything. In fact, I've been thinking about going back to Florida."

"What?" JoAnn grabbed the edge of the nearest chair so hard that her fingers ached. "Where on earth did that idea come from?"

"I. . .was happier living in Florida."

"You weren't happier; you were hiding from your past." JoAnn shook her head. "And where would you stay?" JoAnn looked at

Jeremy. "Tell her how *narrish* she's being for thinking she should move back to Florida."

He took a seat across from Katie and pulled his fingers through the ends of his beard. "Your mamm's right. Moving back to Florida would be a foolish thing for you to do."

"I don't see why. I've saved up some money working in the stamp shop, and I'll look for a job when I get to Sarasota."

"*Puh!*" JoAnn flopped into the chair she'd been gripping. "Jobs are hard to find these days, and you'll be out of money in short order if you don't find a job right away. Besides, you have a good job right here in our stamp shop, and I thought you enjoyed working there."

"I do, but—"

"What about your counseling sessions?" Jeremy asked. "If you move back to Florida, you might lose all the ground you've gained."

Katie fiddled with the edge of the tablecloth. "I can practice the things Dr. Coleman suggested while I'm living in Florida just as well as I can here."

JoAnn reached over and clasped Katie's hand. "What's the reason behind this decision? Are you that unhappy living here with us? Have I said or done something to turn you against me?"

Tears welled in Katie's eyes and dribbled onto her cheeks. She sniffed and swiped them away. "It's not you, Mom."

"Then what is it that's driving you away?"

"I. . .I'm in love with Freeman, but he loves Eunice, and I can't stand the thought of seeing them get married next spring."

JoAnn's mouth dropped open. "Oh, Katie, I had no idea you'd fallen in love with Freeman. Are you sure he's planning to marry Eunice?"

Katie nodded. "Eunice told me that Freeman's going to join the church this fall and that they're planning a spring wedding."

"Have you talked to Freeman about this?" Jeremy asked.

Katie shook her head. "I'd be too embarrassed to admit that I love him. He's never seen me as anything more than a friend." She reached for a napkin and dabbed at her tears. "It hurts so bad to know that he loves Eunice. She's not a nice person and doesn't deserve someone as kind as Freeman."

"That may be true, and I'm sure that it hurts, but you can't spend the rest of your life running from things you don't like," JoAnn said. "I think you need to stay right here and deal with the situation."

Jeremy shook his head. "No she doesn't, JoAnn. If Katie can't stand the thought of seeing Freeman and Eunice together, then we need to support her decision to move." He touched Katie's arm. "My cousin Clarence and his wife, Mae, will be moving to Sarasota, probably next month. Would you like me to ask if they'd be willing to let you stay with them until you find a job and are able to rent a small place of your own?"

"Would you really do that for me?" Katie asked with a hopeful expression.

"Wouldn't have suggested it if I wasn't willing."

JoAnn stood up and pushed her chair aside so quickly that it toppled to the floor. "I can't go along with this! Katie's place is here with us, plain and simple!"

CHAPTER 41

Sell kann ich mir gaar net eibilde!" Katie's dad said as he stared at the newspaper.

"You can't conceive of what?" Mom asked, peering over his shoulder.

"The young English man who delivers our paper every morning was arrested for robbing a convenience store in Goshen. Guess he told the sheriff he needed the money to buy a new car." Dad slowly shook his head. "The fellow had a gun and threatened the store clerk with it, but then another customer came in, saw what was happening, and called for help."

"That's too bad. When a young person does something like that, it hurts not only him but his whole family." Mom clicked her tongue as though she were scolding someone. "Sure wish we could read some positive news in the paper once in a while. It's depressing to hear so many negative things, and it makes me sad to know that there's so much crime and corruption in our world."

Katie cringed. She was glad she hadn't taken Mike up on his offer to ride with him to Sarasota. He was obviously not as nice as he seemed to be. It was better that she'd be traveling with Dad's cousin and his wife.

Mom still wasn't in favor of Katie moving back to Florida, but at least she'd stopped hounding her about it. Since Clarence and Mae wouldn't be moving for another month, that gave Katie plenty of time to get ready to go. She would need to tell Loraine and Ella, too. She just wasn't sure what to do about saying good-bye to Freeman.

Mom touched Katie's arm. "Will Freeman be going to your counseling session with you again today?" she asked, pulling Katie's thoughts aside.

"I'll be going by myself from now on," Katie said. "It's better that's way."

"Would you like me to go with you?"

Katie shook her head. "If I'm going to move back to Florida, I'll have to learn to go places and do things on my own."

Mom opened her mouth as if she might say something more, but she closed it again and reached for her cup of coffee.

Dad looked over at Katie and winked. At least he understood why she needed to move.

~※ ※~

"Are you sure you have time to trim the trees in our yard this morning?" Fern asked Freeman during breakfast.

Freeman bobbed his head. "I'm caught up on things in my shop, so this is as good a time as any to get the trimming done."

She smiled. "If you can get started before I leave for school, I'll hold the ladder for you."

"That's okay," he said with a shake of his head. "I'll make sure the ladder's secure."

"Even so, I'd feel better if someone was here to help."

Freeman clenched his teeth. "I'm not a boppli, Fern, so stop treating me like one."

"I'm not."

"Jah, you are." He reached for a piece of toast. "Sometimes I think you just like telling me what to do."

"I do not! I just don't want to see you get hurt."

"I'll be fine on my own, so just go ahead to school and teach your scholars. By the time you get home, all the trees in our yard will have had a nice haircut."

"All right then," Fern said with a nod, "but please be careful."

"I will."

She pushed her chair away from the table, picked up her dishes, and carried them to the sink. "Oh, I forgot to mention that I talked to Eunice the other day, and she said that since she hasn't been able to find a job, she's decided to start selling candles and scented soaps. I think I might book a party with her soon."

"That's nice," Freeman mumbled around a mouthful of cereal.

Fern glanced over her shoulder. "Have you made any plans to go out with Eunice soon?"

He shook his head. "We broke up a few weeks ago. I thought I'd told you that."

"You did, but I was hoping you'd change your mind and get back together with her."

"Nope."

"Why not?"

"She's too much of a gossip, and she's pushing to get married." He gulped down the rest of his juice and swiped his tongue across his lip. "I'm not ready for marriage. At least not with her."

Fern's forehead wrinkled. "Are you thinking about marrying someone else?"

"Maybe. When the time's right."

"It's not Katie Miller, I hope."

Freeman blew out his breath. "What have you got against Katie?"

Fern shrugged. "I don't have anything against her personally, but I don't think she's the right woman for you." Fern glanced at the clock. "We can talk about this later. I need to go or I'll be late for school." She grabbed her canvas satchel and black outer bonnet then hurried out the door.

❧ ❧

"How are things going for you?" Dr. Coleman asked Katie as she took a chair on the other side of his desk.

"I've been driving the buggy more, and I'm having fewer panic attacks."

"That's good to hear. Are you going places that have caused

you to feel nervous in the past?"

Katie nodded.

"What do you feel has helped the most in conquering your panic attacks?"

"The tapping method, breathing exercises, and homeopathic remedy are helping me relax, and I think facing my fears and talking back to the panic attacks are keeping them from happening so often or lasting so long." Katie clutched the folds in her dress, wondering if she should bring up the subject of moving back to Florida.

"You look kind of thoughtful. Is there something on your mind?"

Katie nodded. She figured she may as well tell him now. "My dad's cousin and his wife will be moving to Florida soon, and I'm planning to go with them."

His eyebrows rose. "How come?"

Katie shifted in her chair, too embarrassed to tell him the reason she was planning to move. "Well, I like it in Florida, and I think I'll be happier there."

Dr. Coleman wrote something on his notepad. "Does this decision have something to do with your mother?"

Katie blinked. "No, of course not. Why would you think that?"

"I saw the way you responded during your first counseling session with me. It was obvious that your mother wouldn't let you speak for yourself, and whenever you did get in a word, she kept interrupting." He placed both hands on his desk and clasped his fingers together. "That's why I asked her not to sit in on any future sessions."

"My mother is overprotective, but that's not the reason I want to go back to Florida."

"What is the reason?"

Katie squinted against the ray of light streaming in the window as she struggled with what she wanted to say. "There are too many things here to remind me of my past. Too many things I'd rather forget."

"You can't run from your past. You'll only take your problems with you." He leaned forward and looked at her so intently that she squirmed in her chair. "You're just beginning to make some progress in dealing with your panic attacks. If you move now, you might lose ground."

"I'll still be able to do the things I'm doing now," she said.

"That may be true, but I think you'll do better if you keep coming here awhile longer. Will you at least think about it, Katie?"

She nodded, although as far as she was concerned, the decision had already been made. When Clarence and Mae were ready to move, Katie would be going with them.

~❦ ❦~

Later that afternoon while Katie was working in the stamp shop by herself, Ella showed up. "Is it true?" Ella asked, frowning.

"Is what true?"

"Are you really moving back to Florida?"

Katie nodded. "How'd you find out?"

"My mamm said your mamm told her when they saw each other at the Kuntry Store a few days ago."

"Oh, I see."

Ella folded her arms. "How come you didn't tell me about this, Katie?"

Katie swallowed hard, hoping she wouldn't cry. "I was going to tell you. I've just been busy and haven't had the chance to speak with you yet."

"Does anyone else know?"

"Just Mom and Dad. Of course I don't know who else Mom might have told."

Ella frowned. "What would make you decide to move back to Florida? I thought things were going better for you and that you were happy living here."

Tears welled in Katie's eyes, and she blinked to keep them from spilling over. "Freeman's going to marry Eunice next spring."

"What's that got to do with—" Ella's forehead puckered. "Oh, now I get it. You're in love with him, aren't you?"

Katie nodded slowly. "I. . .I didn't think I could ever love anyone but Timothy, but I feel so peaceful and content when I'm with Freeman." She reached for a tissue from Mom's desk and blew her nose. "At least, I used to."

Ella slipped her arms around Katie and gave her a hug. "I was afraid you were falling for him, and I tried to warn him not to lead you on, but—"

Katie pulled away. "You—you've talked to Freeman about me?"

"Jah. I knew he was going out with Eunice, and I was afraid if you fell in love with him, you'd end up getting hurt."

"What'd he say when you talked to him?"

"That I was worried for nothing, that you and he were just friends."

Katie swallowed several times until the lump in her throat disappeared. "I. . .I'm so embarrassed. I wish you hadn't talked to him. He probably thinks I'm a foolish little girl who's been trying to take him away from Eunice. I'll bet he wishes that he'd never befriended me." She leaned her head on Ella's shoulder. "I wish I'd never come back to Indiana!"

～ఈ ৯৴～

Freeman had just finished writing up an ad he planned to place in *The People's Exchange* when Penny darted up to him with a ball in her mouth.

He leaned down, grabbed the ball, and tossed it across the room. "Go get it, girl!"

Woof! Woof! Penny raced after the ball, scooped it up in her mouth, and dashed back to Freeman. She dropped the ball in front of Freeman and looked up at him with her tail wagging and her head cocked.

Freeman chuckled and threw the ball again. Penny darted after it.

He was amazed at how quickly she caught on to things. He'd been able to teach her several tricks already—to fetch the ball, roll over, play dead, and sit up and beg. Besides the pleasure it had brought him to train Penny, his customers seemed to enjoy the pup's antics, too. Freeman had begun to wonder if some people came into the shop just to play with Penny.

Woof! Woof!

Freeman chuckled when she dropped the ball at his feet again. "Okay, but this is the last time, girl. I've got to get this ad written up; then I need to get outside and trim up some trees." Freeman tossed the ball, and Penny scampered after it.

He hurried to finish the ad; then he put the CLOSED sign in the window and went out the door. Penny raced out with him and found a place to sleep on one end of the porch.

Freeman went to the barn to get the ladder and lopping shears; then he hauled them across the yard and leaned the ladder against the most overgrown tree. Holding the shears in one hand, he climbed the ladder, reached up, and cut the nearest branch. Then he trimmed two more and leaned out farther to trim a third branch.

"Whoa!" Freeman clung to the ladder as it began to sway. He leaned to the left, trying to regain control, but it was too late. The ladder shifted again; then it toppled over. Freeman tossed the shears aside and reached for the closest branch. He missed and fell to the ground with a *thud*.

A searing pain shot through his chest, and he gasped for breath. *Dear God, send someone to help me, please.*

CHAPTER 42

Eunice was not looking forward to going to the stamp shop, but that's exactly where she was heading. She'd just come from the Lambrights' place, where she'd delivered some candles Ada had ordered. Mama had asked her to stop by the stamp shop on her way home to pick up some cardstock and a few scrapbooking supplies. Eunice dreaded seeing Katie because she knew that Katie was in love with Freeman. She could tell by the look on Katie's face whenever she and Freeman were together.

Eunice had hoped that after she'd told Katie that she and Freeman planned to be married, it would discourage her from hanging around Freeman so much. What Eunice hadn't expected was that Freeman would break up with her that very same night. She hoped she could get him to change his mind, but in the meantime, she was worried that Freeman might start going out with Katie.

When Eunice entered the stamp shop, JoAnn was busy waiting on an English woman, but there no sign of Katie. That was a relief. Maybe Katie wasn't working today. Maybe she wouldn't have to speak to Katie at all.

Anxious to be on her way, she hurried over to the scrapbooking supplies and picked out what Mama needed; then she grabbed a package of cardstock. As soon as the English woman left, Eunice placed the items on the counter.

JoAnn smiled. "Looks like you're going to be busy for a while."

"These aren't for me," Eunice said. "They're for my mamm."

"Oh, I see." JoAnn placed everything in a plastic bag. "Is there anything else you need?"

"No, but I was wondering where Katie is. Isn't she working here today?"

JoAnn shook her head. "Katie's up at the house, packing her suitcase."

"Is she going on a trip?"

"No, she'll be moving back to Florida tomorrow morning."

"Now that's sure a surprise."

"It was to us, too. She'll be living with Jeremy's cousin and his wife until she finds a job."

Eunice smiled to herself. With Katie out of the picture, Freeman was bound to take her back.

~§ ♀~

Slurp! Slurp! Slurp!

Freeman moaned as Penny continued to lick his face. He tried to sit up, but the burning pain in his chest wouldn't allow him to move. He tried to talk, but he could barely breathe. All he could do was lie on the ground and pray.

Clip-clop. Clip-clop. Someone was coming up the lane. *Clip-clop. Clip-clop.* The sound of horse's hooves drew closer.

Freeman gritted his teeth and tried to get up, but it was no use.

Woof! Woof! Penny darted away.

Freeman lay there helplessly as Penny continued to bark. Even if he'd been able to holler for help, no one could have heard him with the dog yapping like that. Well, at least she'd quit licking his face.

Several minutes went by; then someone shouted his name.

"Oh, Freeman, what happened to you?" Eunice dropped to her knees beside him, her eyes wide with fear.

"F–fell," he rasped.

Eunice stared at him with a blank expression for several

seconds. Then she pointed to the ladder nearby. "Did you fall from that?"

He managed a slow nod. "C–can't breathe."

"I'm going to the phone shed to call for help!" Eunice leaped to her feet and hurried away.

Penny flopped down beside Freeman, whimpered, and licked his nose.

Freeman closed his eyes and said a prayer. *Thank You, Lord, for sending help.*

Several minutes went by; then Eunice knelt beside him again. "I called 911, and an ambulance is on the way." She took hold of Freeman's hand. "I was heading to your bike shop to tell you something, but Penny kept barking and looking up this way, so I decided I'd better see if something was wrong."

Freeman's chest hurt so bad, he could only nod in reply. He was relieved when he heard the wail of a siren.

"I'd better go to the schoolhouse and let Fern know what's happened," Eunice said after the ambulance arrived.

Freeman nodded and closed his eyes, thankful to God that Eunice had come along when she did.

CHAPTER 43

W ould you like another pillow?" Fern asked as Freeman settled himself on the sofa.

He winced as he shook his head. "One's enough."

"Are you in pain?"

"A little."

"Should I get you some water and a pain pill?"

"Not right now. I had a pill before we left the hospital."

Slurp! Slurp! Penny, who'd been lying on the floor in front of the sofa, lifted her head and swiped her tongue across Freeman's hand.

"You're a good girl," Freeman mumbled.

Fern took a seat in the rocking chair across from him. "I'm so thankful that Eunice found you when she did. No telling what would have happened if she hadn't come along."

Freeman nodded. "I'm very grateful."

Fern's nose crinkled. "When Eunice came to the schoolhouse to tell me what happened, I could see how concerned she was. It's obvious that she cares for you, Freeman."

"I know." Freeman leaned his head against the pillow and closed his eyes. "I'm really tired. Could we talk about this later?"

A knock sounded on the door. Freeman opened his eyes and groaned. "I hope it's not someone who went looking for me at the bike shop."

"I'll see who it is." Fern hurried from the room, and when she returned a few seconds later, Eunice was with her.

"I was hoping you'd be home from the hospital by now," Eunice said, moving quickly across the room.

"I have something to do in the kitchen, so I'll leave you alone." Fern smiled at Eunice, and then she scurried from the room.

"How are you feeling?" Eunice asked, stepping into Freeman's field of vision.

"Fair to middlin', all things considered."

She took a seat on the end of the sofa by his feet. "I was really scared when I found you lying on the ground."

"I was scared, too." He grimaced as he tried to find a comfortable position. "Don't know what I'd have done if you hadn't come along when you did."

She nodded. "Guess it's a good thing Fern's puppy was barking like that, or I might not have come up to the yard."

Just then Penny leaped into Eunice's lap and swiped her tongue across Eunice's nose.

"Get down!" With a disgruntled look, Eunice pushed Penny to the floor.

Freeman smiled despite the pain in his chest. "Guess I'm not the only one that pup likes to kiss."

They spent the next several minutes in silence. The only noise in the room was the steady *tick-tock* of the clock on the far wall. Freeman wondered if Eunice felt as uncomfortable as he did. Was she expecting him to say that he'd changed his mind about breaking up with her?

Should I change my mind? he asked himself. *She did come to my rescue yesterday, and she does seem to care about me. Still, I'm not sure that's a good enough reason to keep going out with her.*

Eunice inched a little closer to Freeman. "When you're feeling better, maybe you can come over to my place for supper again."

The expectant look he saw on Eunice's face made him want to jump off the sofa, run out to the barn, and hide in the hayloft. But he was in no position to jump or run. "Since I'm gonna be laid up for the next several days, I probably won't be going anyplace," he said.

"I meant after you're feeling better."

"Maybe Fern and I can both come to supper after I catch up with things in the shop," he said, hoping to appease her.

Her mouth turned up at the corners. "That would be nice."

~≈ ≈~

Loraine's steps slowed as she neared the stamp shop. When Ella had told her that Katie was leaving for Florida tomorrow, she'd decided to come over and see if she could talk Katie out of going. She just hoped her cousin would listen to reason.

Loraine stood on the porch a few minutes as she asked God for wisdom in knowing what to say. Drawing in a deep breath, she stepped into the stamp shop. She found Katie bent over a piece of pegboard where some scissors and paper punches hung.

"I hear you'll be leaving us tomorrow," she said, stepping up to Katie.

"That's right," Katie said. "Clarence and Mae are planning to leave sooner than they expected."

Loraine touched Katie's shoulder. "Do you really have to go?"

Katie nodded, and tears gathered in her eyes. "It's the best thing for me right now."

"How come?"

Katie sank into a chair at her mother's desk. "Eunice has spread so many rumors about me, and with her and Freeman planning to get married next spring, it wouldn't be right for me and Freeman to remain close friends."

Loraine's eyebrows shot up. "Wayne and Freeman are pretty good friends, and as far as I know, Freeman hasn't mentioned anything to Wayne about marrying Eunice."

Katie shrugged. "They probably won't let too many people know until the time gets closer, but Eunice told me herself that she and Freeman would be getting married."

"Speaking of Freeman," Loraine said, "did you hear that he got hurt while he was pruning some trees in their yard?"

Katie bolted out of her chair. "When did that happen?"

"Yesterday morning. Eunice's daed came by the taxidermy shop with a fish he wanted stuffed, and he told Wayne that Freeman had been pruning some trees in their yard and fell off the ladder." Loraine's brows puckered. "I guess Freeman ended up in the emergency room with some broken ribs and a collapsed lung."

Katie covered her mouth with the palm of her hand. "That's baremlich!"

"You're right, it's terrible," Loraine agreed. "Eunice's daed said that Eunice told him that Freeman was in a lot of pain the day that it happened."

"Is he still in the hospital?"

"I don't think so. From what Wayne was told, Freeman was supposed to be released some time today."

Katie moved quickly toward the door. "When my mamm comes out of the bathroom, would you tell her I had an errand to run?" She scooted out the door before Loraine could respond.

CHAPTER 44

As Katie headed out with her horse and buggy, she reminded herself to relax, breathe deeply, and stay focused on the road. She hadn't had a panic attack in several weeks, and she sure didn't need one now.

A flock of geese honked overhead and landed in a nearby field. At the same time, a car whipped past Katie, going much too fast, and she gripped the reins tightly, fearing that her horse might spook. Dixie, however, did okay, and so did Katie. She was more relaxed than she'd expected.

Katie hoped Freeman was home from the hospital and that she was doing the right thing in going to see him. She just couldn't leave Indiana without saying good-bye, and she needed to know that he was all right.

When Katie turned up the Bontragers' driveway, she saw a horse and buggy at the hitching rail near the barn. Apparently, Freeman must be home, and he already had some company. Katie didn't want to say good-bye to Freeman in front of anyone else, and she considered leaving a note, along with the banana nut cake she'd brought for him on the porch. But she wanted to say good-bye to Freeman in person, so she quickly dismissed that idea.

She pulled up to the other side of the rail, climbed down from the buggy, and secured her horse. Then she retrieved the container of cake and sprinted for the house.

Stepping onto the back porch, she rapped on the door. A few seconds later, she was greeted by Fern.

"I heard about Freeman's accident," Katie said. "I wanted to come by and see how he's doing."

"His ribs are very sore, but he's getting along okay." Fern glanced over her shoulder. "Knowing my energetic bruder, he'll be back on his feet in no time at all."

"Can I see him for a few minutes? I want to see how he's doing."

"Eunice is visiting with him right now. They're talking about some personal things, so I don't want to interrupt."

"Oh, I see." Katie heard muffled voices through the screen door and figured it was Freeman talking to Eunice. She cringed when she heard the words *love* and *marriage*. Eunice had obviously been telling the truth about getting married next spring. For all Katie knew, they might get married even sooner—maybe right after Freeman joined the church.

She stared at the toes of her sneakers, trying to decide what to do. It had taken courage to come over here, and she couldn't leave without at least letting Freeman know she'd been here.

Katie handed Fern the container with the cake inside. "Would you give this to Freeman and tell him that I'll be leaving for Florida tomorrow and wanted to say good-bye?"

Fern tipped her head as she took the cake. "Are you moving back to Florida?"

Katie nodded. "I'll be living with my daed's cousin and his wife until I'm able to get a job and a place of my own."

"Oh, I see. Well, that's probably for the best." Fern's mouth turned up at the corners. "You were happier there, right?"

"Jah, I was." Katie could barely speak around the lump in her throat. She really didn't want to leave Indiana, but hearing Freeman and Eunice talking about love and marriage made her even more certain that she was doing the right thing by moving back to Florida. "Will you tell Freeman I was here and give him the cake?" she asked in a voice barely above a whisper.

Fern gave a quick nod. "I wish you the best in Florida, Katie."

"Danki." Katie dashed down the steps and raced across the lawn. She quickly untied her horse and scrambled into the buggy. As soon as she took her seat, the dam broke and tears flowed freely down her cheeks.

As she guided Dixie down the lane and onto the road, she could barely see because of her tears, and her throat felt so clogged she could hardly swallow.

❦

"I'm sorry, Eunice," Freeman said, "but there's no point in us going out, because we can never have a permanent relationship."

"Why not?"

Freeman searched for truthful words that wouldn't hurt Eunice too much. "I, um, think we both know that our relationship isn't based on anything more than physical attraction."

Eunice's nose twitched. "Are you saying that the only thing you like about me is my pretty face?"

"It's not that. It's just that—" He blotted his sweaty forehead with the back of his hand and cleared his throat a couple of times.

"You're in love with Katie, aren't you?"

He nodded slowly. "But I don't know if—"

"How can you love her?" Eunice scowled at him. "Katie has emotional problems, and she's so immature."

Freeman's fingers clenched as irritation welled in his chest. He was trying to be nice to Eunice, but he was getting tired of hearing her put Katie down all the time. "Katie's panic attacks are getting better, and she's not immature!"

"Well, if you want my opinion, anyone who'd keep a baby when she should have notified the sheriff is immature," Eunice huffed.

"I'll admit that wasn't a good decision on Katie's part, but she's trying to make good decisions now, and she's able to cope with things a lot better."

Eunice left the sofa and dropped to the floor on her knees in front of Freeman. "Katie doesn't love you, Freeman."

"Maybe not now, but in time, she might. We've become good friends, and—"

"If she loved you, she wouldn't be moving back to Florida."

"What?" Heat shot up his neck and cascaded onto his cheeks.

"I talked to Katie's mamm the other day when I dropped off some candles at Ada's. She mentioned that Katie plans to move back to Sarasota. She wouldn't be doing that if she loved you, now would she?" Eunice looked up at him with questioning eyes and a hopeful smile. "Won't you please give us another chance? I'm sure if we spend more time together—"

"Did JoAnn say when Katie plans to move?"

"Uh—I think she said in a few days, but I'm not really sure."

He breathed a sigh of relief. That would give him time to heal enough so he could go over to Katie's and talk to her. Maybe if he came right out and told her that he loved her, she'd reconsider. Then again, a declaration of love might scare her off.

Just then Fern stepped into the room holding a plastic container with a cake inside. "Katie came by a few minutes ago, and she wanted me to give you this." She set the container on the coffee table.

"Did she say anything else?"

Fern glanced over at Eunice then back at Freeman. "She said she was leaving for Florida tomorrow morning and asked me to tell you good-bye."

Freeman groaned as he closed his eyes and pushed against the pillow. He couldn't believe Katie was leaving so soon. Never in all his twenty-two years had he felt like this. The physical pain in his ribs was nothing compared to the emotional pain in his heart.

~❦~

Eunice smiled to herself. Katie was leaving even sooner than she'd expected, which meant she'd no longer be a threat. Given a little more time, Eunice was sure that Freeman would forget about Katie, and then he'd see Eunice in a different light.

"I think I'd better go and let you get some rest," Eunice said, rising to her feet. "I'll be back tomorrow to see how you're doing."

Freeman opened his eyes and slowly shook his head. "Don't bother, Eunice. It's over between us."

Her mouth dropped open, and her eyelids drooped. "You— you can't mean that."

"Jah, I do. It's your fault Katie's leaving."

Indignation rose in Eunice's chest. "How can it be my fault?"

He shifted on the sofa and moaned. "If you hadn't started so many rumors about Katie, I don't think she'd ever have decided to go back to Florida."

Eunice thrust out her chin and was going to defend herself when Fern stepped up to her and said, "Maybe it'd be best if you went home now. Freeman looks tired, and he needs to rest."

Eunice gave a quick nod and rushed out the door. She hurried to her buggy, untied the horse, and was soon on her way.

"Well," she mumbled, gripping the reins, "I may never have Freeman, but Katie won't, either."

Eunice drew in a couple of deep breaths, trying to calm herself as she pulled out of the driveway. The trees lining the road swayed in the breeze, and the twittering of birds could be heard all around, but she barely took notice. "At the rate I'm going, I'll never find a husband," she mumbled. "Why have all my boyfriends pushed me away?"

Eunice had gone only a short ways when she spotted a dead possum in the road. She guided her horse and buggy around it but had just moved back into her lane when the sunlight caught a piece of metal lying on the shoulder of the road. The flash of light from the reflection temporarily blinded her and apparently startled her horse. He whinnied, stopped dead in the road, and then backed straight into the ditch.

Eunice snapped the reins, but the horse wouldn't budge. She reached for the buggy whip and cracked it over the horse's head. He lunged forward, but the buggy didn't move. The wheels were stuck.

She cracked the whip again, and the horse reared up. Clutching the reins, she tried to get him under control, but he only tossed his head from side to side and stomped his feet.

Suddenly, the buggy lunged forward, rocked back and forth,

and jerked to the right. The next thing Eunice knew, it had flipped on its side, spilling her out.

She felt groggy from hitting the hard ground, but she didn't think she'd been seriously hurt. Her first impulse was to jump up and run after her horse, which had managed to break free from the buggy and was galloping down the road. Before Eunice could make a move, she heard the rumble of buggy wheels coming down the road from the opposite direction. A few seconds later, the horse and buggy pulled in behind her rig. Andrew got out and secured his horse to a low-hanging branch.

"Are you all right?" he asked, rushing over to Eunice.

Inhaling slowly, she nodded and said, "I think so."

He reached out his hand to her. "How'd your buggy end up in the ditch?"

She stood and brushed a clump of dirt from her dress; then she quickly explained how her horse had reacted to the reflection and had backed into the ditch.

"Don't think I can do much about your horse," Andrew said. "He took off down the road like a flash of lightning and is probably halfway to your place by now. I'd be happy to give you a ride home, and then I can come back for your buggy later on."

"Danki." Eunice hoped her smile would convey the feelings of gratitude she felt. This was the second time Andrew had offered his help when she was in need. *Hmm. . .maybe he would make a good husband.*

～❦～

As Freeman lay on the sofa, he decided he had to see Katie, and it had to be now. Gritting his teeth, he winced as he rose from the sofa. He was almost to the back door when Fern stepped out of the kitchen and snapped her fingers. "Just where do you think you're going?"

"To the barn to get my horse."

"What for?"

"I need to see Katie."

"Oh no, you don't." She positioned herself between him and

the door. "You're not up to going anywhere right now, much less hitching the horse to the buggy."

He leaned around her and reached for the doorknob, but a searing pain shot through his ribs, and he braced himself against the wall for support.

Fern snapped her fingers again and pointed to the living room. "You ought to be lying down, and there's no need for you to see Katie today."

"Jah, there is. She's leaving tomorrow morning; you said so yourself." He grunted and held his hands against his sore ribs. "I wish you'd have invited her in so I could've talked to her."

"Would you like me to go out to the phone shed and leave a message for Katie on their answering machine?"

He shook his head. "She might not get the message before she leaves in the morning. I need to talk to her now."

Fern folded her arms and stared at Freeman as if he didn't have a lick of sense. Several seconds went by; then she puckered her lips and said, "You're in love with Katie, aren't you?"

"Jah. I don't know if she could ever love me, but I can't stand the thought of her leaving without me telling her the way that I feel."

Fern moved away from the door. "If you're determined to go, then let's wait until after supper, because it's almost done."

"Us? Are you suggesting that you'll go with me?"

She nodded.

"Huh-uh. I need to speak with Katie alone."

"That's fine; I'll wait in the buggy while you talk to her, but I can't stay here and worry while you go there alone."

Freeman took a few minutes to think things through; then he finally nodded. It would be a lot easier if Fern drove the buggy. He turned toward the living room. "I'm going back to the sofa to rest. Call me when supper's ready."

~※ ※~

When Katie entered the barn after supper that evening, she was greeted by the gentle nicker of the horses in their stalls and the sweet smell of hay.

She seated herself on a bale of straw and listened to the soft cooing of the pigeons in the rafters overhead. She'd come to say good-bye to Dixie and the other animals, but now that she was here, all she wanted to do was sit and cry. She would miss this place—her family, friends, and even the critters who lived in the barn. Most of all, she would miss Freeman. In the months since she'd come home from Florida, she had allowed herself to get closer to him than anyone else. She hadn't even felt that close to Timothy. It had been as if she and Freeman were soul mates. The only problem was that she loved him and he loved Eunice.

Katie moved across the room, reached over the gate in Dixie's stall, and stroked the horse's soft nose. Dixie whinnied and nuzzled Katie's hand.

Maybe it's best that I didn't get to say good-bye to Freeman, she decided. *It would have been too painful. At least this time I'm not running away from the memory of the accident that took Timothy's life. This time I'm going because I can't stand the idea of seeing Freeman with Eunice, which to me is just as painful as losing someone in death.*

Katie backed away from the stall, doubled over, and gave in to her tears. She would never let herself fall in love again. She would be an old maid for the rest of her life.

CHAPTER 45

Freeman woke up with a start. The room was dark, and at first, he didn't know where he was. Then he remembered that right after supper he'd gone back to the living room to rest one more time while Fern cleaned up the kitchen. They were supposed to head over to Katie's as soon as Fern got done with the dishes. Apparently, he'd fallen asleep. What he couldn't figure out was why Fern hadn't awakened him. It made him wonder if she'd let him sleep so he couldn't see Katie. From some of the things Fern had said in the past, Freeman knew that she liked Eunice a lot and hoped Eunice and Freeman would become a couple. He also knew that Fern saw Katie as an immature girl who had too many emotional problems, so it wouldn't surprise him if Fern purposely had let him sleep.

Freeman pulled himself to a sitting position, turned on the gas lamp on the table near the sofa, and groaned when he looked at the clock above the fireplace mantel. It was almost midnight! It was too late to go over to Katie's now. He wished he knew exactly what time she planned to leave in the morning. Now he'd have to set his alarm clock to go off early and hope he would make it over to the Millers' place before Katie left. If he didn't get there on time, he might be making an unplanned trip to Florida.

❦

"I wish you'd change your mind and stay here with us," Mom said tearfully as Katie set her suitcase by the front door.

"I wish I could, but going back to Pinecraft is the best thing for me right now. Maybe someday I'll come home again, but that might be a long time off."

Mom pulled Katie into her arms and gave her a hug. "I want you to know something before you go."

"What's that?"

"I'm sorry if I've seemed pushy or controlling. Since you're the youngest of my kinner, it's been hard for me to let go and allow you to make your own decisions." She gently patted Katie's back. "I hope you know how much I love you and only want what's best for you."

Katie nearly choked on the sob rising in her throat. "I know that, Mom, and I love you, too."

"Your mamm and I will come down to Florida to visit you this winter," Dad said, joining them in the hall. "It'll be good to get out of the cold, snowy weather we'll no doubt have here."

"I'd like that," Katie said as she hugged him. "Maybe I'll even have a place of my own by then."

Beep! Beep!

"That must be Clarence and Mae's driver," Dad said. He picked up Katie's suitcase and opened the door.

She followed him outside, and Mom walked beside her to the van. Clarence and Mae were in the back, but when Dad put Katie's suitcase inside, they both got out to say their good-byes to Mom and Dad.

"Take care of our girl," Mom said, hugging Mae.

"We will," Clarence and Mae both said.

Katie wanted to remind Mom once more that she wasn't a little girl but figured there was nothing to be gained by that. In her parents' eyes, she would always be their little girl.

Katie grimaced at the sinking feeling in the pit of her stomach. *If I never get married, I'll never know the joy of being a mother.* That thought hurt more than she cared to admit. Ever since Katie had been a little girl playing with her dolls, she'd wanted to be a mother. But some things weren't meant to be, and she'd have to learn to accept them and make a life for herself without a husband or children.

"We'd better get into the van now," Clarence said. "Our driver, Bill, is anxious to get going."

Katie gave Mom and Dad one last hug good-bye. She was just getting ready to climb into the van when a horse and buggy rumbled up the driveway. She waited to see who it was, and her breath caught when Freeman climbed down from the buggy.

"Thank the Lord I'm not too late," he said, walking slowly toward her.

"Too late for what?" Dad asked, looking at Freeman.

"Too late to speak to Katie." Freeman stood at her side. "Could we talk in private for a few minutes?"

The rhythm of Katie's heartbeat picked up speed. "Well, uh, we were just about to leave."

"I don't want you to go until you've heard what I have to say."

Katie looked at Dad, hoping for his approval. He stuck his head into the van and said something to their English driver. Then he turned to Freeman and gave a nod. "Bill said he'd wait another five minutes."

Freeman took Katie's arm and led her over to the porch. "Can we sit down? My ribs are really hurting."

She felt immediate concern. "You probably shouldn't be out of bed. What were you thinking, driving your buggy over here like that when you just came home from the hospital?"

"I didn't drive myself. Fern's waiting for me in the buggy."

"Even so, it's not good for you to—"

Freeman put his finger against Katie's lips. "I need you to listen to what I have to say."

Katie nodded and motioned for him to take a seat in one of the wicker chairs on the porch. Once he was seated, she sat in the chair next to him. "What'd you want to say?"

Freeman grimaced, as though in pain.

"Are you hurting really bad?" she asked.

"Jah, right here." Freeman placed his hand against his chest. "Why are you going back to Florida, Katie?"

She swallowed a couple of times, hoping she wouldn't break down in tears. "I. . .uh. . .think I'll be happier there."

He crinkled his nose. "I don't want you to go, Katie, and well, I wanted to say that if you ever decide to love again, I. . .I'd like to be the one."

Katie's heart began to pound, and her mouth felt so dry she could barely speak. She'd never expected to hear Freeman say such a thing to her. "What about Eunice? I thought you were going to marry her."

Freeman shook his head vigorously. "I never planned to marry Eunice. She may have wanted it, but I can't make a lifetime commitment to someone I don't love. Truthfully, I don't think Eunice really loves me, either. I think she's just looking for a husband, and in due time she'll find someone else—hopefully someone she really loves." He reached for Katie's hand and gave her fingers a gentle squeeze. "It's you I love, and after I've joined the church this fall, I'd like us to be married." His face sobered. "That is, if you'll have me."

A wide smile spread across Katie's face. "I love you, too, and I'd be honored to be your wife." The words came out in a wondering tone as the meaning of his words sank in. Freeman loved her, not Eunice.

Freeman stroked Katie's cheek as he gazed into her eyes. "You're the girl—I mean, the woman for me. I've known it ever since we were kinner." He leaned closer until their lips were almost touching.

Beep! Beep!

Katie's eyes snapped open, and her gaze went to the van waiting to take her away. "I'll be right back!" she hollered over her shoulder as she tore across the yard. When she reached the van, she leaned inside, grabbed her suitcase, and shut the door. "I'm not moving to Florida," she said, smiling at Mom and Dad. "I'm staying right here, and when the time is right, I'm going to marry Freeman."

Mom looked at Dad, and Dad looked at Mom. Both of their faces broke into wide smiles.

Katie handed her suitcase to Dad then hurried back to the

porch and took a seat beside Freeman.

"Were your folks happy to hear that you're staying?" he asked.

Katie nodded and smiled. "I used to think that God never answered any of my prayers, but I've come to realize that He answered every one—just not always the way I wanted Him to." She reached over and boldly took Freeman's hand. " 'God hath not given me the spirit of fear, but of power, and of love, and of a sound mind.' He's answered my prayers and helped me deal with my panic attacks. Best of all, He's given you to me."

Freeman leaned close to Katie, and this time there was no horn honking to stop his tender kiss.

Being careful not to cause further injury to Freeman's ribs, Katie gave him a gentle hug. "I pray that all of my cousins will be there on our wedding day," she whispered in his ear. "And I pray that God will give us many years together as husband and wife."

Katie's Banana Nut Cake

2 cups flour
1⅔ cups sugar
1 teaspoon salt
¾ teaspoon baking powder
1½ teaspoons baking soda
⅔ cup shortening
⅔ cup sour milk or buttermilk
3 eggs
1 teaspoon vanilla
1½ cups mashed bananas
⅔ cup chopped nuts

Mix all ingredients thoroughly and pour into a greased and floured 9 x 13 x 2 inch pan. Bake at 350 degrees for 35–40 minutes.

DISCUSSION QUESTIONS

1. Katie Miller had a difficult time accepting her boyfriend's death, and she went through a period of depression. Has someone you know gone through something similar? If so, how did you try to help that person work through her or his depression?

2. List some ways you can help someone going through depression. What should you not do when someone is depressed?

3. Did Katie's folks do the right thing by sending her to live with her grandparents after Timothy died? Do you think Katie's parents were supportive or too controlling?

4. When Katie returned to Indiana, her depression turned into anxiety attacks. At first Katie tried to hide the attacks, feeling embarrassed and confused by her unexplained symptoms. Have you or someone you know ever suffered from anxiety or panic attacks? If so, was the person experiencing the attacks embarrassed by the symptoms? Did that person tell someone about the feelings or try to hide them?

5. Why it is important to share your feelings with someone when you're depressed or experiencing some other kind of emotional problem?

6. What are some ways you can help someone dealing with anxiety or panic attacks? Is there ever a time when a person can deal with these kinds of attacks alone, or does the person always need the guidance of a trained professional?

7. When Loraine miscarried, she was deeply saddened, although she accepted the miscarriage as God's will. What are some ways you can help someone who has lost a baby?

8. When Katie found a baby on her porch and decided not to notify the sheriff right away, she told Freeman about it. Did Freeman do the right thing when he agreed to keep Katie's secret? What would have been a better way for Freeman to help Katie?

9. Is there ever a time when it's all right to gossip or talk about someone's problems?

10. Eunice was jealous of the attention Freeman gave Katie, so she gossiped about Katie and tried to make her look bad. What should a person do when she knows someone is gossiping about her?

11. What life lessons did you learn from reading *A Cousin's Prayer*?

12. Were there any verses of scripture that spoke to your heart? If so, in what way might you use that scripture to deal with some situation in your own life?

13. What did you learn about the Amish way of life that you didn't know before?

About the Author

WANDA E. BRUNSTETTER enjoys writing about the Amish because they live a peaceful, simple life. Wanda's interest in the Amish and other Plain communities began when she married her husband, Richard, who grew up in a Mennonite church in Pennsylvania. Learning about her Anabaptist great-great grandparents increased Wanda's interest in the Plain People. Wanda has made numerous trips to Lancaster County and has several friends and family members living near that area. She and her husband have also traveled to other parts of the country, meeting various Amish families and getting to know them personally. She hopes her readers will learn to love the wonderful Amish people as much as she does.

Wanda and her husband have been married over forty years. They have two grown children and six grandchildren. In her spare time, Wanda enjoys photography, ventriloquism, gardening, reading, stamping, and having fun with her family.

In addition to her novels, Wanda has written two Amish cookbooks, an Amish devotional, several Amish children's books, as well as many novellas, stories, articles, poems, and puppet scripts.

Visit Wanda's Web site at www.wandabrunstetter.com and feel free to e-mail her at wanda@wandabrunstetter.com.